A CLIFF
OF FALL

A CLIFF OF FALL

*Selected Short Stories
and Novellas
1970-2000*

Norval Rindfleisch

Copyright ©1999 by Norval Rindfleisch.

Library of Congress Number: 99-91896
ISBN #:   Hardcover   0-7388-1390-7
          Softcover   0-7388-1391-5

All rights reserved. No part of this book may be reproduced or transmitted in any form or by any means, electronic or mechanical, including photocopying, recording, or by any information storage and retrieval system, without permission in writing from the copyright owner.

This is a work of fiction. Names, characters, places and incidents either are the product of the author's imagination or are used fictitiously, and any resemblance to any actual persons, living or dead, events, or locales is entirely coincidental.

This book was printed in the United States of America.

To order additional copies of this book, contact:
Xlibris Corporation
1-888-7-XLIBRIS
www.Xlibris.com
Orders@Xlibris.com

CONTENTS

IN LOVELESS CLARITY 11

A CLIFF OF FALL 35

THE SUMMER OF
    HIS DISCONTENT 59

THE DISSERTATION 75

OF STREETCARS, STRANGERS, CHESTNUTS,
    AND CHILDHOOD 111

A TRIP TO THE COUNTRY 127

THE PARTNERSHIP 153

GIFTS 179

ACKNOWLEDGMENT

With gratitude, to the editors and publishers who said yes to the previous publications of these stories: (the late) Charles Angoff of THE LITERARY REVIEW, (the late) Baxter Hathaway, co-founder of EPOCH and publisher of ITHACA HOUSE; William Abrahams, editor PRIZE STORIES: The O. Henry Awards; Ritchie Darling, publisher THE NORTHERN NEW ENGLAND REVIEW PRESS; Jean Ervin, editor and publisher THE MINNESOTA EXPERIENCE.

"Memory believes before knowing remembers. Believes longer than recollects, longer than knowing even wonders."

LIGHT IN AUGUST
William Faulkner

IN LOVELESS CLARITY

The city of St. Paul is built like Rome on seven hills along a river. The hills are rather puny, and the river, dirty with refuse, is narrow and unimposing except at flood time when it overflows its banks and carries in the breech of its current massive slabs of ice. Each morning in the summer sewers flush the night's accumulation into the river, and contraceptives like unweighted parachutes (from that citadel of Black Protestantism upriver, Minneapolis) toss and turn and swivel languidly just below the surface. The mighty Mississippi in the childhood of its length has just begun toward the Gulf of Mexico, yet it is already, glacially speaking, senile and shrunk to a rivulet. Its thin trickle is mocked by the distant valley ridges which were once the lips of a gigantic flow that drained a continent.

The West Side, built on one of those hills overlooking the river (dominated by that section euphemistically called Cherokee Heights after the Indians and the high bluffs), is perhaps the most uniformly dull residential section of that traditionally safe but sleepy city. It slopes ever so slightly away from the Mississippi to the limestone cliffs and then continues to slope gradually for about two more miles to the farthest limits of the old river's edge, to the Dakota county line and the countryside beyond. There are huge caves carved in the limestone cliffs which reveal in their echoing emptiness the prehistoric energies of primitive man, and stored in some of the caves for aging are barrels of beer and quantities of cheese and mushrooms which reveal in their organization and arrangement the genius and practicality of civilized man.

It is Sunday noon. We are going there, to the West Side, (up from the river, past the caves) for dinner, to my father's childhood home now occupied by his older sister, Aunt Esther, her husband, Uncle Otto, and my cousins, two girls, Roberta and Marlys, and a boy, Donald, who at seven years of age is the shame of the family and the only evidence of Aunt Esther's failure at anything large or small.

When my father was raised on the West Side far above the limestone cliffs near the city limits, the house was relatively isolated. The few acres they had with two cows and some chickens formed a kind of quasi-farm. My grandfather had emigrated from Germany in the 1880's and continued his trade as a tailor in this country. He never bothered to learn English except for those few words necessary to carry on business. He wisely married an American bride, some twenty years younger than he, who served as his interpreter and point of stable adjustment in the new and alien world which he would have preferred to remodel along the lines of old country discipline and order.

They had three sons and a daughter. The sons married early, but the only daughter, Aunt Esther, remained at home, became a proficient legal stenographer, and supported her parents in their retirement and nursed them in their sicknesses. Then she married Uncle Otto, to everyone's relief, in her middle thirties and before it was too late had three children in quick succession. Grandfather was hit by a car at eighty-nine years of age and when Grandmother died six years later, Aunt Esther, for services above and beyond the call of duty (and after all the forgotten wounds of childhood had been reopened), inherited the old house and assumed the leadership of the family.

Now the old home and Aunt Esther's uncontested leadership have become the focus of family unity. She has forged a reluctant coherence with these Sunday dinners. Once a month from late fall through spring we go home, as it were, to her unity dinners, one brother and his family at a time. Her feasts represent our cloistered line of defense against a crumbling world first of depression and now of war.

The struggle in Europe and the Pacific has been raging for a little over a year now. Sugar and meat are rationed; tires are impossible to buy. Gasoline quota stickers decorate the lower right-hand corners of every car windshield and a red C sticker can lend a new prestige and dignity even to a dilapidate Model A Ford. Everything that seems of value is scarce or conscripted and the adult world, that outer world of business and doing things, has been either channeled into the war effort or has been patriotically, reverently suspended out of respect for the holy madness that has seized the world.

That feeling of having been left behind, of having been cheated out of some grand destiny pervades my family's spirit. The depression turned the national sympathies inward toward the midlands, and this concern made significant the prosaic terms of daily survival. The war has suddenly redirected those sympathies outward toward foreign lands. While everyone else has gone to sea to engage the enemy in the death struggle, we watch from the safety of a distant shore. No one in my family is old enough or young enough to serve. We have become peripheral.

Winter is entrenched, has taken a deep hold in the earth so that it seems that spring will never come. We are in the fifth layer of snow since November. It is packed tight of its own weight, and the crust has crystallized. It seems that all beauty, and joy, and love have been banished by the arctic blasts which sweep down through Canada and grip a nation already caught in fury and terror.

II

Although it is bitter cold, my father's old Plymouth surprises us by starting. My brother, Hank, and I are pleased that we do not have to shove it. We drive the four slippery miles across town with deliberate caution. When we arrive, my father, who does not presume upon good fortune, leaves us off at the path shoveled in the plowed snowbank below the from entrance. He drives two blocks father so that he can park the car on a downhill slant.

The house is narrow, with unpainted shingles and a sharp peaked roof; it is set back on a lot which rises thirty feet above the street. The houses across the way are built on the street level and their back yards fall away to the alley of the street below.

Hank, now an honors senior in high school and the pacesetter of our generation, solicitously assists my mother up the slippery steps. Although Uncle Otto has shoveled and sanded the walk, they proceed cautiously gripping the pipe railing on the right. I try to run up the steep embankment. My mother tells me to stop. She is afraid I will ruin next summer's lawn.

Out of habit we go around to the rear entrance although we are expected to arrive at the front door on formal occasions. Besides the front door sticks and the wind whips strongly around the corner of the house. The stoop is precariously small, exposed, and has no railing.

Uncle Otto greets us in the entry. He opens the door from the kitchen and stares at us as he looks for my father.

"Where is he?" he says. "Where's the Republican?" He squints and looks behind me pretending my father might be hiding there. He shakes his head, bemoaning my father's absence.

We stamp the snow from our feet. My mother insists we take our overshoes off in the entry so we won't track the kitchen. We bump into each other leaning over.

"He was afraid to come. I know. I understand. He can't stand defeat," he mocks. Then he turns to me as I take off my coat.

"Your father is a high-strung, sensitive man. The other night on his way home from work he dropped by for an argument and left like a whipped dog with his tail between his legs."

"Don't worry, Uncle Otto. He'll be here. He just went to park the car on a hill," Hank says. "He wouldn't miss an argument with you for anything."

Uncle Otto wears a white shirt open at the collar. He is short, thick-chested, and bandy-legged. It seems as though the lower half of his body is either under-developed or wasted away. His pin striped trousers hang loosely from his hips.

He has already been drinking beer, but he looks to my father's arrival as justification for whiskey which they will drink secretly, as is their custom, either in the basement or in the back entry out of sight of all children. He fidgets uneasily, eagerly spoiling for a debate. He has probably remembered an important point or learned a new argument since his last encounter with my father.

Uncle Otto has been a carpenter and furniture maker from his childhood, but he dates the beginning of his moral and political existence (they are the same with him) from the moment he joined a union and registered in the Democratic Party. He has a narrowness of sympathy—for the common man only—which the depression made broad through massive unemployment.

He is a craftsman of great skill. His knotty hands work with that slow, plodding patience which tolerates no errors. His deliberate caution and his slowness of intelligence are often mistaken as mature thoughtfulness, and his occasional obtuse insensitivity is often interpreted as self control or moderation, but the opposite is true: he is quick to anger especially when the issue is politics.

Uncle Otto loves the popular radio culture of Jack Benny, and Fibber McGee and Molly. He is humble before the brilliance of Dr. I.Q. and overawed by the Lone Ranger and the frontier justice he dispenses daily to the common man of the days of yore. In Uncle Otto's mind there is a singular parallel between the Lone Ranger and Franklin Delano Roosevelt, his greatest and only hero, the defender of the widow, orphan, and laboring man.

My father is Uncle Otto's logical opponent. He is a white collar worker, an accountant and bookkeeper who has found it convenient to subscribe to the politics of his employers. He has had three jobs in the last ten years, but he has never been unemployed for very long.

He is a Republican in the fullest sense of the word. He is still loyal to Herbert Hoover and holds John L. Lewis in supreme contempt. Just as laboriously as he tries to find a foreign cause for the depression (it *must have* been caused by foreigners—there is nothing wrong with the American economy—it is after all *American*), he tries to find a domestic cause for the war. It is the warmongers, Jews, and Easterners who have delivered the national destiny into the hands of the Communists and the Anglophiles.

For a while he was a follower of Father Coughlin. We used to go to mass at the Cathedral (located across the river at the foot of Summit Avenue where the Hills and Weyerhaeusers still reside, or rather where they still exist in a state of transcendental endowment) which was one of the few places where the *Social Justice* was available. But my father had too much good humor to follow Father Coughlin all the way. He drew back from the brink of reactionary involvement before Pearl Harbor.

In their arguments my father attacks the power and corruption of unions; Uncle Otto defends collective bargaining to the death. According to Uncle Otto the struggle against the Axis powers is a smoke screen to divert attention from all the really important domestic issues. Hitler and Hirohito are pansies to be fought with one hand while the rest of our massive strength is to be directed toward an immediate confrontation with the National Association of Manufacturers.

Political debate is a game to my father. He has been effectively emasculated by his relatively full employment and the status of his white collar. He does not feel with the power of his whole being like Uncle Otto the real consequences of any political or economic policy. He has never been on strike or relief; he has never cringed in anguish and fear before an arbitrary boss.

His detachment has made him more nimble, more flexible. He wins most of the points in their arguments, but he never wins the argument. His intelligence is quicker and he has read more widely than Uncle Otto, but he loses every debate because he always capitulates, acquiesces, to the moral and emotional force of Uncle Otto's proletarian earnestness.

Aunt Esther enters the kitchen and greets us individually with her best sales smile. She cups her hands under my chin and tilts my head upward. Then she turns abruptly to her dinner preparations. My mother volunteers to assist her and we are chased out of the kitchen. My father enters and is quickly ushered by Uncle Otto to his work bench in the basement.

We are all somehow diminished in Aunt Esther's presence. We

have been intimidated by her energy and strength. She has the largest of the large noses which are characteristic of my family. We grow older each year in continual apprehension that maturity will prove we are indeed the children of our parents. Hank is already beginning to look like a loser.

After her late marriage and the children, Aunt Esther grew restless especially during those times Uncle Otto was on strike. She never shared his absolute faith in collective bargaining and the duties of a housewife did not fill the void left when she relinquished her professional responsibilities as a legal stenographer.

She began selling greeting cards shortly after Roberta's birth and the business has grown steadily over the years. Her technique, of which she is justifiably proud, is to establish a "plant," one of the girls in an office of twenty or more workers, whom she will supply with free cards. The duties of the "plant" are to circulate the sample boxes of cards and then to take the orders which Aunt Esther quickly fills. Low prices, personalized service, and the uncanny ability to pick the right girl as a "plant" have been Aunt Esther's secrets of success. As a consequence of hard work and her system, she controls the sale of greeting cards to the office staffs of perhaps thirty large companies throughout the city. She has recently diversified into cosmetics and has already developed a considerable clientele, many of whom call her at home to place orders.

Aunt Esther was one of the last to have her hair bobbed when that was the style. It is years now since bobbed hair went out, but she persists, has made it her own—the unforgettable signature of her personality—and it along with a calculated formula of colorless clothes and hats gives her the appearance of dignified shabbiness so necessary in her kind of sales work. The girls who buy from her feel they are helping someone worthy of their patronage.

She has been remarkably successful. It is rumored that she makes more than Uncle Otto. My mother is quietly envious of her success especially since her recent purchases of wall to wall carpeting, new living room furniture, and a spinet piano. The piano is especially galling to my mother who has considerable musical talent but only the dilapidated piano of her childhood upon which to perform. Neither Roberta nor Marlys plays despite the several years of intensive lessons which Aunt Esther has lavished upon them. In hopes of getting full value for her purchase, she encourages my mother to play whenever we visit, but my mother often refuses to go close to it, protesting that she just doesn't feel like playing. Aunt Esther never pushes or nags. She does not understand the artistic temperament. She believes that all artistic achievement results from inspiration. She respects the unpredictable vicissitudes of feeling in my mother because she knows she will get her money's worth in the long run.

Aunt Esther has her own form of inspiration. She is intensely religious. Each morning after she has disposed of the children either to school or into the hands of a responsible neighbor or baby sitter, she attends mass. For the rest of the day she trudges about town on foot or via street car selling her wares, believing each moment of her waking hours that true faith will be rewarded with material success. But she is not a fool; she knows that God helps those who help themselves. The profits over the years have vindicated her faith, although my mother spitefully murmurs that child abandonment is too high a price to pay for economic security.

III

Now we are summoned to dinner. Aunt Esther stands beaming at the head of the table directing each of us to our assigned places. We stand obediently behind our chairs waiting for Uncle Otto and my father, whose footsteps we hear on the basement stairway. As the basement door opens, their voices burst forth in good-natured argument.

When they have assumed their places, we all clasp hands in a circle of unity and Uncle Otto says grace. I have been placed between Roberta and Marlys. My father sits at the foot of the table; across from me sit my mother and Hank. Aunt Esther and Uncle Otto sit tandem on the piano bench at the head of the table.

Donald has been fed in the kitchen and has been banished to the living room where he plays strange games no one seems to understand. Donald's manners are bad enough, but the main reason he has been fed early is that his toilet habits are unpredictable. Aunt Esther, believing that to presume a desired effect will produce it, has obstinately refused to put rubber pants on him. He cannot be trusted at a table with guests.

As Uncle Otto stands to carve the roast, Aunt Esther returns to the kitchen and in a flurry of trips completes the conveyance of food, still steaming, to the table. The dinner is always the same; we are having green gelatine with grated raw carrots imbedded in thickened suspension and topped with mayonnaise. Only my mother and Aunt Esther will eat this salad. The quality of the pot roast is beyond her control; it is a war cut from a canner cow—tough and stringy. Aunt Esther has overcooked it to make it palatable. It has been roasted hard; the meat has shriveled away from the bones which have been bleached white (with blackened marrow ribs) by the heat. The potatoes have been peeled and cooked whole and the carrots have been partially boiled, then put in with the meat to brown. They are not thoroughly cooked, however, and they skitter unpredictably across my plate when I try to slice them with my fork. Crowning the meal is that thick, pasty pan gravy that Uncle Otto pours indiscriminately over his entire plate.

Everyone is hungry. There is little talk the first half of the meal—only the sounds of eating. Uncle Otto eats at a furious pace, his mouth not three inches from the plate. He holds his fork as if it were a hammer and occasionally loads food on his knife and stabs it into his mouth. My mother catches my eye and directs me toward Uncle Otto. "Don't shovel," she says with her eyes. She considers all of my failures as reflections upon her. After ten minutes we begin to slow down as though to catch our breath. The rate of our eating diminishes. Uncle Otto cuts some more roast and we pause to pass our plates. Aunt Esther begins her casual table talk.

We rarely talk about any of our uncles or their families. All recent information has already been exchanged. Aunt Esther tries to direct the conversation along lines of personal interest, away from public issues or controversies. She knows that my father and Uncle Otto will argue about anything just for the sake of arguing.

When she turns to Hank, I know before she opens her mouth that we are going to consider again the various aspects of the joint theatrical project of Christian Brothers' High School and St. Joseph's Academy entitled "The Lady of the Veranda."

"Now what was it again that you did in the opera, Hank?" she asks.

"It was an operetta," he corrects her. "I was the stage manager."

"Weren't there quite a few youngsters that we know in the production? I thought I recognized some names on the program, but I couldn't tell who was who with the wigs and costumes."

"Well, I think you know Fritz Ehrling and Buddy Scheffer. They're from the West Side. Then Rita Mertz and Joanne Carstairs." He blushes when he mentions the girls' names.

"Is that the Carstairs family that lost their son at Guadalcanal?" Aunt Esther asks.

"He was Joanne's older brother, a Marine. She says he was reported missing in action. They still think he might be alive," Hank says.

"I heard he was killed in action," my father says bluntly between bites. Hank flushes.

"I only know what Joanne told us. She says he was reported missing in action. She said the telegram said *missing in action*."

"That's probably what they told her," my father says. "But I know the boy's father and what *he* said. Bob Carstairs was killed in action." My father fights a piece of meat.

"Well, whether he was killed or is missing, it's tragic. I feel with all my heart for that poor mother," Aunt Esther says.

"He could be missing," Hank argues, angry that he has been repudiated by a more reliable source of truth. He is ashamed that he may have accepted uncritically a story of romantic wistfulness. My father rises to Hank's pitiful challenge.

"Awful goddamn small island to get lost on. You can almost throw a stone across it."

"I mean, they could have got dog tags mixed. He might still be alive. Somebody else might have been killed and they thought it was him."

"And I suppose he got hit on the head and has amnesia or thinks he is somebody else and that's why he hasn't written for close to a year now."

"Leave the boy alone," Uncle Otto says. "He might be missing in action. You don't know for sure."

"Well, if he is missing, then it's because they can't find all the pieces," my father replies brutally.

"Rudy. For heaven's sake. We're eating dinner," my mother cries. "If you must wrangle, go down the basement."

But my father is angry.

"I'm just getting sick and tired of him contradicting me every time I say something. This is just one of a dozen times in the last week. If he wants to enter adult conversations, then he'd better start thinking like an adult and not like some moonstruck fool."

"He was just telling us what this girl told him," Uncle Otto says.

There is a silence. My father does not answer. He begins to eat again. Hank picks at his food to cover his humiliation.

The serving bowls are passed around for seconds. When Marlys takes more potatoes, Aunt Esther says,

"Marlys, eat everything on your plate. You haven't touched your meat."

"I can't chew it, Ma. It's too tough."

"Either eat your meat or there will be no more potatoes," Uncle Otto says with sudden anger. Marlys reluctantly begins to stuff her mouth with the meat. Her jaw moves up and down, exaggerating the difficulty of chewing. Aunt Esther resumes the discussion of Hank's operetta.

"It certainly seems a shame that with all the work you put in on the play that you could only have four performances."

"Somebody suggested that we put it on for another weekend and it was almost set. Some parents agreed to guarantee the expenses, but Brother Anthony put the kibosh on the whole thing. He wanted to know if the parents were going to guarantee our homework done on time, too."

"What's a kibosh?" Roberta asks, but before Hank can answer, Marlys chokes and gags. Her mouth opens wide and she rushes her head over her plate and delivers a round, symmetrical ball of chewed meat and potatoes. She smiles sheepishly and brushes the tears from her watering eyes.

"Marlys, if you are not hungry, you may leave the table now," Aunt Esther says. Marlys gets up from the table without a murmur and shoves her chair in, then turns on her heels for the living room. She does not seem unhappy that she is being disciplined. As she leaves, my mother looks at me again and throws me a glance which says, 'There, but for the grace of God and my vigilance go you.'

"What exactly are the duties of the stage manager?" Aunt Esther asks, knowing that continuity is the only way out of her embarrassment.

"Well, actually the stage manager is the most important single person in any production. Once the show is ready for the stage, the director turns everything over to the stage manager who is the absolute boss. He is responsible for every prop, every cue, every scene change, every actor being at the right place at the right time . . . " Hank exults in his importance, in the knowledge that everyone on the production looked to him as the real star, the unsung hero of "The Lady of the Veranda."

"Besides that I sang in the chorus and helped design the set," he continues eager to seize this opportunity.

We hear a scream from the living room. Marlys races around the corner. She holds her nose delicately as if she is politely drinking a cup of tea.

"Pew, pew. He's done it again, Ma," she tattles. Aunt Esther tightens her lips, pressing her face into a frozen smile. "He's gone to the bathroom in his pants again."

Roberta jumps from the table, dashes into the living room at her sister's heels. She spells loudly and emphatically,

"P.U. P.U. It's Number Two."

They return to the dining room. Roberta's voice is full of disgust. She begs Uncle Otto.

Uncle Otto sits bent in suspended fury. He swallows the food he has been chewing. Then he thrusts the bench back from the table.

"Goddamn that kid. Goddamn him. Goddamn him." Spittle sprays across his lips and his eyes bug wildly.

We sit stunned by his violence. Aunt Esther prays aloud in bold supplication to cover his blasphemy (or is it to protect herself from the backwash of his damnation?)

"God's name be praised in our house. God's name be honored in our house. God's name be praised in our house."

With each incantation she makes the sign of the cross. She smiles her set smile and continues to eat as though nothing has happened, or rather she continues to chase the remnants, the minute fragments of food, across her plate, catching them and pressing them in the crevices of her fork.

Uncle Otto wraps Donald in a newspaper and carries him upstairs to the bathroom. Roberta sits down again at the table. Her face is ugly with anger. She blurts,

"He does it on purpose. He saves up all day so he can make everybody *sick* at dinner."

"That's enough, Roberta. We'll talk about something else." Aunt Esther smiles her tight smile. She addresses my brother again.

"How did you make the stage so misty for the last scene when the mysterious lady leads Sir Michael to the lost family treasure? It was a really fine effect."

"We dropped this big curtain made out of something like cheese cloth from the deepest batten on the stage. It's called a scrim. Then we set the lights up at different angles. The Lady of the Veranda danced slowly across the stage behind the scrim." He pauses. "That created the effect of mist and shadows that everyone admired so much."

Roberta is too humiliated to be still. She interrupts, turning to us in pleading explanation.

"He did it at school all the time because the little snot didn't want to go."

My brother is annoyed.

"We set the lights at about thirty different combinations and angles before we got just what we wanted."

"Then Sister sent a messenger to my room and I had to take him to the girls' bathroom and clean him up and then take him home," Roberta continues. Aunt Esther's smile disappears. She glares at Roberta who seems to wither before our eyes. But she persists in her explanation, weakly.

"He can't go to *any* school. Even the public school expelled him and the nuns won't take him back."

Roberta's voice breaks and trails off. She jumps from the table and runs wailing up the stairs to her bedroom.

We hear the stinging slap of leather on flesh and Donald's howls. After several licks my father stirs in his chair and then pushes himself away from the table. He goes into the living room and yells up the stairwell.

"Otto. Otto. Do you want coffee with your dessert?"

The thrashing stops. We hear Uncle Otto's footsteps. My father shouts again,

"Otto, do you want coffee with your dessert?" Donald's simpering moan trails down the stairs.

Suddenly Aunt Esther bolts upright, her mouth sagging in alarm.

"Oh, has he hurt my boy? Has he hurt my little Donnie?" She runs from the room past my father and calls ahead of her as she stumbles up the stairs.

We sit silently for a few moments. Then Hank says,

"Now that all the dirty work is done, she can be the loving mother again."

My mother nudges him to be quiet. She stands up and begins clearing plates.

"Well, Marlys honey, would you like to help Auntie Bea serve desserts?"

Marlys follows my mother into the kitchen. Uncle Otto, his forehead covered with sweat, returns and sits as my mother and Marlys serve the desserts and coffee.

Now all is predictable, automatic. My mother has a headache and goes into the living room to lie down on the sofa. Uncle Otto disappears upstairs for his nap and my father draws a chair close to the radio where he will sit all afternoon through the concert and the Catholic Hour.

Aunt Esther returns once Donald is securely asleep and begins the preparations for tomorrow's calls. Roberta, Marlys, and I finish clearing the table and begin the dishes in the kitchen after which Aunt Esther will give us enough money to go to the movie and have a treat.

Hank is going to the third reunion of the cast of "The Lady of the Veranda" to be held at the home of the soprano lead over on the East Side. He borrows carfare from my father and hurries to the car stop three blocks away lest he be late and fail to share those poignant moments of recall which a resinging of the entire score is certain to evoke.

When we go into the dining room to collect from Aunt Esther, she requires a last chore before she will let us go. I must carry a stack of card boxes from the small bedroom off the dining room (which she has converted into a storeroom) to the dining room table. She makes several groupings of the boxes in a spatial arrangement which corresponds to the order of her Monday deliveries. When we receive the money, Aunt Esther puts me in charge and adds a bonus of a quarter to our total which we in turn squabble about all the way to the theater.

Now we eagerly seek the refuge of the darkness which we know will dispel the clarity of the winter's sun and where we can hide our glaring shame. We abandon ourselves in this plot of others' joys and woes with the certain knowledge that we shall be delivered from all impending calamities, from every haunting doom.

It is the story of a beautiful night club singer who has a depression trauma: she wishes to marry for money rather than love. Her mother made the foolish mistake of marrying for love and both her parents worked themselves to death supporting the products of their love.

Two men are in love with her. One, the worthy lover, happens to be a fine dancer and this talent along with the heroine's production numbers adds variety to the progression of the plot. The other lover is the hat check boy, unworthy of her love by talent, looks, and station in life. The hat check boy is in turn loved by the cigarette girl who deadpans her way through the entire movie.

The plot thickens when the hat check boy wins the Irish Sweepstakes and suddenly becomes wealthy. But he does not wear his new affluence well. He makes an ass of himself and we are asked to believe that because he did not "earn" his wealth, he does not know how to spend it.

He sets out to court the lovely singer who now realizes that she is caught in a conflict of heart and head. Her heart yearns for the dancer who has gone off somewhere with his pride. Her head dictates that marriage to the newly rich hat check boy will end her depression trauma forever.

But the heart wins out over the head. The hat check boy realizes that money cannot buy love unless you are worthy of it to start with. He finally accepts the cigarette girl who has chased him without respite throughout the movie.

Honesty is rewarded; perseverance is rewarded. The dancer marries the singer; the hat check boy marries the cigarette girl and then the two young husbands sing and dance themselves to a recruiting office and are last seen marching in uniform out the other side into a hastily staged sunset. They are joined by the girls in a grand finale of patriotic songs and although I get the message (am convinced even of its truth) I wonder why two single thirty year old men haven't been in the service all the time.

IV

And now the sureness (and accuracy) of my vision falters.

It is growing dark as we leave the theater. Street lights have been turned on. The descending shadows seem to soften the cold hardness of the winter's glare. There is no wind; a stillness has settled on the streets. As we make our way along the icy paths and streets, I feel a gradual release from the bondage of my shame.

Perhaps it is not the darkness alone which has mitigated the cold, yellow objectivity of a Sunday afternoon. Because we cannot long sustain the clarity of a loveless gaze, we seek to transfigure the squalor of our lives as if we had always believed in the mythic, Perfect Circles of our better selves, or as if we had never doubted the final triumph of the Ideal over the Real.

From the entry, where we are hanging up our coats, we can hear the drone of voices. Although we have missed the Catholic Hour, we have arrived in time for the Rosary broadcast from a local station. In the living room Aunt Esther kneels before the radio. Uncle Otto is behind her and my mother half sits, half kneels on the edge of an easy chair. We reluctantly join in the antiphonal prayers for peace. We squat behind my father who kneels at the far side of the room from Aunt Esther. My lips mumble the words without conviction, but when I look at Aunt Esther, I see her head thrust in forthright challenge and I am impressed. It seems as though she is looking God squarely in the eye. She answers the voice of the priest loudly in precise, clearly articulated phrases. I decide that if she does not have a faith to move mountains, she has incredible gall, either quality to be greatly admired. We are in the fourth joyful mystery.

The prayers are over, the radio turned to an obscure local station where Uncle Otto has discovered yet another transcribed repeat of a complete episode of "The Lone Ranger," which will come on in fifteen minutes. Uncle Otto and Donald have already settled in chairs close to the radio. Aunt Esther and my mother, who is now fully recovered from her headache, go into the kitchen and begin removing the platters of food, which Aunt Esther has already prepared, from the refrigerator. She has sliced the pot roast and added lunch meats and cheese. There is a bowl of potato salad and the several gelatine salads, now cleansed of mayonnaise. My mother carries an armful of bottles—olives, pickles, mustard, ketchup, mayonnaise—from the refrigerator. Then she begins to whip the cream for the desserts. It is all arranged smorgasbord style. When Aunt Esther carries the pitcher of nectar to the table, we realize with delight that we are having a summertime picnic in the middle of winter.

My brother arrives from his afternoon of happy recapitulation of the finer moments of "The Lady of the Veranda." He is still flushed with excitement and sings as he hangs up his storm coat. The song, from the third act, reflects the radically masculine posture of the male chorus in opposition to the radically feminine female chorus. The occasion of plot which justifies this explosion of emotion is an argument between the hero and the heroine over the probable and preferable sex of their children if and when they marry. The blocking of this scene was his masterstroke as stage manager. All the boys were to one side of the stage and all the girls to the other; they faced each other in physical and symbolic confrontation.

Hank acknowledges our presence with dignified condescension, then he crosses the kitchen to the table of food. He rubs his hands in eager anticipation (as well as in imitation of the manner of the villain of "The Lady of the Veranda"). He surveys the food carefully and proclaims loudly,

"Ah, thrift, thrift, Horatio. The funeral meats are set forth coldly at the wedding feast."

He quickly steals a slice of cold beef before my mother can stop him. Roberta, who has been watching him in admiration and bewilderment, says,

"What is *that* supposed to mean?"

"It is a line from Shakespeare, from *Hamlet* to be specific, which I have rather cleverly applied, extemporaneously, to our picnic supper." Hank is in a rare mood.

"Well, what does it mean?" she says.

He raises his hand to signal her attention.

"Object lesson to illustrate." He picks up one of the green gelatine salads and a knife from the table. "First, your mother, my dearest Auntie," he bows toward Aunt Esther and clicks his heels together, "slicks the mayonnaise onto the left-over potatoes." He pretends to flick the blade across the top of the shivering mass. Then he snaps his wrist directing the imaginary mayonnaise into an imaginary bowl.

"Next, we smother the naked salad with whipped cream."

Hank goes over to the table and ladles three heaping tablespoons from the bowl which my mother has placed behind the nectar pitcher. He selects a spoon and holds the plate before him and raises his eyes toward heaven as though he is making an offering to appease the angry gods. Then he presents it for our inspection.

"Lo, the bitter salad of despair hath become the sweet dessert of hope and nothing hath been wasted." He adds a dramatic aside behind his hand and out of the corner of his mouth so Aunt Esther won't hear. "The mayonnaise hath already found its way into the potato salad."

Hank spoons a mouthful. Some whipped cream catches on the tip of his nose. He stretches his tongue and licks it off, a talent of such prodigious dexterity that I am awed and envious each time he does it. Roberta giggles and my mother pretends to scold him for making off with a dessert and an excessive amount of whipped cream. He swaggers slowly into the dining room, eating as he goes. He turns in final commentary on his explanation.

"It's like transubstantiation," he says obscurely to Roberta who has no idea what he is talking about.

We pile our paper plates high and with our silverware and glasses of nectar carefully make our way through the dining room to the card table which Uncle Otto has set up just inside the archway in the living room. Roberta places her food on the table and goes to get a deck of cards. It is our unspoken custom that we will play cards as we eat. We do not mention the game because we always argue about its proper name. My cousins call it Rap Rummy and I call it Thirty-One.

Aunt Esther approaches and from a coin purse withdraws fifteen cents for each of us and places the coins in neat piles on the table. She leaves three nickels in the fourth position for Hank who she knows will join us in his good time. He will eat alone and then kibitz at my father and Aunt Esther's game for a while, but he has not yet been invited to play with them so he will reluctantly demean himself by joining us.

My father sits at the end of the dining room table eating and warming up a deck of cards for his game with Aunt Esther. They will play Sixty-Six, a strange hybrid of Euchre and Pinochle. Uncle Otto and Donald sit by the radio eating from plates balanced unevenly on their laps. The women are the last to eat. Aunt Esther takes her plate to the dining room table. As she sits, she vows to give her baby brother a lesson at cards as evidence that she is still the boss around here. We laugh when she calls my father a 'baby brother.' My mother takes her plate into the living room, places it on a side table and then sits at the piano and begins running scales, quietly so as not to disturb anyone, to loosen her fingers.

We begin our game. In our first two hands I rap quickly and catch Marlys without even a matched pair. Hank joins the game, but as a concession to Marlys' losses he must place a nickel in the kitty before we will deal him in.

My mother now bursts into song. She plays a rhythmic virtuosity piece, "Kitten on the Keys" to warm us up and we hear the thunderous chords of her rendition of "Bye, Bye Blues." She plays the first several notes slowly with majestic pomp and emphatic repetition. It is a false start, though, for she suddenly changes tempo and rushes through the song in happy release from the despair to which the lyrics bid a fond farewell.

We can tell from the 'card German,' the only foreign language spoken in my family, that my father is defeating Aunt Esther in their first game. She has called upon the Lord in heaven to assist her, and she has damned the Jews, the universal scapegoats, all to no avail, but she smiles despite her bad luck. As my father deals a new hand, she leans across to our table and says to Roberta,

"Ask Auntie Bea to play 'The World is Waiting for the Sunrise.'"

It is her favorite song. Perhaps she thinks it may have some influence on the cards. Roberta excuses herself from our game and walks across the room to my mother's side. As my mother continues to play, Roberta whispers in her ear, and my mother nods her head, but I know she will not honor Aunt Esther's request for at least another song or two.

After "Alice Blue Gown" and "Beyond the Blue Horizon," (we are in the 'blue' period of my mother's musical development) we are bathed in the idealism and hope of a new dawning. My mother embellishes the piece with occasional runs and rhythmic improvisations. Aunt Esther says, shaking her head in admiration,

"She plays that song with *such* feeling."

When my mother is done playing, she takes up her plate and silver and begins to eat. Her timing is perfect, for as the last notes of the piano are fading, the trumpets on the radio proclaim our return to the days of yesteryear. Uncle Otto turns the volume up. He puts his glasses on, an odd habit apparently intended to assist his hearing or to keep his imagination in proper focus, and then he leans closely to the radio.

As we continue our card game, I listen out of the corner of my mind to the unfolding plot. The Lone Ranger and Tonto are camped outside of Canyon City in a secluded clump of trees. Tonto is out rustling up wood when the Lone Ranger, busily administering to Silver's needs, is surprised from behind and told to raise his hands. He discovers that the rifle aimed between his shoulder blades is wielded by a boy of fourteen years, who mistakenly has concluded that the Lone Ranger is one of the outlaws who has been harassing his family in a thinly veiled attempt to make his widowed mother sell her homestead quarter.

At this point in the dialogue young Jeff is surprised from behind by Tonto who disarms the youth and holds him awaiting orders from the Lone Ranger. In his understanding and great compassion, the Lone Ranger orders Tonto to release the boy, who overwhelmed by this unexpected mercy and already convinced of the essential goodness of the marked stranger, unburdens his difficulties to the two attentive listeners.

They ride together to the boy's home where the Lone Ranger, with that marvelously resonating baritone, quickly wins the confidence of the boy's mother and his sister. The rest of the exposition is completed. It seems there is a range war in the Canyon City area. Jeff's father was killed fighting for his right to be a free yeoman farmer in fulfillment of the dreams of Thomas Jefferson, after whom his son is named. The villain appears to be a certain cattle baron, Rancher Gillis, who has hired outside gunslingers to do his harassment while he poses as the sympathetic neighbor willing to pay a fair price for the land.

Then the Lone Ranger sends Tonto to town to buy supplies as a pretext to eavesdropping. Tonto overhears the villains and reports back to the Lone Ranger.

"Me hear Rancher Gillis talk to tough hombres," Tonto says. "Him say him buy mortgage from bank. One missed payment and him foreclose."

Their suspicions are confirmed.

And then the Lone Ranger in that deep, re-assuring voice says, "Listen to me, Tonto. I have a plan." His voice trails off into a crescendo of music. We return to the present.

During the commercial my father on the verge of another triumph shouts across the room. "Hey, Otto. I hear the Lone Ranger shot Tonto last week." He plays a card following Aunt Esther's lead.

Uncle Otto turns the volume down and takes off his glasses. He stares at my father. "What are you talking about now, Republican?"

"It's true, it's true. He shot him right between the eyes with one of those silver bullets." He points his forefinger between his eyes and flicks his thumb hammerlike, then lands with a trump on one of Aunt Esther's aces.

"I heard about it just the other day," he laughs. "After all these years the Lone Ranger finally discovered that 'Kimosabe' actually means sonovabitch."

He breaks into his stuttering donkey laughter as he completes Aunt Esther's downfall. My mother admonishes him to guard his language before the children.

"Aw, Pa, that joke's as old as the hills," Hank complains.

Uncle Otto returns to the radio with an unsympathetic "humph" which reflects his utter contempt for my father's sense of humor. But Hank, catching my father's spirit, points his thumb toward Donald, bent with his father in profound involvement, and announces our reconciliation.

"Anyone who listens to "The Lone Ranger" can't be *all* bad," he says and even Roberta smiles a partial forgiveness.

"Why do they call him the *Lone* Ranger?" Roberta asks. "Tonto is always with him and he has a nephew, too."

"Indians, even good ones, are not counted as people in American history," Hank says cynically, "and Dan has been tossed in as a sop to the moronic twelve year olds who listen to the stupid program."

Uncle Otto does not appear to hear him.

"Notice that he is the *Lone* Ranger, not the *lonely* Ranger," my father says. "My guess is they call him *Lone* to emphasize that he is unmarried, free of burdens and responsibilities."

Roberta does not seem satisfied with either answer.

We move quickly now toward resolution. The Lone Ranger's plan works perfectly. The Rancher Gillis falls for the ruse and discovers himself trapped. In fact, the plan works so well that the Rancher Gillis unwittingly reveals himself as the greedy villain. When all seems lost, he resorts to his gun which is instantly shot out of his hand by the Lone Ranger. The hired gunslingers prove to be cowards, and the Sheriff, who has been too weak to confront the wealth and power of Rancher Gillis in the past, is now able to jail the whole gang until the circuit judge arrives to conduct a fair trial.

That would be enough, but there is one final scene. The widow, her children, the good townsfolk, and the Sheriff assemble to thank the Lone Ranger and his faithful Indian companion. Someone, however, is still confused. A voice asks,

"And who is the masked stranger?"

The Sheriff answers (with a touch of impatience and disbelief in his voice),

"Why, *that* was the *L-o-o-one* Ranger."

We hear the Lone Ranger's final distant urging to the great horse, Silver. As his voice fades once again into the past, a shiver goes down my spine and I am swept along by this scene of recognition and farewell. It seems as though, through the power of this fiction, we have all been somehow wondrously translated into a remote allegorical drama. As I look about me I see my father, Good Humor, braying laughter and my mother, Fine Arts, returning to the piano. There is Aunt Esther, Ambition and Industry, waiting patiently for the ever renewing possibilities of a new shuffle, cut and deal, and Uncle Otto, Common Man himself, leaning over Radio listening to the Good News of Eternal Justice.

And I, now helpless to resist, am moved to believe (if only for the moment) that Truth and Beauty and Peace and Love (Ah, Love) reign upon the face of the earth.

A CLIFF OF FALL

"Oh, the mind, mind has mountains; cliffs of fall
Frightful, sheer no-man-fathomed."

Hopkins

Father Schauf was up and dressed and ready for mass before six o'clock. He had moved a chair away from the dresser into the hallway to be closer to the heat from the stove. Using the edge of the light from his room as it splashed over into the hall, he read aloud in Latin from his breviary articulating each word and stopping occasionally to listen to the quality of a pronunciation as it resonated for a moment after he had stopped speaking. He was usually pleased with what he heard.

He looked from his breviary down the hall to the flames that flickered behind the isinglassed door. The stove had been left in the hallway near the head of the stairs and the doors of the other bedrooms had been closed off when the first priest had moved into what was then a farmhouse. It had been his impractical speculation (and one of his most enduring legacies) that the heat would be channeled into the open bedroom, thus leaving more room in the bedroom and spreading the heat over a larger serviceable area. It seemed to reach the door and hang vaguely and indecisively upon the threshold. It rarely entered. In colder weather Father Schauf undressed in the hallway and danced across the icy linoleum rug to his bed. Whenever he wished to read, he moved a chair into the hall or crawled into bed.

He marked his place in the breviary with a ribbon, closed the book, and leaned forward out of the chair to return to the bedroom. As he entered the room, he felt the wall of chilled air. He placed the breviary on the dresser top along with the other dozen or so books and pamphlets, each carefully marked for future reference and each deferred to some later time for closer examination.

Father Schauf had finally reconciled himself to the coldness of the room. He had inherited it along with a score of other miscalculations from the priests who had preceded him at St. Joseph's. In the enthusiasm of his first months he was going to have the parish house remodeled and the church redecorated, but his ardor cooled as other more pressing matters took precedence until he finally decided to defer the remodeling because he just didn't have enough money. He simply accepted the inconveniences as part of the tradition of the parish, the temporal signs, the heritage of the spiritual struggles of one of his predecessors with the "facts" of the human condition.

Now it was time for the morning unveiling. He went to the window, opened the curtain, and raised the shade. He stooped and rested himself, suspended his body on stiffened arms and the balls of his hands pressed against the sash. In the blear light of early morning, he could see the low rain clouds. The gray and black patched farmland stretched to the horizon. Occasionally, an island of trees, a windbreak of uniformly spaced cottonwoods and ash protecting a house or barnyard, interrupted the endless flow of land. In the distance a cattle truck moved slowly, marking (tracing as it moved) one of the plane dimensions of an ordered, static, Euclidian universe.

The land and weather permitted no excesses. Season moved into season gradually. Within a week of winter, fall was forgotten; within a week of summer, spring was forgotten. True, the land grew green in summer but only briefly. The black and brown and gray fields were covered with growing verdure by June, but by the end of July at the height of summer, the oat and wheat beards mounting above the green stems had already begun to return the earth to its natural color. Then the oats, flax, and barley were harvested and fields were already being plowed again. By Labor Day the corn fields were dominated by the brown tassels and the leaves were fading into pale yellow. There was no time for nature to experiment in brilliance. The earth did not flame out with violent oranges and reds.

Father Schauf felt that his parishioners had been formed by a corollary of that law that had cast the land into its bland and homogeneous mold. His flock, centered at Amburg but with two mission congregations at Ravinia and Salemn, was uniformly flat and gray like the land. There were no extremes. There seemed to be a singular incapacity among his people for great virtue or great evil. Only the trivial, the slight offenses (even the serious sins were relatively unimportant except, of course, in the eyes of a perfect God) managed to accumulate, to gather gradually but slowly into a force of moral attrition.

It was this undifferentiated venial world that was his enemy. Experience had taught him that his greatest struggle was to keep his sense of proportion, not to lose his powers of discrimination. The great temptation was to reduce everything, to see everything in his boredom as trivial and trite. (The confessional alone had taught him the overwhelming logic of Purgatory).

He looked across the room with pain and gnawing anxiety at the galley proofs of the diocesan newspaper hanging over the back of his bedside chair. They were to be returned by noon to the printer seventy miles away. He still had three of the long sheets to read and correct by ten o'clock if he hoped to make it on time. He sat, turned the shade of the wall lamp to direct the light to his lap, and took up his reading where he had left off at midnight the night before. There was still a half hour before he would have to leave for church.

Although he had expected some kind of diocesan "intellectual" responsibility to supplement his parish duties when he was first transferred to St. Joseph's, his appointment as proofreader came ironically. His assignment to the post of assistant copy editor by the Bishop had a twist to it that reflected Father Schauf's failure from the very beginning.

It happened soon after he arrived and because he had made a fool of himself. He had been invited to the Bishop's for dinner as was the Bishop's custom with priests newly appointed to his diocese. He had heard little about the Bishop. He knew that he was called the "Owl" by some of the younger priests in the diocese. Father Schauf had not yet discovered whether or not it was a term of approbation. He had also learned that the Bishop was somewhat pompous and formal (because his predecessor had been most informal) and that he had an incredible reputation for fund raising.

Father Schauf arrived at the Bishop's residence punctually at six o'clock. He had, in fact, arrived fifteen minutes earlier, but he drove around the neighborhood and then into the commercial center of the city and back again before he parked.

He was admitted by the housekeeper and sent to the library where he found another priest, a Father Cullen, mixing a drink from a portable bar. Father Cullen was attached to the Bishop's residence. He was in charge of the Newman Club at the State University and taught English and religion at Sullivan High School. The two priests introduced themselves and shook hands.

"Have a drink, Father," Father Cullen said as he introduced the bar with a toss of his hand. "If you don't mind, I have to finish reading an assignment for class tomorrow."

"I have to admit I am happy to see somebody else," Father Schauf laughed nervously. "I've never been here before."

Father Cullen nodded, crossed the room to the sofa, and resumed reading a book he had apparently put down prior to Father Schauf's arrival. Father Schauf sipped his drink and then asked:

"What's he like?"

"Who? The Owl? Oh! He's O.K. He won't bite you," Father Cullen said. "Drink up! Don't worry, he's not as bad as everyone says," he added with a smile and returned to his book.

"Thanks a lot," Father Schauf laughed and drank his highball quickly and mixed another. He walked about the room, casually examining the contents of the library. He looked across the room occasionally at his fellow priest. Father Cullen wore his reddish blond hair in a crew cut style. His body was thick, muscular, and his face was beginning to accumulate the flesh of his thirty to thirty-five years of maturity. An athlete going soft, Father Schauf decided. It took another drink and two tours of the room before Father Schauf ventured to interrupt the uncommunicative Father Cullen.

"If you don't mind my asking, where is our host?"

"Probably fund raising," Father Cullen answered flatly, without irony and without looking up from his reading. Then he cocked his head toward the doorway. There were footsteps on the carpet.

"Speaking of the _____," Father Cullen said, closed his book, and stood up as the Bishop hurried into the library. The Bishop smiled an insipid greeting as Father Schauf knelt to kiss his ring.

The Bishop's face was round and plump. He wore rimless glasses, the kind Father Schauf had always associated in his mind with bankers and accountants. Most of his hair was gone on top except for a faint remnant, a wisp of hair that stuck up intensifying his hurried manner. The Bishop poured a glass of sherry and said,

"I hope you don't mind that I have neglected you so notoriously, Father Schauf, but I have been gone and since you are a Midwesterner, I didn't think you'd have any trouble. It's the Bostonians I worry about. I get one every so often." He paused and smiled faintly. "They think this is mission country like Africa or China. No one understands them with their 'idear' and heah' and feah'. The parishioners think their priest speaks Latin as a native tongue for a month or so, and our Boston priests think the faithful out here are all Indians—genuine, unadulterated aborigines."

The Bishop walked to the window and back as he talked. Father Schauf smiled ambiguously. He decided the Owl wasn't so bad after all. He seemed to have a sense of humor.

There were several priests from Boston currently in the diocese. Father Schauf had met one, Father Donohoe at St. James in Covington. To Father Schauf's ear Father Donohoe spoke like the Brooklynese he had heard in the "Bowery Boys" movies of his childhood, but he judiciously refrained from commenting and let the Bishop ramble, uninterrupted, until a dinner bell chimed.

When they entered the dining room, Father Schauf noticed its conspicuous elegance. The room was carpeted from wall to wall. There was a huge floor to ceiling window that overlooked a flower garden, now only rows of stubble cluttered with dead leaves. From the ceiling hung a sparkling chandelier showering its light on a long mahogany dinner table set with expensive linen and china. He did not know the meal was to be so formal. Although Father Cullen seemed to accept everything as normal, Father Schauf could not avoid a growing apprehension. He was impressed but he withheld his opinion for fear he would seem a gusher or a false flatterer. The Bishop continued his talk, his light meaningless banter. Father Schauf decided the Bishop was a paradox: a rare combination of conversational superficiality and rigid formality of manner.

After the grace the Bishop pressed a button on the floor with his foot which signaled the pantry for the first course and which also prompted someone to turn on a stereophonic phonograph flooding the room with an excerpt from the "Nutcracker" suite from loudspeakers concealed somewhere in the walls or ceiling.

"You are in the musical position, Father Schauf," the Bishop said. "The multi-directional effect is maximal in your seat."

Father Schauf felt conspicuous and uncomfortable. He felt he should get up and offer his seat to the Bishop.

"Father Cullen and I are off center," he continued. "He gets mostly strings and I get the brass."

Father Schauf nodded but said nothing again. Then the housekeeper brought in a tureen of soup and bowls which the Bishop began to ladle serving Father Schauf first.

"I am modern, too," the Bishop said pointing to the ceiling with the ladle.

"Do you mean the music, Your Excellency?" Father Schauf said.

"No, I don't," the Bishop said with a frown. "I meant the stereophonic equipment. I meant the electronic aspect." The Bishop began to spoon his soup. Then it seemed, as Father Schauf recalled it all later, that the Bishop suddenly turned upon him without provocation, almost as though he had been briefed on Father Schauf and was deliberately probing a weakness.

"What do you think of the music, then? I suppose it is too old fashioned for you?" he asked.

"It is good dinner music, Your Excellency," Father Schauf answered ambiguously, trying to be accommodating.

"It is Tchaikovsky," the Bishop said testily.

"I know. The Waltz of the Flowers, I believe."

"I take it, in your judgment, that Tchaikovsky is only dinner music?" he demanded.

Father Schauf blundered an answer.

"I didn't mean to imply that. I like some of Tchaikovsky but he is notorious among music critics as superficial and sentimental. I can't speak for all his music. I'm not an expert."

But the Bishop would not let the matter drop. They continued to eat silently for a few minutes when he turned on Father Schauf again.

"I suppose you prefer Stravinsky or those noisemakers. He hesitated trying to remember. "Bartok. Prokofiev. Shostakovitch. I can't see they make anything but noise."

Now Father Schauf became defensive. Why couldn't the Bishop just drop it? He had translated the conversation into a split between generations, as a split between tradition and progress—an over-simplified dialectic of opposites that did violence to the truth and turned a simple discussion into an argument of blacks and whites.

"Actually, I find that if you listen closely and often, there is much beauty and depth in modern music. I'm eclectic, neither traditionalist nor modernist." He answered as benignly as he could. The housekeeper cleared the table and served the main course. As the Bishop began to eat, he smiled as he struck upon what he thought was an irrefutable argument.

"They were communists, weren't they?" he asked. "Prokofiev

and Shostakovich. Members of the Communist Party." Then he exploded. "Reds!"

Father Schauf answered calmly in the voice and manner of a teacher in serious discussion, not angry, but concerned with the truth. He disregarded the Bishop's baiting rhetoric.

"That is perhaps true, but I don't think that has any bearing on the music. The political opinions, the philosophy, even the disposition of a composer are not necessarily reflected in the art object." He paused for a moment and then clinched his argument. "Take Tchaikovsky, for example. He was morbidly neurotic, and it is believed a latent or actual pederast. There is also a strong suspicion that he committed suicide under salacious circumstances."

The Bishop looked confused. Father Cullen almost slid under the table from shock.

"Neurotic? Pederast? . . . "

The Bishop hesitated for several moments.

"I see," the Bishop said finally with a nod acknowledging that Father Schauf had trapped him.

He changed the subject and shifted the conversation to Father Cullen. For the rest of the meal he politely avoided Father Schauf and then dismissed both priests abruptly after dessert. The Bishop had an appointment with a professional fund raiser.

Father Schauf had won a battle but lost the war.

It wasn't until the next morning in the cold, critical light of day that Father Schauf realized fully what a fool he had been. Anxiety and a few drinks had resulted in acts of arrogance and pride. What did he care one way or the other if the Bishop liked sentimental music? He wanted to go on his knees before the Bishop and beg his forgiveness, but time and space did not allow such a dramatic mitigation of his guilt. He made a vow to cultivate humility in everything he did.

A week later Father Schauf received a short and characteristically formal letter from the Bishop. He was informed that "in order to put your dialectical skills to practical use" he was to assume, immediately, responsibilities as assistant copy editor of the diocesan newspaper. It had amounted to little more than a proofreading job, and although it had been Father Schauf's bitterest and most frustrating duty, he accepted it without complaint in the spirit of humility he had vowed to practice.

Now he sat reading the long, uncut columns, checking the set type against the thin, yellow, onionskin sheets of typed copy. It was growing lighter outside. Soon he would go downstairs and get ready to leave for the church to prepare the altar for seven o'clock mass.

As he sat proofreading, he was startled by the sudden whir of an electric motor from somewhere downstairs. He looked at his watch. It was only six thirty-five. Mrs. Johnson, his housekeeper, usually arrived at seven-thirty to prepare his breakfast and clean the house. He bolted from his chair and hurried across the room and down the hall to the stairway.

At the bottom of the stairs he turned to his right toward the noise. In his study he discovered Mrs. Johnson vacuuming. He watched her short, squat body working like a piston driving the wand into the corners. Mrs. Johnson loved her vacuum cleaner. It seemed to Father Schauf that all she did was vacuum, vacuum, vacuum. Every day without fail. It was a wonder there was any nap left on the rugs.

He cupped his hands around his mouth and shouted.

"Good morning, Mrs. Johnson."

He felt he was struggling against a great wind. She could not hear him, and he refused to shout louder, to lose his dignity before a vacuum cleaner. It suddenly struck him that, from behind, Mrs. Johnson looked like a sausage—fat, round, nondescript.

The whir of the motor drowned his voice again. His eye caught the electric cord, trailing behind her to the plug. He took a step into the room and bent to the floor with his knee, reached forward with his right hand and grasped the cord. He stood up in a single motion, pulling the plug from the socket. The motor stopped instantly, but Mrs. Johnson kept right on working, pumping the nozzle into the rug, for several seconds before she realized the power was off.

It occurred to Father Schauf that had someone been watching, his action might have appeared like a genuflection, one of those sloppy, hurried genuflections characteristic of his careless, incompetent altar boys. When she finally turned around grumbling, he assumed a casual attitude by leaning against the door, crossing his legs, and twirling the plug nonchalantly in a lazy arc.

He sensed a certain humor in the scene. He knew that she would tell everyone, by way of illustrating her industriousness and diligence, and the effect of his action would heighten his reputation for humor and wit. They would laugh and talk about him with the pride they usually reserved for their children who had gone away to college to become clever, and intelligent, and incomprehensible.

He could not help but feel that they regarded him, as a person that is, as a kind of prize bit of livestock, a genuine blue ribbon pet in which they took great paternalistic delight. He knew that, in conversations, they flung him in the teeth of their Protestant friends who could hardly retaliate with an amusing story about the slow, somber, plodding Rev. Peterson, the Lutheran minister.

There was no question about it. What little success he had was the result of the "class," the urban sophistication they attributed to him, but it made his distance from them even greater. It ruled out any intimacy between equals. The inequality was sharp and clear. The irony of it all was that he wondered who patronized whom. He often felt that they with their practical intelligence laughed at him. Certainly they took great pains to explain the mechanical workings of the parish house and church as if anything prosaic was beyond his ken.

Mrs. Johnson put her hand over her mouth and squealed.

"Father," she blurted when she recovered from her surprise, in a scolding tone as if he were a naughty child. He had difficulty pretending to be angry, restraining the self-mocking undertone of his seriousness; he had difficulty taking Mrs. Johnson seriously under any circumstances. He had inherited her along with a cold bedroom and a defunct toilet when he came to the parish. She kept the house clean and cooked breakfast and dinner. Supper he had to make for himself or eat out.

Mrs. Johnson was an uncertain fifty to sixty years of age. Father Schauf decided she did look most exactly like a sausage. The fat layers folded under her chin minimizing the separateness of her head. Her hair was streaked with gray unevenly and cut high in back in the masculine style of the Twenties. She had a permanent reddish-purple color high on her cheeks. Only her glasses—modern, sophisticated, intelligent—belied the fact that she might well have been a sausage.

Father Schauf never doubted the humanity, the essential dignity of his parishioners, but he often doubted, or rather wondered in awe, how a person like the bland and venial Mrs. Johnson had ever been sexually viable. His imagination, his charitable willingness to believe anything good about his fellow creatures was hard put to visualize Mrs. Johnson as sufficiently attractive even to a completely indiscriminate Mr. Johnson to result in six children. But six children she had and eight grandchildren. Humanity was capable of far more outlandish accomplishments than Father Schauf had ever dreamt of in his meager experience, and this he knew was his central limitation. Too much of his life had been vicarious, by word of mouth. Too much had to be guessed at through the facade of words that were rarely adequate, rarely direct. His whole life had been lived by the word not the deed and he had been isolated too long in studies.

He tried to appear stern. He looked at his watch and then held his wrist out to her, pointing to the hands.

"It is six thirty-five. You are approximately one hour early."

Mrs. Johnson shrugged. She had never paid any serious attention to him. He had suggested changes when he first arrived, but she continued the old habits after dutifully acknowledging his new orders with the ceremonial and meaningless "Yes, Father." He had made mistakes in the beginning too. He had been too jovial, too playful in his early attempts to win her over. He had wanted immediate popularity too eagerly. Once before in the first few months she had frightened him silly and to cover his embarrassment and fright he responded in comic exaggeration.

He was reading in the study one morning when she entered behind him in her silent way and suddenly turned on the infernal vacuum cleaner. He jumped up, whirled around, and crossed the room in a feigned stagger, grasping his heart with both hands and panting for breath. Her jaw dropped and her eyes opened wide. He collapsed into a stuffed chair across the room, took out a handkerchief and began to wipe his forehead. When he looked at her gaping at him, he could not suppress an open laugh. From that moment on Mrs. Johnson was never certain whether he was serious or joking, and so she continued to do just about what she had always done. The tone of their relationship was set with that incident, and he could not help but temper even his most serious orders with some joking or self-mockery.

Besides, he had come to feel that Mrs. Johnson regarded him as a fool, as an utter incompetent that God in his mysteriousness had endowed with the ultimate power. There were a hundred incidents that Father Schauf preferred not to recall that seemed the evidence of her attitude. She seemed a silent critic whose expressionless gaze and complete indifference stood as continual reminders of his failure to understand or be understood.

In her phlegmatic way, she explained to Father Schauf why she had come so early. She had a chance to earn a little extra money at the Co-op cleaning pheasants. The morning shift began at seven. Because the hunting had been excellent, there were over two thousand birds waiting to be cleaned from yesterday's kill. And what was she going to do about his breakfast and dinner? Well, she thought he could have cold cereal for breakfast and she was just about to ask him about dinner. But why didn't she ask him before? She didn't think he minded. Then he shrugged indifferently. He certainly wasn't going to make an issue of such a superficial matter.

She left to vacuum the living room as he sat at his desk. He removed the sacramental wine from the lower right hand drawer and poured some into the tubular vial he used to fill the cruet. On his desk were two sheets of paper: one with the notes he had made for announcements on Sunday, and the other blank—the total result of three days of thoughtful consideration of next Sunday's sermon.

From the beginning the sermons had been difficult. The reluctance of anyone to speak at length was exasperating. They shrugged, they grunted in monosyllables, but they rarely carried on a conversation. They lived in a world of action where husband and wife, and children responded to the rhythm of habit and work, where vague suggestion was taken as statement of intent. He couldn't even think out loud anymore.

Once at a card party he had suggested that the brushing of an elm branch on his roof over the bedroom was distracting. He was only half serious and he mentioned it in a joking context. One evening about a week later and without any forewarning, three men in a pickup drove up in front of the rectory and unloaded a ladder. They went around to the rear and placed the ladder against the house under the elm. It was nine-thirty at night and Father Schauf was reading in his room.

Later, whenever he told the story, he confessed he had never been so frightened in his life. He heard bumps outside the window and footsteps across the roof. Then he heard the saw followed by an enormous clump on the roof. For a moment he thought someone was dismantling the rectory right about his ears. At the time he couldn't remember having ever mentioned the elm branch. When his desperation and curiosity had overcome his fear, he pulled up the shade and threw open the window.

Out on the lawn was the president of the Holy Name Society directing two other members, one on the roof and the other in the tree. "Sorry, Father," he said taking off his hat in respect. "Didn't mean to disturb you." Then they all apologized and briefly explained that because of cultivating they couldn't get by any earlier. As their flashlights danced in his eyes, he realized they meant earlier in the week as well as in the evening. He thanked them and withdrew still trembling half in rage, half in fright.

How was he ever going to communicate. They lived in a world of action and he had been prepared to cope only with a world of ideas. All of his studies had been ultimately and essentially linguistic disciplines. In the beginning was the Word, but also in the beginning was the light—the light of energy expended in gigantic creation, the energy of grace and love. He understood the Word, but they knew the Light.

What good was the language of philosophy or theology? How could he possibly find some common ground of understanding without compromising himself and implicitly patronizing them?

Analogy was the answer, but his experience was so meager. In three years he had barely begun to immerse himself in their world. Oh, they understood the planting and reaping metaphor. Whatever you sow, thus also will you reap. Unless you get hailed out, of course. He didn't believe their stories of hail the size of baseballs until he walked into a corn field shredded to bits by round clumps of ice still lying in the furrows hours later.

Oh, Lord. He had tried to learn their way of life. In his first year, he had dutifully accepted every invitation to Sunday dinner. Wherever he went it was always the same—a heavy meal which he overate out of kindness, a seat close to the heater set at eighty degrees, and two hours of polite questions on his part and polite grunts and nudges on theirs. Until once out of sheer boredom, to escape the stares of the stone chorus of nodding heads, he volunteered to help the farmer and the vet, who had been called in the emergency, to treat the frothy bloat in a young steer.

Outside the cold air was a welcome relief. He stood on the fringe of the action as they cut the Hereford calf from the others in the feed lot and into the barn. The vet was a huge, young, crewcut Kansan who had been educated in Texas. Father Schauf guessed he was six-feet-three and two-hundred-twenty pounds at least. He spoke a twang with a drawl, but what endeared him to Father Schauf was that he spoke—incessantly to the animals, to the farmer, and to Father Schauf.

They had given Father Schauf an old jacket to cover his clothes, so he ventured close and even helped swing a gate when they ran the animal into an empty stall. He began to ask questions and instead of the usual one syllable answer, he got intelligent and detailed responses. They put a ring halter into its nostrils, ran the rope over a rafter and then down the outside of the stall where the farmer pulled down on the rope yanking the head of the steer high into the corner. He watched their crude efficiency with fascination, asking questions each step of the way.

The animal's sides were swollen and it was frothing. He learned from the vet that the cause of symptoms was unknown but that death was imminent unless treated immediately. Why did it hit only one animal out of twenty, each with the same food and environment? Nobody seemed to know. There was no question that the killing gas that was pressing against the heart and lungs came from wet, alfalfa or silage corn. There was probably a virus involved somewhere but it had never been isolated. The treatment was simple enough: relieve the gas pressure and neutralize, with dextrose, the thickened green sputum that blocked the canals of egress.

Father Schauf stood a little distance from the work. He listened with pleasure to the jargon as it rolled from the vet's lips. The vet jammed the steer with his hip against the wall as the farmer pulled down on the rope, stretching the head and neck of the animal straight up in the corner. Then he punched a needle into what Father Schauf thought was the region of the kidneys.

"What's that for?" Father Schauf asked.

"I'm lettin' the gas out of its stomach," the vet answered.

"What is the stomach doing way back there and up so high?"

"Well, that's where the good Lord put it."

The steer gave a violent lurch and the vet jammed it with his shoulder and drove it back, tight against the wall. As he spoke, he leaned against the animal and talked over his shoulder.

"I can tell you've been educated somewhere, but you never had a good course in animal amatory. No sir." He smiled over his shoulder. Father Schauf realized that they had never been introduced and that the vet did not know he was a priest because his collar was covered.

"No, I haven't, but I think I might recommend just such a course for the curriculum." He paused and asked, "What's happening now?"

"Why, gas is comin' out of this end of the needle almost asphyxiating me. Whew!" He shook his head. Father Schauf listened closely and heard the hissing sound. The needle looked like one of those Father Schauf had used to pump up footballs when he was a young.

"What do you do next?" Father Schauf asked. The steer lurched again and the vet lost his footing.

"I don't think I'll do anything if you just stand there with your hands in your pockets trying to get my education for nothing."

Father Schauf laughed. "What can I do? This is as close as I've ever been to a cow." The vet reset his feet and drove his shoulder into the steer again.

"Well, first of all this is one helluva strange cow, and secondly all I need is unskilled labor. No specialist required." Father Schauf stepped forward and the vet eased off the steer.

"I want you to step around here on the other side of this here ole cow," and he pointed to the spot on the wall-side just forward of the hind legs.

"I won't get kicked, will I?" Father Schauf asked apprehensively.

"Not if you stand in front of his leg," the vet answered sarcastically. Father Schauf took the position.

"Now," the vet said with a wide smile, "this is the tail."

"I know that much," Father Schauf said with nervous laughter.

"Your job will be to grasp the tail like this, twist it, and shove it forward driving the steer's head into the corner, there."

"Oh, it's a steer," Father Schauf said. "I know what that is, too."

"Why, you'll be getting your Ph.D in no time. Now you all grab on here and use a little weight to keep this ole cow still."

Father Schauf was surprised to discover that what he had been told to do worked. The steer was caught in a vise of cross pressures.

Once Father Schauf was set, the vet attached a tube to the needle and to the end of a bottle of dextrose. When he inverted the bottle the amber fluid flowed slowly into the steer's stomach. Then the vet shoved a long black rubber hose down the gullet of the animal and eased it back and forth pumping the thickened mucous out and releasing the gas that had built up behind the lungs and heart. An acrid stench filled the stall. Father Schauf's eyes began to water.

Then he was told they were all done. As he eased off the steer it seemed to Father Schauf that the animal almost politely stepped aside to allow him to pass. But the steer's weight shifted and it stepped backwards onto Father Schauf's foot, all seven hundred pounds.

As Father Schauf limped to the farm house for coffee and lunch, he noticed his trousers were spattered with manure. Later he threw them out rather than have them cleaned. In that first year he was overly fastidious. The vet and the farmer preceded him into the kitchen. He paused to wash up in the entry. When he entered the kitchen without the jacket, the vet stared at his collar and then jumped up from the table in respect.

"Why, Gawd a'mighty, a preacher," he exclaimed in astonishment. Father Schauf limped to the table and managed a wan smile.

"No, only a crippled priest."

There was no doubt that the incident helped him. The story of his injury circulated rapidly. The next morning the high school football coach called and wondered if Father Schauf would like to use the whirlpool for treatment. Complete strangers smiled hello as he limped down the street. But that was the last time Father Schauf went out to Sunday dinner. He discontinued the practice by politely refusing all invitations. He confined his "immersion" into local experience to occasional visits after confessions on Saturday night to the vet's office on Main Street. There he listened to the farmers, all neatly scrubbed and dressed, complaining—forever complaining—to the loquacious young vet and then listening shrewdly in hopes the vet in his great love of talk would inadvertently outline a treatment they could administer themselves.

But his difficulties didn't arise only because of the disparity between his background and theirs. It was partially the result of his own temperament. He simply disliked the language and devices of persuasion, of rhetoric, as manipulative and deceptive. In Father Schauf's mind they were tantamount to lying. Once his theology instructor had entered the classroom late. He walked to the front of the class, whirled around toward the students, paused deliberately, and then detached his collar and with care placed it on the corner of his desk. Then he announced dramatically and with great emotion in his voice, "There is no God." Father Schauf, repulsed by the artificiality of the device, refused to engage in the discussion although he would normally have been one of the most articulate debaters.

Whatever effectiveness he had as a speaker or a teacher had resulted from his natural, unaffected delivery of what he believed to be true and logical. Fortunately, before coming to Amburg, his audiences had been more responsive. His first sermons in Amburg, however, had been received with cold indifference. His first effective sermon, or at least the one upon which several of his congregation had commented, had been a shameful compromise of his standards.

The Bishop had requested that a sermon on the evils of communism be delivered sometime during the month of September. Father Schauf wrestled the whole month with the language he believed relevant. He wanted to do his best job. He wrote and rewrote, and then at the last minute he threw the whole thing out. It was too historical, too philosophical even though he had grounded the sermon on a well-known parable and quoted liberally several of the more popular Catholic radio and television speakers.

Finally, in last minute panic he reduced his entire argument to terms he knew they would understand: Thou Shalt Not Steal. He proceeded to elaborate upon the infringement of totalitarian states upon the rights and freedoms of individuals, especially upon the rights of private ownership of property which he used as a concrete illustration. They could at least understand the loss of property; perhaps, he hoped, they might understand how the state could "steal" such precious rights and freedoms as worship and speech.

They understood that sermon all right, but he didn't believe his own argument. He knew that his entire position could be demolished and he felt sick and angry at himself for the snobbism implicit in his compromise of logic and language. He was appalled when several of the men of the parish commented favorably on the sermon at the Tuesday Holy Name meeting. Then a farm wife, a nervous, shrewish woman who had said little or nothing to him since he had arrived, called unexpectedly at the rectory one evening and used his sermon as a pretext to unload upon Father Schuaf an hysterical harangue of the most confused and frighteningly incredible political sentiments he had ever heard. Apparently she thought he held the same apprehensions about government, labor, Negroes, taxes, and foreign aid as she held. The only response he could give was to gently lessen her fears and sympathetically qualify her rambling and chaotic assertions and then to diplomatically change the topic of conversation.

Since then Father Schauf had limited his sermons to obvious comments on the gospel, but even these simple commentaries were becoming more excruciatingly difficult. He no longer tried to guess how they might respond. His rhetoric, whatever he did, invariably had ambiguous or unpredictable results.

He was ready, now, to leave for church. He opened the closet door in his study and selected his heavy winter coat and overshoes. For some reason his feet were always cold. He slipped the tubular bottle of wine into the outside pocket of his coat and left the house through the kitchen. He opened the side door just off the pantry, leaving Mrs. Johnson to her last chores and her day of pheasant plucking.

Outside the wind was blowing. The low rain clouds had vaulted high. It would be colder now, but it seemed as though the rain was over. Bending into the wind, he walked across the yard, really only a closely cut empty lot of weeds that separated the rectory from the church and which Father Schauf whimsically called his "farm," and around the back of the church to the sacristy door.

After he turned on the church lights, he set about immediately preparing the altar. Of one thing he was certain: his altar boy would be late. He removed the green felt altar cloth and stood the framed prayer cards up in their proper places. He fixed the cruets, put the missal on its stand on the epistle side of the altar, and then lit the candles for low mass. Then he prepared the chalice in the sacristy and began to put on his vestments.

Father Schauf's altar boys were deplorably bad, but try as he would it was simply impossible to find time for practice. It was difficult enough for religious instructions. His parish covered three school districts and the bus schedule which served each precluded any early morning or late afternoon classes or practice.

He had managed to schedule religious instruction classes but not without dissent and grumbling. He tried to be democratic, but first one group objected to Saturday, then another group didn't want Sunday, and nobody wanted the evenings. Sunday was impossible for him anyway because he had to say mass at two locations and wouldn't have time to supervise the instructors. They finally accepted one week night for the high school students and Saturday morning for the grammar school children. He knew that those who lived on the farms were angry for some time because of the schedule. He heard by way of rumor that they believed he had favored the town folks unfairly.

He abandoned his plans for altar boy practice for fear of aggravating his already strained relations with the rural parishioners. He used the boys from Amburg as much as possible for daily mass, but they were few and in order not to overburden those who were adequately prepared, he had to use boys who were careless and irresponsible. Often he said mass without a server. Sometimes old Raymond Madsen, one of the few daily communicants, would volunteer to serve, hacking and spitting phlegm throughout mass and requiring oral instructions each step of the way. Father Schauf preferred an incompetent server or no server at all to old Raymond.

At five to seven his sleepy and disheveled altar boy arrived. After dressing slowly, the boy wandered onto the altar to prepare for mass. He wandered back into the sacristy when he discovered that his duties had already been done. His surplice was bunched high in back. Father Schauf pulled it down, then took the boy over to the sink, wet his hair, and combed it with his own comb.

He was ready to enter the altar for mass. Now, all his petty triumphs and failures were peripheral in the light of the eternal sacrifice. Father Schauf may have doubted himself, but never Christ or the grace which flowed from the mass. He did not feel he was unreasonable in demanding at least a simple dignity in its execution. He was not overly concerned with an elaborate and formal exactitude. He did not expect perfection. He smiled with others at the standing joke about a certain wealthy parish in the Cities where four altar boys in colorful cassocks were used even for the daily low mass and where on Sunday there was such an elaborate use of bells and altar lights which chimed and dimmed so often it was rumored they employed a stage manager to keep everything straight.

"I go unto the altar of God." It had been "Introibo ad altare Dei" when he was an altar boy. He articulated the prayers at the foot of the altar with deliberate accuracy, trying to convey in the tone and inflection of his voice the exact meaning and feeling of each. Because this particular altar boy was almost worthless in his responses, Father Schauf answered each of his spoken prayers silently with the words the altar boy was supposed to say aloud. Once when he was depressed and short tempered, he lost his patience with a server and answered every response himself, loudly drowning out the boy's feeble attempts.

As he ascended the steps to the altar, he was distracted by one of Mr. Madsen's coughing fits. It seemed the old man would never catch his breath. Father Schauf continued the prayers with a conscious effort to keep his mind on the meaning—the Kyrie, the Gloria, and then the Epistle. He extended his left hand to signal the change of the missal and was surprised to hear the altar boy scrambling behind his back to remove the book on the proper cue. Then the Gospel and the Credo.

The boy missed the cue for the cruets, so Father Schauf stood with the chalice at the top step of the Epistle side until the boy realized that it was the Offertory. At the center of the altar he faced the congregation and spoke the words, "Pray brethren, that my sacrifice and yours be acceptable unto God," and he answered himself silently, for he knew the boy couldn't even pronounce the response reading from the altar card let alone memorize it.

The altar boy missed the first two responses of the Preface and slurred the last two. "Lift up your minds and your hearts," the priest said. "We have lifted them unto the Lord," he responded for the congregation. The boy picked up the bell in anticipation and then rang the "Sanctus" correctly which suggested to the priest that perhaps the boy's performance might be an improvement over the effort of the day before.

In the intention of the mass Father Schauf remembered his parents as usual and prayed for the special intentions of Father Willett, the pastor of one of Father Schauf's neighboring parishes. It was the geographical proximity of their assignments which had brought the two priests together. Over the past year Father Willett had become his closest and most frequent companion. But just a week before, they had had an argument which had cooled their friendship.

Father Willett was not the kind of friend Father Schauf was drawn to naturally. He was thin and nervous. Everyone called him "twitchy fingers" in description of his continual wringing of hands. Father Willett was precise and exacting in his speech, prissy and shrewish in temperament, timid and distant in his relationships with everyone, fellow priest or parishioner. But friends they had become, drawn to each other out of isolation and loneliness.

The argument was petty. It was about a new holy day that had been added to the liturgical calendar. Father Schauf argued that qualitative additions might be significant but simply to add another opportunity for grace to the liturgical year was like trying to measure God out in buckets, quantitatively. Poor, timid Father Willett was shocked by the analogy. Father Schauf felt sick at heart for being so argumentative and so insensitive. He prayed for the virtues of patience and self-control.

The boy did not see the priest extend his hands over the chalice as the last bell cue before the Consecration. He craned his neck looking for the signal that had already passed. He did not know that when the priest blessed the host and then leaned over that the words of consecration were about to be pronounced. He did not hear the words "This is my body," and he did not hear the priest, after a moment of silent terror, repeat the words in Latin:"Hoc est enim corpus meum." He did not see the trembling hands, nor did he see the contorted face fighting the tears of self-pity and despair. His eye caught the reflection of light when the chalice was raised for adoration. He grasped the bell and with six quick, short, late bursts rang the Presence of God upon the altar.

THE SUMMER OF HIS DISCONTENT

The summer my older brother, Hank, came home from college with the liberal chip on his shoulder and a smouldering discontent in his eyes, Great Aunt Kate had her seventy-seventh birthday in the first week of June, and at the party we drank grape nectar toasts to her health, and, because she was always teaching even then in the twelfth year of her retirement, she had us offer toasts also to some of her heroes and heroines. So we drank to their memory two or three times to fix firmly in our minds names about which we would surely be quizzed sooner or later. There wasn't much we did with her that did not end up in some kind of literary, moral or historical lesson, so we humored her and she wisely kept her instructions brief.

On the afternoon of that particular birthday we drank toasts to the memory of Harriet Tubman, who we gathered was the president of a railroad that ran underground all the way from Alabama to Canada, and Emma Goldman, who fifteen years later I learned was some kind of communist and advocate of free love; to Frederick Douglass, the Great Slave, and Woodrow Wilson, the tragic professor. We drank to the health of Eleanor Roosevelt, who was still alive, a beacon of reason and compassion in a darkened world; and finally to Franklin Delano Roosevelt, who had died too, she said, in April (the month of the death of the Great Emancipator) in the time of the lilacs' bloom.

We drank those historical toasts, my younger brother Benjy and I, sitting at the picnic table on the side lawn to the nodding approval of my grandfather's youngest sister, Aunt Kate, who, following Grandmother's early death, had raised my mother, nursed Grandfather though his final sickness to death, and taken care of the old family house in its declining years until my father took over and remodeled it. By the end of the party, Benjy wore a purple, crescent-shaped moustache across his face, its tips reaching almost to his ears.

It was a time of post-war optimism and triumph. I was in the seventh grade, Hank was in college, and little Benjy had just turned six. Technically Aunt Kate was living with us then, though actually we went to live with her after Grandfather died and my mother inherited the old family house. Aunt Kate stayed on as if nothing more had happened than her world had once again been invaded by somebody else's children.

She was a retired high school history and English teacher who had never married. She wore her yellowing gray hair parted in the middle and drawn tightly back to a bun, which she swirled and fastened each morning before a mirror with hairpins that she held between her lips and took one at a time with her free hand and then plunged into the growing mass at the back of her head. Her dresses were long, almost down to her ankles, and for a while in those years after the war when the old fashioned became fashionable, perhaps to compensate for the shortened victory dresses, her wardrobe came briefly back into vogue. She wore steel rimmed glasses that set tightly and high upon the bridge of her nose except when she used the bifocals for reading and then they slipped down and away, loosely, toward the tip of her nose.

I learned over the years from my mother the history, or rather, the mythology of her life. She was the third child of Irish immigrants who had found their way to a homestead farm in southern Minnesota along the upper Mississippi River valley just after the Civil War. She was the only one in the family to receive an education in the sense that she attended secondary school and teachers' college and then went on to teach for forty-five years in the Midwest—in Chicago, Madison, and St. Paul.

In her day, she had been an active suffragette and a continuing defender of women's rights in politics and the workplace. She was a lifelong political liberal. Her assimilated sense of Victorian justice had been fused with the democratic spirit of her frontier childhood, and so she became, while teaching in Wisconsin, a Progressive in the LaFollette tradition. "Fighting Bob" brought her to Wilson, to the partial fulfillment of liberal ideals in the first term and to the tragically futile defense of humanity and peace in those last dying years of the second. A LaFollette Progressive, a Wilson idealist, she became a passionate New Dealer in 1932. No one lived more intensely and with greater expectation and anxiety than Aunt Kate in those First Hundred Days. In her teaching career she had had a profound influence in some vague, imprecise way on one Democratic governor and two federal judges, who were originally Republicans but were not claimed by her until they went "beyond party" into the courts.

She was a believer in "liberation theology" before it had even acquired a name. Though loyal to the Church, her finest moral stand was taken in defiance of it. She had read THE GRAPES OF WRATH and had been deeply moved. When it was made into a movie and was about to arrive at the neighborhood theater, it was denounced and condemned from the pulpit. The week before its opening an advertising truck with a blaring loudspeaker went up and down the street selling the movie's realism as lurid eroticism.

On the opening night she was the first in line with her fifty cents at the ticket office. She was not going to hide her light under a bushel. She recommended the movie to everyone she met and seemed personally offended that the Church had mysteriously decided to condemn compassion and a powerful call to social responsibility. She was outraged by the shabby advertising campaign and wrote a letter to the editor of the local newspaper in protest and calling for a boycott of the theater if the management persisted in its crass and vulgar methods.

She was always reading or instructing. I suspect now that she had a lesson plan for each of us, devised to stimulate our moral and intellectual growth, linear and upward, though I must have frustrated her because, in retrospect, my own development seems to have been irregular and circular and often regressive with vast stretches of wasteland between small steps of progress. She didn't seem to notice, I guess, because she patiently and consistently kept working at me for almost ten years without any apparent improvement on my part or disappointment on hers. We used to wedge next to her in her chair when we were small enough or at her feet as we grew older, and she used to read aloud long passages from the American classics: the lyrical scenes of Huck and Jim floating free on the Mississippi; the shadowed forest meeting between Hester and Dimmesdale; all of UNCLE TOM'S CABIN a scene at a time like the adventure serials at the movies on Saturdays, and at one time or another massive dosages of Emily Dickinson and Whitman. She also read from the evening newspaper aloud from the front page through the want ads to whoever would listen. Hank and I had our turns and then Benjy squeezed into the chair next to her and listened raptly to what he didn't understand.

The day before Aunt Kate's birthday, I had been somewhat miraculously promoted, deemed fit to continue to the next level of incompetence though Sister Frances told my mother that she had serious reservations about my maturity. Aunt Kate's party was again a success; as was her custom, she gave us presents, one dollar apiece. And following her party was the crowning glory of my emancipation: opening day at the municipal swimming pool.

The only cloud on my summer horizon was the imminent return of Hank from St. Thomas (Aquinas, of course) College. Although his first year had been mediocre to say the least, this, his sophomore year, had revealed a gradual but profound transformation, almost a transfiguration he had changed so radically. All the way home from the pool, I shuddered to think what changes he might have undergone since Easter vacation.

I could tell something was happening when he came home for Thanksgiving. He had decided to major in political science and minor in philosophy. He said things like "Let us commence to proceed," and he called the sunrise "Aurora." Sometimes he was full of "a priori assumptions" and sometimes his behavior was dictated by "overwhelming amounts of empirical data." He was in revolt against the blind authoritarianism of a bankrupt generation of Victorian hypocrites (perhaps something of an anachronism but he used it as a generalized term referring to any condition of calcified moral or political opinion).

During Christmas vacation he was oppressive. He had several pet phrases that he invented or borrowed and he used them whenever he could. Sometimes he manipulated a conversation to make his epigrams seem like spontaneous wit. Sometimes he quoted himself (he always held two fingers of each hand above each ear to indicate quotation marks) and then added a little note of explanation of his profundity. One of his favorite epigrams was "the antithesis of conformity is madness." Once when someone told him it wasn't necessary to footnote his wit, he borrowed the phrase and used it cuttingly. "I'm not an idiot. You don't have to footnote your wit." He liked "irrevocable" and "essence" and "provincial" (in the caustic sense of the word denoting limited or not cosmopolitan) and he spent two whole weeks on inherent. Benjy and I were "inherently provincial."

Hank wanted to put Christ back into Christmas by purging the season of its commercial and pagan elements. He announced rather melodramatically, like Zarathustra coming out of the desert or the woods, "that Santa Claus was dead." Santa Claus and Christmas trees and colored lights simply weren't rational.

My mother almost had one of her anxiety attacks. She pleaded with my father, "He's trying to rob Benjy of his childhood." But she really didn't have anything to worry about. Good old Benjy, the child of her middle years and the comfort of her old age, was so excited he hardly noticed that Hank was home for the holidays. By Easter he had gone "political" and evolved into a full fledged Christian radical. Without abandoning his faith he understood socialism, secularism, labor unions, homosexuality, evolution, and civil rights issues demanding complete separation of Church and State. He was a Catholic in the liberal tradition of freedom and social justice, and he looked to the leadership of German and French intellectuals. According to Hank the entire American hierarchy was a flop. I didn't understand much of what he was saying at the time, but he repeated himself so often over the years that I grew into an understanding despite my slowness of intellectual development and general indifference to political and theological matters.

Although Hank was a great believer in the equality of everybody, I don't recall that in practice he applied the principle of equity to Benjy and me. There was something paradoxical in his democratic attitudes. It was as though he, a self-styled intellectual aristocrat, proclaimed in the spirit of noblesse oblige (from his Olympian heights) that the rest of the world—the vulgar masses—were indeed equal (at least theoretically) to him. At the same time he inconsistently argued that one great poem, one scientific achievement was worth the sacrifice, if necessary, of ordinary or unproductive people like post-menopausal women or retired mailmen.

Because of the "bomb" and the emerging underdeveloped nations, Hank belonged to a different species of Liberal from Aunt Kate and a species which today has already been supplanted at least twice. In fact, he classified her as one of the calcified moral and political hypocrites who had made a mess of the world. In his new enthusiasm he didn't distinguish her from Father, who was a conservative Republican. Hank was a sworn enemy of the "bourgeois mentality" and yet he dismissed the whole of dialectical materialism with the condescending concession that Marx and Engels were useful social critics whose observations "were not entirely incompatible with Christian moral theology" but whose theory of history was just plain "bunk." The world according to Hank was populated by idiots, gross materialists, and damned fools. There were also a considerable number of phony bastards.

When Hank arrived home, our peaceful world of free and easy vacation, which had just begun, was transformed into argument and agitation. He fought with Father over politics and economics. Father dismissed him as an inexperienced Keynesian—a big spender without a pocketbook, and he began ridiculing Aunt Kate behind her back as a quaint anachronism. He teased Benjy into tears and antagonized me with his quibbling and captious, arrogant superiority.

He was brimming with ideas and feelings that he could neither fully understand nor implement. There were few genuine activist opportunities in those post-war years when everyone seemed sick of idealism and eager for comfort, except perhaps opposing McCarthyism. As a consequence we, Benjy and I, were submerged by his energy and dominance and made the unwilling accomplices in his misdirected plots, in his frustrated and futile groping for a place in the sun. He wanted to escape from under the ominous shadow of Father's generation and the fading memory of Aunt Kate's, and because she seemed the weaker of the two, he spent a good deal of his time trying to assert his identity and will at the expense of hers. He failed rather shamefully at every attempt.

The first incident occurred about a week after his arrival. Hank had grown bored with behind the back insults and had been soundly outshouted by Father in an argument on deficit spending and the unbalanced budget. One morning Hank and I were playing ping pong in the basement and Benjy had plunked himself into one side of an old orange crate and threw his legs over the partition to watch. He usually got stuck in that awkward position and I often threatened to leave him sitting there trapped by his own ignorance until I exacted some promise of what is now called "behavior modification" in the future. Suddenly Hank stopped the game and went over to Benjy. He walked around the box nodding his head, while Benjy's head which had been following the action of the game began to gyrate round and round as he followed Hank. Then he dumped Benjy out of the crate and onto the cement floor and sent me for a hammer and saw.

"Whatch'doin", Hank?" Benjy asked.

"I'm not sure yet, but if you don't blow it, I think we're going to play a joke on Aunt Kate."

I returned with the hammer and saw, and Hank began to reconstruct the crate by taking out the partition. He found two old pillows in my mother's storage closet under the stairs and stuffed them into the bottom of the box as it lay longwise on the floor and then with thumbtacks he covered the outside with dark brown wrapping paper.

When he placed Benjy into the top opening and had him stretch out flat except for his bent knees, I could tell that Hank had made a miniature casket. He dumped Benjy out again. He covered the old pillows with an sheet and tacked the dark wrapping paper over the top to cover Benjy's legs. When he had finished, he put Benjy back into the box, covered his face until it was pasty white with talcum powder that I had retrieved from the bathroom, and folded his hands together with a rosary across his stomach. Then he instructed Benjy not to move a single muscle, not smile even a little bit.

We carried Benjy ceremoniously up the stairs and set him down on a coffee table in the living room. Then Hank sent me outside for some flowers, and when I returned, he began arranging them in water glasses and sent me to find Aunt Kate.

When she entered the room and saw Benjy laid out on the coffee table, she folded her hands in front of her and sighed as she walked slowly toward him. "Oh my, Benjy is dead." She pursed her lips and looked around at Hank and said, "Did you see this, Hank? Benjy is dead."

She patted Benjy gently on the forehead and said, "It is too bad for us, but he is certainly in heaven, a little angel in heaven to pray for us." She clicked her false teeth.

Then Benjy could control himself no longer. He giggled. "I ain't dead, Aunt Kate. I ain't dead." He lifted his arm and wiggled his fingers. "See, I can move."

"Oh, my," she cried in mock relief and clasped her hands under her chin. "Oh my, Benjy isn't dead. Why, look at this. Benjy isn't dead at all."

Then Hank said sarcastically, "It was a joke, that's all, only a joke."

"Well, I certainly am glad you told me. I would never have

been able to figure that out by myself." She turned on her heel and went to the kitchen to make a cup of tea.

In early July, just after the Fourth, Hank had the first of his two summer guests—a tall, handsome Negro from Bermuda who did not go home for summer vacation in order to take one last course in theology before entering a Jesuit seminary. His name was James Billington—Jimmy—and he spoke with the finest British accent I have ever heard. Hank was disappointed that Jimmy was accepted so readily by the family. Perhaps had he been an American, Protestant, uneducated, and from Chicago, we would have thrown him and Hank right out of the house. I do not wish to overstate the liberality, the toleration of our family. It was simply better than Hank had expected and, after all, Jimmy was British and an incipient Jesuit at that.

In any event, Benjy took a great fancy to him. He followed poor Jimmy all over the house, outside, up the street and down. He sat next to him in the car and ate next to him at the table. Benjy was taken by Jimmy's voice. He hung on every word that Jimmy uttered and began imitating the accent. According to Benjy, Jimmy spoke "high class" like a duke or a butler.

What time Benjy did not monopolize, Aunt Kate did. She and Jimmy began talking casually at first, and then later in long discussions about books they had read. They talked about writers like Dostoevski and Sophocles and others whose names I could not pronounce either . Because Hank had not read the works under discussion, he participated vaguely, asking questions now and then. Aunt Kate and Jimmy said he was a good catalyst which, I discovered after looking it up in the dictionary, was a nice way of saying that Hank contributed to an interaction without being essentially involved. Hank was like the straight man in a Socratic dialogue, always drawing the wrong or the naive conclusion and invariably playing the role of the straw dummy which existed only to be knocked down.

Hank's second guest arrived a week after Jimmy left. He was a Mexican youth studying public administration and his name was

Sus. Before he came, Hank was very particular that we call him Sus, but didn't explain why to Benjy and me. When Sus arrived, we discovered that his complete name was Jesus Armando Rodriguez y Aguilar. Benjy said,

"Do you mean his real name is Jesus?" and his eyes widened in disbelief.

Hank said, "Yes, if you must know. But it is not proper to call him Jesus. Besides, it is pronounced Hay-suice. Just call him Suice as in juice."

But Benjy was not about to let such an opportunity for blasphemous impunity pass him by and he ran around the house shouting,

"Jesus, hey, hey, Jesus, let's play bullfight, Jesus."

Sus taught Benjy the roles of the picador, matador, and the bull and, however he tried to convince Benjy that the matador was the main attraction, Benjy always wanted to play the bull. Benjy bragged about his new visitor to his friends and our neighbors. "We got a real Jesus staying at our house and you can call him Jesus without swearing."

After Sus left, Hank started after Benjy who ran to Aunt Kate and hid behind her chair next to the radiator. Hank demanded that she turn him over to get what he had coming to him for ridiculing his friend. But she suggested that, perhaps, Hank was the only one to interpret Benjy's action as ridicule. But when Hank wouldn't leave Benjy alone, she said to him,

"You let that child alone. You may be proud of your toleration of foreigners, but do not feel that because you have imposed a difficult relationship on a six-year-old child, he will respond in the same manner and with the same affectations that you have so studiously cultivated."

But Hank knew how to take care of Benjy. He got an old straw hat and a cane from the attic. He dressed like a carnival barker with the hat cocked and he shouted out of the side of his mouth while pointing at Benjy with his cane, "Come one, come all. See Benjy, the little boy with the big mouth," and Benjy grew red with rage and humiliation.

My mother began to worry about Hank. She asked Father what had gotten into the boy and wondered if it was healthy for a nineteen-year-old boy to spend all his time reading books and arguing. Wouldn't a job do some good? Hank spent much of each day at the public library reading his self-imposed list. He would come home excited and in his excitement he made notes to himself which served as reminders of the new reading he was to do to follow up his present progress. Once I saw one of his notes to himself. He had planned to read during the third week of July all of Shakespeare and St. Augustine.

In late July my father got him a job at the Country Club as a waiter on Thursday, Friday, and Saturday nights. Hank rubbed his hands and proclaimed his eager anticipation to seize this opportunity to observe "the vulgar bourgeois mentality in all its drunken nudity." By the end of the first weekend he had met and fallen for the daughter of the local Chevrolet dealer, who was working as one of the hostesses to earn spending money before returning back East to college in fall. Hank began picking and squeezing his pimples before a mirror, washing himself in toilet water, and brushing away the enamel of his teeth to make them flashing white and his breath halitosis free. His disciplined reading program was abandoned and he disappeared from the unhealthy atmosphere of the home. He quit browbeating Benjy and me and bickering with Aunt Kate and to my mother's relief he began pursuing a "normal" vacation program. But it lasted only a month, for the Chevrolet dealer's daughter dropped him cold for the champion high diver of the summer Aqua Carnival, and Hank returned to his reading list vanquished and humiliated.

The last incident of that summer was like the first, Benjy's mock funeral—senseless, almost malicious. It was the result, perhaps, of his disappointment in romance though there were probably larger causes. His dissatisfaction, his discontent with himself and the world made him do things not directly related to his scorn. It was almost as if he had discovered how to mock, to deride, to ridicule, and he didn't care whom or what he attacked so long as he could relieve the tension of that enormous gap between his ideals and the facts of a sordid and unjust world that needed immediate correction or remaking.

Benjy used to say mass for Aunt Kate in imitation of Father O'Callahan. He had been given an old dish towel on which he had drawn a large cross with a crayon. He pinned it around his neck and it flowed down to the edge of his tennis shoes—a somewhat oversized chasuble. He used the long coffee table, his funeral catafalque, as the altar and a Sears catalogue as an enormous missal. A cardboard box turned on its end sufficed as a pulpit. He conducted his mock ceremony with utter seriousness and, to Aunt Kate, it had the dignity and grandeur of the prayer and sacrifice it imitated.

Benjy's ceremony was pretty much limited to the movements of the priest that were clear and expressive as they appeared to him from a distant pew. It was, in fact, little more than the reading of the gospel and a halting sermon about giving more money to the support of the parish, an offertory collection, and a series of whirling, hand extended blessings accompanied by prayers of nondescript linguistic origin. There were no principal parts, no Offertory, Consecration, or Communion in Benjy's ritual—no sacrifice of agony or death. It was superficial and, above all, innocent of the mystery and terror of the love of God for man.

Hank decided to orchestrate Benjy's mass, to jazz it up a little. They practiced several times in secret and then delivered their mass before Aunt Kate and me in the living room. Hank served at the mass himself and answered each of Benjy's prayers or movements with a shouted "Amen" or an "Alleluia" and then he rolled on the floor at least once in imitation of the Holy Rollers, or what he thought was the manner of the Holy Rollers, scurried back to his kneeling position, rang the dinner bell he had borrowed, and then with the switch of an extension cord blinked the spotlight he had directed from a floor lamp at Benjy's back for rhetorical effectiveness.

Hank even wrote a sermon—no more than four or five lines because Benjy couldn't read—to the effect that fornicators and adulterers would not enter the Kingdom of Heaven and that although your seed was cast all over the place—among the thorns, on the rocks—some of it was bound to land in the belly of a wanton woman which was better than on the stones or in the brambles because bringing forth any fruit was better than none at all, although there was the question of good and bad fruit which had to be decided upon at the judgment day.

Whatever Benjy did, Hank went through his theefold ritual, a shout and roll, the ringing bell, and the blinking lights. His spirits were high for the two days of practice sessions and, when they delivered the mass before Aunt Kate and me, he nearly lost his balance, he was leaning over so far laughing. He almost choked when Benjy gave the sermon which was a confused version of what Hank had intended to be gibberish to start with. All through the ceremony Benjy beamed with pride and delight in happy ignorance of the travesty of innocence Hank had committed.

When the mass was over Hank said,

"What did you think of Benjy's mass, Aunt Kate? Pretty good?"

She was still sitting in her reading chair. She thought for a few moments and then with the newspaper folded across her lap and her head cocked in her brightest school teacher manner, she answered him with the kind of systematic and pedantic language that she knew he understood. Hank should never have given her an opportunity to teach or preach.

"I have difficulty locating precisely the object of your scorn. At first I thought you were mocking the mass, but I know for all your insolence you still have some faith. Then I thought you were mocking me. I thought that perhaps the sermon was directed as a ridicule of my, should we say, single state. But it couldn't have been ridicule. I have never been so complimented. Imagine a seventy-seven-year old virgin having a sermon on adultery directed solely at her."

She paused to reflect and then she really bored into poor Hank. "No, it wasn't the mass and it wasn't me. I think you have done an effective job of ridiculing your little brother's finest prayer and highest aspirations. See, he stands there now in naive excitement, thinking you have done him a favor, thinking his little mass has been improved by your participation, for he worships you, you know. I don't know why, but he does. In conclusion, I thought your whole performance was remarkably petit-bourgeois. I am disappointed. I thought you had a larger spirit of rebellion."

When she had finished her analysis, Hank protested, "I did not ridicule Benjy. I did not."

I could tell he was angry and embarrassed and guilty. Color rose to his face and he began to pace back and forth across the living room rug trying to think of arguments to refute her, but he was defeated and he knew it. His rebellion was not large enough and he knew that too.

"I did not ridicule Benjy," he said again, and then loudly and defiantly. "I am not petit-bourgeois."

But Aunt Kate would not answer. She had returned to her reading, had shut him off completely. Hank finally muttered,

"Aw, nuts, you can't do anything around this dump," and stomped angrily out of the living room and up the stairs to his room.

It was now an empirical reality that even Hank recognized. He was just not ready to take on someone who had publicly defied the weighty authority of the Roman Catholic Church. After Hank left the room, I said to Aunt Kate,

"Hank's kind of a smart aleck, isn't he?"

She looked up from the paper and said, "Not really. He is only arrogant, intolerant and opinionated, but he often has the right opinions and the right sentiments. I think, perhaps, he is an idealist." She seemed to be looking off into the distant past. "He confuses the intensity of personal discovery with originality. He has not learned that beauty is as important as truth and that beauty and truth are often very old, indeed." Then she added: "His greatest deficiency is that he is not very well read."

"Aunt Kate," I said, "would you read something to Benjy and me?"

She smiled, pleased that I had asked.

"What would you prefer?"

"How about that scene when Hester meets Dimmesdale in the shadows of the forest and little Pearl dances in the sunlight?"

"I believe we have had enough of that for one day," she said.

"Enough of what, Aunt Kate? Enough of what?"

"Enough of Hester's sin. We just had a somewhat confused sermon on the subject."

"Well, anything you want then," I said.

Benjy and I sat on the floor. She went to her bookshelf and selected an old, worn volume of poetry and returned to her chair. She began with Benjy's favorite poems by Emily Dickinson, which he acted out, mixing the figurative and literal levels in his pantomime. He became simultaneously a horse and a train as he galloped and chugged and blew steam alternately. Then he staggered around the living room as the Little Tippler, drunk on air and debauched by dew. During the next poem he climbed up next to Aunt Kate and huddled closer as she approached the ending when he shivered all over as if on cue to the words "zero at the bone." Benjy shuddered and announced solemnly:"I hate snakes." The next poem was clearly for me because it had a message. "The soul selects her own society . . ." she began, and it is strange that after all these years though I can't remember much about the poem beyond its first line I have always believed that the soul, like the great ships of the sea and Holy Mother the Church, is of the feminine gender.

THE DISSERTATION

> And when his bones are dust, his grave a blank,
> His station, generation, even his nation,
> Become a thing, or nothing, save to rank
> In chronological commemoration,
> Some dull M.S. oblivion long has sank,
> Or graven stone found in a barrack's station
> In digging the foundation of a closet,
> May turn his name up, as a rare deposit.
> LXXXIX, Canto the Third
> DON JUAN

William Brosnan's dissertation, "The History of the Critical Evaluation of the Major Novels of William Dean Howells," was officially accepted in early October, two weeks before he collapsed and died of a massive coronary occlusion and three months before his thirty-eighth birthday. For Brosnan the dissertation was the culmination of ten years of epic struggle against and final triumph over the English department's imposing obstacles: the nine-hour qualifying examination; two years of course work beyond the baccalaureate; hours of orals covering the substance and historical background of over seventy books; a false start on a dissertation topic which collapsed when his major advisor left for Harvard; years of research and the compilation of over three thousand file cards of notes; and then most formidably the writing, revision, editing, rewriting, and revision again and again and again of the dissertation itself.

It was a decade of agony, of struggle to consummation attended, unfortunately, by a variety of insidious psychosomatic disorders: terrifying spells of shortness of breath; palpitations of the heart; a chronically nervous stomach requiring periodic barium x-rays to check the possibility of developing ulcers; and a sinus condition accompanied by continual postnasal drip,—also known as catarrh or the scholar's disease.

And his wife, Virginia, no less then he, lived for ten years in the shadow of the dissertation. She bore him two children in the shadow of the dissertation and worked as a technician in the University Clinics lab in the shadow of that dissertation. She worked and waited and waited and worked in the shadow of the dissertation. She had typed the entire manuscript and had, in effect, re-typed it twice because of mistakes and revisions. After he finished his course work, she agreed to continue working so that he could devote more time to research and writing. They decided that he would carry a half teaching load at the University Extension Center and a part-time job as the evening librarian in the Modern Fiction Reading Room until the dissertation was completed. They had not anticipated eight years.

When he had incorporated the last revisions recommended by Professor Shelbourne, then resubmitted it to the Committee, William and Virginia Brosnan allowed themselves a minor celebration. It had been a joint accomplishment. The dissertation was the work of faith and mutual effort upon which their marriage was based. Years of struggle and fear and defeat had been finally completed. She would share equally in the fruits of his victory. How many others had quit, fallen by the wayside, rationalized their failure. The doctorate was uncreative, they had said, a bore, an obstacle course for the fact grubbers, grinds, and pedants. How many had left the University to complete the doctorate at a school where the requirements were less rigid! The attrition rate of doctorate candidates was incredible, perhaps the highest in the country. The vast majority who had entered the program with high hope and more ability than Brosnan had lost the faith. But not William and Virginia Brosnan. They had stuck it out, persisted, endured to the very end, and they had triumphed, almost.

Then they were delivered of their burden. When they received the notice that the dissertation had been accepted, they felt suddenly emancipated. They had done their duty, paid their homage to the gods of the mind. Their identities had been confirmed; the dissertation was the external sign and symbol of an internal condition. It was as though an indelible mark had been stamped upon the souls of William and Virginia Brosnan. They no longer needed to worry about being second rate.

II

He described the pain as indigestion. It shot down his left arm; then it seemed to grip his chest like a vise. When he began gasping for his breath, she ran across the hallway to the Coleman's apartment, and they helped rush him to the emergency room of the Clinics. Once in the Coleman's car the pain seemed to lessen and he began to breathe freely again, but when they entered the waiting room, he was convulsed by the final, fatal seizure.

Virginia Brosnan had achieved, through no fault of her own, a perfectly existentialist condition: the labor of her husband's life and thus the labor of her own life (the doctorate though negotiable is not transferrable) had come to naught. She had helped her husband in his Sisyphus-like struggle. She had encouraged him to shoulder his boulder to the crest of the hill, but, alas, his feet had slipped. She stood by impotently and watched as the stone rolled back crushing him ignominiously in the mud. Unlike Sisyphus, the god, William Brosnan, mere mortal, had no second chance. There had been a certain dignity in the struggle, but in the face of the certain and inevitable defeat that is the common lot, it simply didn't seem fair—even absurdly fair—that he should have come so far to be defeated and that she should be denied the right to pursue his half finished goals to some sort of fulfillment or realization however transient. Instead of shaking her faith in the rational order of things, her husband's death had quite a different effect. In her deep grief she raged against the dark, revengeful personal God of divine election which she had dismissed as an anthropomorphic fiction twenty years before.

In a week, she resumed her job in the lab. Although Brosnan had G.I. insurance, she realized she would have to bear the whole burden of family support now. Several professors, old friends, former fellow students wrote notes of sympathy. She was kept busy answering them for weeks. The concern expressed by many in the English department led Mrs. Brosnan to believe that a corollary of their sympathy would be some official recognition of her husband's efforts.

At one point, she expected they would grant him the doctorate posthumously at the December graduation. She filled out in her husband's name and filed the forms for the doctorate. But the application was rejected because Brosnan had not retaken his French and German language examinations. A small box was checked in the form response and the University policy was explained in the double asterisk footnote. There was a five year delimiting date on all language exams. Brosnan had intended to take them again, of course, and she wrote explaining the circumstances. The official response was again a coldly impersonal rejection.

What had been shock, then sorrow, then self-pity, then benumbed indifference now turned into anger and indignation. She called the department but was referred to the Dean of the Division of Humanities. She made an appointment with him, but if the nonexistent, non-architect of the universe was completely indifferent to her husband's death, so was the existent University and the more than real (the larger than life) earthy and corpulent, cigar chewing Dean of the Division of Humanities.

She argued, she quibbled, she pleaded, she cried and she raged, but the dean held his ground—explained that the regulations were necessary to protect the integrity of the doctorate. There could be no compromise of excellence. But she argued and cried some more until he thundered in final dismissal of her appeal "that the University did not grant doctorates either previously or posthumously." And he didn't expect a change in policy for some time. When the policy was changed, he would call her.

Her friends told her it didn't seem fair. She called Professor Shelbourne, but he was about to retire and had little influence in the department—had had little influence for some time. He was, in fact, referred to by the middle level age and tenure group as "the old fraud" (or the "old fart" depending upon the degree of hostility and point of view). He was kind and sympathetic but he could do nothing for her.

III

In due and proper course, Virginia Brosnan became the problem of Donald Tyndal, associate professor and Secretary of the Department of English. He had been appointed two years before as a compromise alternative to the candidates presented by the new critic faction and the historical-biographical group. He had managed to steer an independent course. He mocked enough sacred cows to endear himself to the students, yet he was a sound scholar and critic. His book on Twain and American Humor was good (even sporadically humorous itself) but not that good and, of course, American humor was hardly major. In brief, he was solid without threatening anyone.

The secretary had several responsibilities the most important of which were the scheduling of classes and the chairmanship of the graduate admissions and scholarship committee. He was, generally speaking, everyone's trouble shooter especially when it came to unpleasant matters like Virginia Brosnan. Though there was no increase in pay, appointment to the position was evidence that the appointee was being groomed for more important positions—perhaps as a Dean in the Division or in the College. The consensus was that Tyndal had done an excellent job in his first two years. When Virginia Brosnan called the department office once again, this time asking to discuss an important matter, it was natural that she be referred to him. It was late November, a month after her husband's death.

Tyndal was hurriedly briefed over coffee in the bookstore by Professor Watling, the distinguished currently rotating chairman of the department. Between slurps of hot, instant coffee he passed on to Tyndal all the official and unofficial factual, opinionated, and hearsay information about Virginia Brosnan. First of all, and most importantly, she was a pain in the ass. She had called everyone from the Dean down to assistant professors without tenure, trying to cajole or wheedle someone into bestowing the doctorate upon an urn of ashes which she would, undoubtedly, carry forward at the appropriate moment. What the hell she wanted now was beyond him, but she was probably just carrying on Brosnan's tradition of nagging persistence. They had been here since before the Flood and would probably be around after the Conversion of the Jews if somebody didn't do some thing, he complained. "I think the dissertation was finally accepted just to get rid of them. Good Lord, the Brosnans were in half-ass residence longer than most of the faculty. A smart aleck petition was circulated a few years ago by some bright undergraduate to extend him tenure." Finally, Tyndal was assured he could handle the problem but that it would be best to seize the initiative because according to the Dean she could be a genuine, one hundred per cent bitch. And let me know how you make out, he concluded by squeezing his paper cup into a ball and scoring two points in the waste basket.

It was a 5:15 appointment because she worked until five. Normally Tyndal would have left the campus by 3 o'clock. He used the time to catch up on his paper grading. Toward four it began to drizzle. By 5 o'clock there was a cold, late November downpour with flakes of snow blowing and twisting through the rain. She arrived about five minutes late.

Tyndal was not exactly surprised by her appearance, but he had expected a more aggressive, vibrant woman. Virginia Brosnan struck him as dull—responsive but certainly not a persistent pain in the ass as Professor Watling had described her. She was not ugly—but neither was she attractive—rather skinny, with colorless short hair. She wore a brown suit under her raincoat. Her face was thin and sharp. The bridge of her nose arched sharply and prominently between widely spaced, bulging eyes.

She carried a package wrapped in newspaper. As he helped her with her raincoat, she placed the package on the floor. He offered her a chair and as soon as she lighted a cigarette, she picked up the package and began unwrapping the newspaper. Then she slipped what appeared to be a manuscript out of a plastic bag. While they talked, she sat holding the black volume tightly in one hand, then the other as she changed smoking hands. She stretched forward occasionally to tip the ashes into the tray on the front edge of Tyndal's desk.

Tyndal picked up a pad of paper and a pencil and pretended to take notes during their conversation. He felt uneasy, fraudulent, like a quack doctor pretending to professional competence. He leaned back in his chair. She took another cigarette from the package in her purse and lighted it from her first cigarette.

"What time is it?" she asked suddenly. "I'm sorry I'm late. I hurried but I had to finish something at the lab. I don't like to leave the children alone too long."

"Five-twenty," he answered looking at his watch. He looked at her closely. She seemed over the shock of her husband's death; she seemed, in fact, quite rational and controlled. The reports of Professor Watling and the Dean seemed exaggerated. Perhaps, she had settled down. He decided he would be as realistic as possible. He placed his pad and pencil on the desk, folded his hands across his knee, and spoke to her candidly.

"Mrs. Brosnan, I have to be completely frank. There is nothing I can do for you. There is nothing that can be done by anyone. It's a closed matter so far as the department, the division, and the University administrations are concerned. I won't try to justify their decision. It seems to me an exception could have been made in your husband's case, but they have chosen not to do so and that is that."

He finished his little lecture and felt he had made his position firm and clear. She said nothing for a few moments, then she placed the manuscript on his desk and began pushing it toward him.

"I didn't come about that. I don't even care about that anymore."

He stared at the manuscript as it came across the desk toward him.

"I want to know what I have to do about getting Bill's dissertation published."

In order to gain time to think, he picked up the thick, black volume and slowly and reluctantly opened the cover and read, "This dissertation submitted in partial fulfillment of the requirements for the degree of doctor of philosophy in the Department of. . . ." He read the title and the abstract and then began to answer her, groping for words and reasons as he went along.

"I don't know whether it's a publishable book; I mean, I don't know whether there is sufficient interest in the topic to warrant publication. Much of the history of criticism of this period has already been covered by the James dissertation. Though this is the first treatment of Howells, it is not the first treatment of the critics who reviewed Howells. Many also reviewed James and that material has already been published."

He broke off and paused, fumbled for his pad and pencil again and pretended to write something to himself. He did, in fact, copy the title of the dissertation and the date of its submission.

Brosnan's dissertation was the last of a catalogue of topics beginning "The History of the Critical Evaluation of . . ." that began in the late thirties following Professor Wren's conversion to new criticism and his famous purge of the old-line biographical-historical scholars from the department. It was an outmoded topic when Brosnan began it—even Professor Wren had become bored by it and had gone on to other matters before his retirement, but Professor Shelbourne and William Brosnan had apparently come upon this new direction after it had already become a dead end.

"Publication," he continued, "isn't that important anymore with all the information retrieval systems. In due course the dissertation will be microfilmed through the inter-university microfilm service and will be available to anyone interested in Howells or the history of criticism in that period. It will, of course, be catalogued and will become part of the permanent library collection and, finally, it will become part of the Howells' bibliography."

He broke off again. This time she spoke in apparent disregard of everything he had said.

"Where would I send the typescript? What publishers might be interested in this subject? May I send it to more than one publisher at the same time?"

She was looking at the floor. Her hands came together and she began to work them in and out. All of the intensity and despair that he thought she had under control were returning. Tyndal realized that they were not discussing just the possible publication of a dissertation; they were talking about Brosnan himself. Brosnan had no identity except what membership in the academic community had conferred upon him—and immortality in the academic community was, in her mind, equivalent to publication. William Brosnan was his dissertation now that he had been struck dead in the thirty-eighth year of his pilgrimage.

William and Virginia Brosnan's dream had been his dream also, and the dream his wife had shared with him as they struggled through college and then graduate school on the G.I. bill and her job. But he was annoyed that Mrs. Brosnan should impose upon him the burden, the disposition of her husband's legacy. She had appealed to him as an intermediator and now he felt a vague responsibility to do what he could to save William Brosnan from oblivion.

"Bill thought once he might submit it to a few publishers." It seemed as though she were pleading with him but the tone of her voice though more intense was still flatly mechanical.

"Well, I suppose the best procedure would be to work up a letter of description and inquiry and send it along with an abstract of the dissertation to several publishers. There's no point in sending the typescript itself unless there is an interest."

She dug into her purse for a pen and pad and began writing down everything he said as though she were taking notes in a classroom lecture.

"Now the university presses are really the only publishers that might be interested in your husband's work. It would be a waste of time to send it to commercial houses."

"What publishers would you recommend?" she asked.

"Certainly the University Press should be your first query. Then I would send letters of inquiry to at least six or seven other university presses after you have checked their catalogues to see what each seems to be publishing especially in the area of your husband's dissertation, for example, American novelists, late nineteenth century. You might also try to find out what articles and books have been published about Howells recently."

She reviewed what he had told her from her notes, asked a few questions, and snapped her pad closed and thrust it into her purse. She stood up and gathered her coat, reinserted the dissertation into the plastic bag, and announced her departure.

"Could I give you a lift home. It's raining and my car is nearby."

"If you're going that way. I live south, about two miles."

"Right on my way." He hurriedly cleared papers from his desk into his attache case.

"It's really not very far," she commented apologetically. "Bill used to walk to school when the weather was nice. He used to love to take long walks."

Outside it was still raining. He let her in the car and walked back around to the driver's side. He pulled cautiously into the heavy traffic and drove slowly until he reached the first one-way south. Then he drove more boldly, occasionally changing lanes for better position. She said nothing for two or three minutes. She stared ahead of her into the rain, the flashing lights, and the flapping windshield wiper. She clutched the dissertation with both arms folded across her breast. In time she spoke quietly as though she felt reluctantly responsible to structure their time together.

"Did you get your Ph.D. from the University?"

"No. Berkeley. I've been here five years. My first and only job not counting the service and teaching assistantships." He laughed. "Can you believe that? I didn't get a legitimate job until I was almost thirty-two years old. Why, there are fellows I served with in the army who are ready for retirement soon."

"You know Professor McAllister pretty well, I suppose," she said disregarding his efforts at levity.

"Yes, of course. I was his assistant in setting up the interdepartmental committee in the humanities."

"Bill thought he was a brilliant teacher." She paused and decided to shift her burden to her lap. "Bill identified with him very much until his orals." She took out her cigarettes and lighted one. She inhaled deeply and then proceeded to tell him a story, the purpose of which he did not grasp until later.

"Bill worked so hard preparing for his orals. He made his list up carefully distributing the works into five fields. He read a biography of each author and selected critical studies. I quizzed him over and over again. He could identify any line of poetry I asked. He knew the dates of composition and publication of each work. He knew every character—even minor characters from every novel and play. He could identify any allusion or historical or linguistic reference.

"One work that he knew particularly well was "The Deserted Village" which Professor Shelbourne brought up very early in the first session. Bill answered two or three questions when Professor McAllister interrupted to ask what was the average size of a full-grown ewe in 1780?

"Bill had no idea and he was dumbfounded. He tried to guess but he didn't know the size of any sheep in any year. Professor McAllister asked him several more questions about the enclosure movement, its economic origins. All the questioning had something to do with the size of sheep and the amount of grass they consumed. Bill was so rattled he could only stutter and stammer and he became so confused that he could hardly remember anything the rest of the afternoon.

"That night he was more depressed than I had ever seen him. He knew he had failed. We almost quit several times before but we came closest to giving up that night. He kept repeating all evening,

'What was the average size of a full-grown ewe in 1780?' The next day in the stacks he found the unpublished dissertation that Professor McAllister had obviously alluded to. It was entitled 'The Economic Origins of Late Eighteenth Century Pastoral Poetry,' and Bill spent the entire day reading it."

By the time she had finished her story, they were within two blocks of her apartment. After he let her off, he drove west about a mile and then turned south again on the expressway. Half way home he burst out laughing. "Good God," he cried aloud. "What was the average size of a full-grown ewe in 1780? . . .Good God! The Economic Origins of Late Eighteenth Century Pastoral Poetry." He shook his head again. "That goddamn McAllister," he laughed again.

But before he reached home, his laughter had abated.

He knew that he had been moved—essentially—by Virginia Brosnan.

IV

The memorial service for William Brosnan was officially scheduled for the English Common of Wycliffe Hall at two in the afternoon on Wednesday, the twenty-third of January. It was an official decision that resulted in Tyndal's co-ordination of a de facto committee of graduate students and faculty to handle the details of the secular service. The decision was made by the chairman himself, Professor Watling, after a lengthy reconsideration of the department's and the University's traditional policy. It was based upon the individual merits of the case in hand, and, as was clearly explained later at the first departmental meeting in January, was not to be construed as a precedent. After all, he added facetiously, the University was neither a church, a social welfare agency, nor a funeral parlor. But in the case of W1illiam Brosnan (who though only a few months dead was by the fact of his demise as eternally dead as Chaucer or Shakespeare) an exception could be made.

But he had considered the change in policy earlier, by the

time of the Christmas party just before the end of the fall term. About halfway through the party, Professor Watling found Tyndal.

"And how is Mrs. Brosnan treating you, Don," he smiled.

"Not bad. All she wanted was help in submitting her husband's manuscript for publication."

"Well, you did a fine job. She has already written me a note of appreciation for all you did for her. You have taken the pressure off."

"Temporarily. I don't think anyone is going to publish the dissertation."

"I quite agree. Now, I've just been talking to Shelbourne and we think the department ought to do something concrete for Bill Brosnan and his wife."

He seemed deadly serious now. He grasped Tyndal confidentially by the elbow and led him to a quiet side of the room. He continued to squeeze Tyndal's arm as he spoke. Tyndal thought for a moment that he was about to be touched for a contribution to the William Brosnan Memorial Scholarship Fund.

"Everything is unofficial just yet, but we think a small memorial service would be appropriate. All the details haven't been worked out. I'd like to have you expedite the matter. Perhaps, a faculty and graduate student committee headed up by you. Shelbourne will help, of course, and we'll talk to Mrs. Brosnan to see what she wants."

"I'll do what I can," Tyndal shrugged.

"Dan Perkins, the head of the graduate English club, should be of some help. You know him, of course. He's a top student and has done a fine job with the teas this year."

"I think he'll do very well. But do you think he'll cooperate. He doesn't seem like the type."

"I've already sounded him out. He is still very appreciative of that graduate fellowship we gave him instead of the teaching assistantship. He felt it might be difficult to get other students interested though. You know, because Brosnan has not been a full-time student for several years. And though he didn't know Brosnan too well, he said he'd do what he could. He even suggested the Common

Room for the ceremony. Mrs. Brosnan probably won't go for a service in the chapel. Shelbourne feels pretty certain she won't want anything religious, no clergy or anything. Brosnan was a renegade Catholic. They were Unitarians for a while but have had no affiliation for several years. Besides this has to be strictly English department."

"I'll think about it over vacation." Tyndal wanted to appear reassuring "I might come up with an idea or two."

"Good. Good." Professor Watling smiled and turned away toward the bar.

Tyndal mixed himself another drink and a light one for his wife. After three more drinks the problems he envisioned of implementing a secular memorial service for William Brosnan began to fade along with his critical faculties and his sense of balance. But his problems returned the next morning in objective perspective. It all seemed so ridiculous. How could he begin to plan the details of a secular memorial ceremony? For the entire Christmas vacation he was plagued by visions of a grotesque and tasteless ritual in which nothing went according to plan. One night he had a nightmare in which he was robed like a Druid priest. On his head was a papal miter and in his one hand a scepter. With the other hand he was blessing an urn, ostensibly filled with the ashes of William Brosnan. Upon closer scrutiny he discovered that the urn was the very Grecian Urn about which Keats had composed his ode. Virginia Brosnan dressed in black was kneeling a few feet away from the urn.

He remembered the ending of the dream vividly for several hours after he had awakened. Following his blessing and incantation, he began reciting lines from the "Ode" which in turn led to the recitation in a grandly theatrical style of famous lines from great poems and Shakespeare. The final lines that he recited were from Marvel.

> The gravel's a fine and private place.
> But none, I think, do there embrace.

and they signaled a conclusion to the ceremony and the symbolic liberation of Virginia Brosnan whose mourning clothes suddenly fell from her shoulders revealing her in an attractive, stylish, short red dress with garish accessories. She turned with a beatific smile to meet her future as Tyndal woke up.

On the first day of classes of the winter term, Tyndal looked up Dan Perkins' schedule and asked one of the secretaries to deliver a note asking Perkins to meet him at the Student Union cafeteria for coffee at two.

Perkins was a young man of inexhaustible good humor. In the one course he took from Tyndal, Perkins revealed an incisive mind, a quick wit, and cruelly objective prose style that verged upon mockery. Though his body language conveyed the sense that testing was a waste of his time to deal with such drivel, he always answered the question precisely and accurately.

Perkins' classroom contributions, his perceptive and searching questions, became the focus of Tyndal's course that term. And there was a great deal of laughter, of healthy give and take, of spontaneous wit. It was with serious misgivings that Tyndal waited over coffee for Perkins' arrival.

Perkins was just a few minutes late. Tyndal sipped his coffee and watched Perkins wave, hang up his coat, and then get in line for coffee. Perkins was a tall, thin, and impeccably dressed graduate of Yale via one of the New England preparatory schools. He called everyone "sir" with explosive gusto and he was always smiling. His hair was short and parted high on one side. His thin, sharply angular face was decorated by a pair of small, circular steel-rimmed glasses. When he loosened his jacket to sit down with his coffee, Tyndal saw that Perkins was wearing a purple brocade vest. For a moment he thought he recognized a vague resemblance between Perkins and the young Rudy Vallee.

"Well, I guess we have a problem for which I sincerely apologize," Tyndal smiled.

"That's O.K., sir," Perkins smiled. "It's not your fault. In fact, it's my own damn fault. I should never have accepted this graduate English Club nonsense last fall. And after accepting it, I should not have done such a fine job with the teas." He paused to sip his coffee. "The truth is, my downfall can be traced to the high tea, complete with cucumber sandwiches, that I engineered in honor of Mr. Watling just before the Thanksgiving vacation." He shook his head in mock self-pity.

They laughed together for a few moments, and after a brief and awkward pause, Tyndal turned directly to the business at hand.

"I assume that Mr. Watling has spoken to you already, so all I want to do is review the tentative arrangements. It's scheduled for the twenty-third of this month. That's the day of the weekly tea. We thought we could have it at two. Then you would have time for the tea at three-thirty. In fact, I had hoped to correlate the two, that is, perhaps Mrs. Brosnan could be a guest at the tea. Is that O.K. with you?"

"Yes, sir, but that's no problem. What exactly do you want me to do about the ceremony?"

"We wanted to create the effect that this is a joint faculty-student memorial. If I call her and make all of the arrangements, it will seem that everything is from the top, as it were, rather than a tribute from across the board."

"Then I can expect to contact her at some time in the near future?'

"I will call her today, probably this evening. She works days, here at the Clinics. In fact, if you have to meet her to talk about anything, you will be able to get hold of her right here on campus. After I have called, I had hoped you would follow up with a call. Find out exactly what she wants, then we'll get together and work out the details."

"Sounds simple enough. Anything else I should know?"

"Well, she has two children, a boy and a girl. She's trying to get her husband's dissertation published. I've been helping her with inquiries but I don't think there will be any positive results." He paused. "And I suppose you ought to know that everyone thinks she's a neurotic bitch. I didn't find her too bad. Pushy and persistent. Pathetic." He shrugged off further objections, Then he added,

"Maybe you ought to look at his dissertation before you call her. It's in the stacks. On Howells."

"Thanks for the negative side." He smiled again.

"I can't tell you how much I appreciate your help in this matter, Perkins." Though his voice revealed genuine emotion, Tyndal was afraid he might have implied a note of forced sincerity, but Perkins received his gratitude with good grace and a joke to cover their mutual embarrassment.

That very evening he called Mrs. Brosnan at her home.

"The department has decided upon a memorial service for your husband," he said. There was a pause of several moments, then the same,, mechanical voice.

"When?"

"On the twenty-third, we thought, in the early afternoon if that's convenient for you?"

"What day is that?"

"Wednesday."

"I'll have to get off work and take the children out of school for the day."

"Would you prefer to have it in the evening? We hoped to make it part of the academic day. More people will have a chance to attend. I am sorry if Wednesday is an inconvenient day."

"Wednesday the twenty -third will be all right," she interrupted. He paused to adjust to the abruptness of her response.

"One of the graduate students will call you in the next day or so to talk over the ceremony. His name is Dan Perkins. He knew your husband."

"When will he call?"

"I don't know exactly, probably tomorrow night."

"All right."

Two days later Perkins met him in the departmental office and the two retired to Tyndal's office.

"Well, sir," Perkins smiled as he sat down. "I think I've got all the information we'll need to proceed on the specific level."

"You've talked to Mrs. Brosnan, then?"

"I've not only spoken to her, sir, but we've had two meetings over coffee. I have read the dissertation and I've spoken in some detail with Professor Watling. I think we're all set except for you, sir. You're going to have to do something in the ceremony itself."

"Me? What could I possibly do?"

"Now, don't you fret, sir," Perkins smiled. "We've given you the easiest job of all."

"Who is we?" He tried to smile.

"Why, Mrs. Brosnan, Professor Shelbourne, and, of course, Professor Watling."

"I thought we were going to do this together."

"We are, but I'm trying to take care of as many of the details as possible so you won't be burdened. I've found out what she wants and I've been checking with those who will be helpful. I just haven't gotten to you yet. Nothing is set unless you approve anyway, sir. I hope you don't think I've been presumptuous."

"No. No." Tyndal felt useless, almost foolish, but he knew that Perkins was only doing what he had asked him to do. That Perkins was more efficient than he had anticipated was a reality to be appreciated not criticized. "What do you want me to do?" He smiled openly, trying to reassure Perkins of his cooperation.

"Sir, you have the honor or reading the abstract and of placing everything into its proper historical context. You come on first."

What abstract?"

"The abstract of the dissertation,, of course! That's what she wants for the ceremony. Selected readings from `The History of the Critical Evaluation of the Major Novels of William Dean Howells'."

"Good God, No!"

"Good God, Yes, sir!" Perkins was beaming.

Tyndal grasped his hair with both hands and pretended to tear it out melodramatically. Perkins laughed out loud. After Tyndal had recovered he asked,

"And what is my job again?"

"You will open the ceremony by reading the abstract and commenting on what an important contribution to the history of criticism and scholarship the dissertation is."

"Is that all? And then what happens after I make a fool of myself?"

"Why then there are four others, following you, including me, who will each have an opportunity to outfool you."

"And what, pray tell, will the other four be doing?"

"As I envision it all, sir, you will open up the ceremony with the abstract, then Dawson will read a selected passage from 'Lycidas'"

"Dawson? Who's Dawson?"

"He's an undergraduate. Philosophy major."

"Not the Dawson of the poetry reading contest. Third prize as I remember."

"The very same complete with every Dylan Thomas affectation and mannerism of voice. I tried to get Melbourne or that girl who won second prize, but they wouldn't have anything to do with it. Melbourne once said he would read for twenty dollars, but I told him we were running on a low budget."

"Let me guess the rest of the format. Dawson then is going to read passages from several of the great elegies. These readings will be interspersed among the selections from the dissertation that you and Professor Shelbourne and Professor Watling will read."

"Exactly. Mrs. Brosnan picked the poems and passages, each from an important literary period. 'Lycidas,' 'Adonais,' and *In Memorian*, all of which, obviously, were written in memory of the death of a relatively young man. The wasted potential bit. Professor Shelbourne will be last. He will preface his reading with some personal recollections and reflections. Professor Watling and I will read short sections to give everyone the idea of the development." Perkins sat back obviously pleased with the work he had accomplished on such short notice. Tyndal thought for a moment and then asked.

"That's what she really wants?"

"That's what she wants, sir."

"Well, I suppose we had better give her what she wants."

V

One afternoon, a week later, Tyndal sat in his office, trying to grade papers. It was a gloomy midwinter day; the snow had shrunk and hardened and turned a dirty grey. He couldn't concentrate on his reading. He put his pen down, walked to the window, and peered down into the quadrangle.

As he vacantly watched students hurrying along the paths, disappearing into and around buildings, he brooded about the shape his life had taken. Over the past few years, he realized how artificial his every action had become, virtually an imitation of art. His broad reading background made it difficult for him to feel or do anything without acute self consciousness. He continually saw his own experience refracted through the prism of literary or historical analogy. He rarely had a bowel movement, for example, without thinking of Bloom straining in a Dublin privy. Recently, it seemed, that his life was becoming, even more remotely, an imitation of the critical principles derived from the study of literature and art. His days were full of metaphorical epiphanies and peripeties.

The students in each new class reminded him of students he had taught before as a graduate assistant before he finished his doctorate or in the first few years of teaching at the University. In the middle of a class he occasionally lapsed into a startling deja vu. For perhaps a whole minute he experienced a verbatim duplication of a discussion he had conducted four or five years before.

He walked away from the window toward his desk and stopped, staring at the papers yet to be read. He wanted to go home right then and there, but he had vowed as a form of self-discipline to remain every afternoon until he had finished most of his preparation for the next day. As the school year progressed, it became more difficult to keep his vow and he yearned, guiltily, to leave earlier each progressively dreadful winter afternoon.

His office was, like a monastic cell, drab and coldly functional, a high narrow room whose windows opened upon the quadrangle through one of the slits in the fake turret of what was supposed to represent a battlement of a medieval castle. Though imitative and impractical, the gothic architecture of the University symbolized the asceticism and the higher aspirations of the intellectual world. Tyndal had lived according to those ideals through graduate school and through the first years of teaching. He believed the academic community was the last refuge of the mind in a world of gross materialism, commercialism, and military and industrial domination of the American experience. He still believed in the mind and what the University stood for—the pursuit of truth, but in recent years (two years before to be precise) since he purchased a home in a small suburban community, he had been building a separate world for his wife and children, one in which he had no identity as a professor. It was a secret world to which he escaped and where he lived incognito. He was simply another husband who commuted to the city. He had come to enjoy the delights of middle class materialism, of wall-to-wall carpeting, color television, of cocktail parties and sizzling steaks.

He saw himself as a kind of contemporary Wemmick, but in Tyndal's case the two worlds were equally satisfying, equally rational. The old dualism seemed to obtain. The one world satisfied the body, the other the mind. But deep down he felt he had sold out, betrayed his own ideals and those of his profession. However rational and ordered his bourgeois life might be, it was still predicated on the conception of the human body as a pleasure machine. Materialism was essentially a calculated hedonism. Each day in class he preached one set of values, and each night he deserted those values for a mindless domestic, sensuality. Each afternoon he brooded over his failure as intensely as he grew excited in anticipation of leaving his monastic cell for the delights of suburbia.

He was rescued temporarily from his dismal contemplation by a knock on the half open door, which began to swing open before he could answer.

"I was just walking by and thought I'd just stop by and say hello." A smiling Dan Perkins, overcoat over one arm, brief case under the other, stood hesitantly in the doorway.

"Come in. Come in. I was just hoping someone would interrupt me. I can't read another paper. Freshman Comp." He pointed to his desk. "Really dreadful. Everyone, even distinguished service professors, has to teach a section—one of the main selling points of the University. I leave the door half open on purpose so that I will be interrupted."

Tyndal sat behind his desk as Perkins walked across the room to the chair Tyndal had, with a wave of his hand, offered him. Perkins slumped lazily into the chair, dropped his overcoat and brief ease to the floor and begun unbuttoning his vest. Then he pulled his tie knot down and unbuttoned his shirt and collar.

"Do I feel loose, sir, really loose. I just finished a test on eighteenth century poetry. Did you know, sir, that Alexander Pope was four feet, six inches tall and that Queen Anne had seventeen children, none of whom survived childhood?"

"Is that so?"

"Yes, sir. Just two insignificant facts among the myriad of irrelevancies over which I have just demonstrated complete mastery."

"You must be just about through with your course work, aren't you?"

"Actually, except for a few courses that are given in alternate years, I was pretty much done last fall.

"Have you decided on a topic yet?"

"Not really. I thought I would do something with Eliot, but I heard you have to pay by the line for quoted materials so I gave that up. I think maybe I'll do something with William Dean Howells. I feel as though I'm almost an expert already." Again Perkins' face broke into a grin.

"Well, you could do worse, and the field's not crowded."

"I'm not going to hurry. I think I'll just look around for a year or two. Maybe teach. Join the growing army of ABD's."

"Don't wait too long. It's easy to let it all slide."

"Never fear. Actually, I've got a great topic already, but I need an imaginative and progressive committee." Crew wings of laughter formed around his eyes. "I was wondering if you'd be willing to be my dissertation adviser. It's in American Lit."

"Let's hear your proposal first. Then I'll tell you if I'm interested."

"Already I can tell you're too conservative. I don't think you're going to be too excited. I've only got a tentative title so far. I haven't settled on specifics yet, but as I see it, it's title will be 'Penis Envy in Emily Dickinson.'"

"That's absurd. Outrageous."

"Oh, I don't know about that. There's the 'narrow fellow in the grass' and some worm imagery."

"That's not enough material for a course paper."

"I know. That's the problem, but the topic isn't as absurd as you think. I've heard worse. I know a guy in sociology who did a study of the adjustment problems of retired YMCA secretaries."

"You don't have to go out of the English Department to find ridiculous theses. Just last week I heard of one that's almost unbelievable, but I understand it's been accepted at a certain distinguished university somewhat east and north of here. It was entitled 'A Vindication of Lord Byron in the Matter of Incest' or something like that. It seems that the author discovered a letter written by Augusta revealing, cryptically of course, the date of one of her periods. Assuming that her periods were regular, the author asserted with mathematical certainty that she was indisposed at the time the alleged intercourse took place."

"What does that prove?" Perkins interrupted. Anyone willing to lay his sister is not about to balk at a slight organic indisposition."

"But you haven't let me state his main argument. He concedes that Byron, the man, could be immoral, even incestuous, but Lord Byron, the noble English peer, would not have been unfastidious."

Perkins slumped back in his chair with a jerk, pretending to have received a fatal head wound. When he recovered, he leaned forward on his chair and put his elbows on Tyndal's desk.

"I don't believe a word you've said. I don't believe a goddamn word. You're putting me on."

Tyndal raised his right hand and then placed it on his heart. "I swear it's the truth. I swear I have fairly characterized the substance of the dissertation topic. I consider my source to be highly reliable."

"Great God, I'd rather be a pagan suckled in a creed outworn than believe somebody got a Ph.D. for that pile of manure. Besides, I don't believe any of it. I don't want to believe any of that revisionist nonsense. Give me back the old, dirty Byron. In fact, I can see him now, in appropriate period costume, sitting on a couch, leaning with amorous intent toward his semi-reluctant semi-sister, his eyes peering down her ample bosom." Perkins stood up, outlining with his waving arms the portrait he had just described. "As he looks, he whispers satanically into her ear the immortal words of Lady Macbeth, `Tush, tush, Augie Baby,' he says. `A little water clears us of this deed. How easy is it then!'." Perkins exploded with laughter, falling backward into his chair. Tyndal laughed along quietly with him, but he was troubled by Perkins' unwarranted derisiveness. In a few minutes, however, he managed to get away from Byron.

"Speaking of dissertations and our impending project," Tyndal asked, "I was wondering what our mutual friend William Brosnan was really like as a person? I never really knew him. I saw him occasionally. He had finished his course work before I came. I understand you knew him."

"A serious question." Perkins' smile disappeared. "A serious question deserves an objective answer. Let me see. Where shall I begin, with a generalization or a narrative story of our somewhat sporadic relationship?" Perkins took off his glasses and began polishing them with his handkerchief. He put them on and folded his handkerchief neatly as he spoke. "I think I will begin with a generalization: William Brosnan was the living embodiment of the derivative mind. He was humorless bore who couldn't detect a metaphor in a poem unless it had become a cliche or had been footnoted and explained. He was an expert at academic oneupsmanship. You know the bit, sir. There's no possessive in

Finnegans Wake or How can you begin to understand that poem unless you've read 'Teleological Aspects of Absurdity' by Professor I. M. Parochial in the fall number of Obscurity magazine. In short, my evaluation of William Brosnan, which I might add is the consensus judgment of those who knew him, is that he was an unimaginative pedant who couldn't interpret a line of literature without reading a minimum of two secondary sources and an academically orthodox biography of the author."

Tyndal was surprised by the savage passion with which Perkins delivered his tirade.

"I didn't know you felt so strongly about him," Tyndal said. "Had I known, I would never have asked you to help. I'm really quite sorry.'

Perkins smiled again.

"Oh, I don't feel that strongly, sir. I suppose I should admit that I live in a continual state of holy terror that I might become, in time, a William Brosnan myself. My hostility is really only a futile gesture against my own destiny." Perkins suddenly stopped and fingered the knot in his tie for several-moments.

"Say, are you sure you don't mind shooting off like this, sir? You must have better things to do than listening to me running off at the mouth."

"No. No." Tyndal dismissed any objections he might have with a wave or his hand. "I find your comments always perceptive and often amusing. I don't mean to change the subject again but I have a question I would like to ask. I'm afraid it verges upon the personal."

"Go ahead so long as it isn't about my sex life. I haven't had much lately."

"No, nothing that personal. I was just wondering why you use the formal address 'sir' all the time. Your speech is, if you will pardon the trite diction, riddled with 'sirs.'"

Perkins shook his head despairingly.

"Can't help it, sir. It's an ingrained habit. Picked it up in prep school. It's the price I pay for the free ride I have had since I was fifteen. You see, I was minding my own business back in Hazardville, Ohio, when my junior high school English teacher decided I was brighter than the average moron. In turn, she informed the local Congregational minister, who, as a loyal alumnus of a well-endowed New England prep school, recruited me with a full scholarship. It was there the habit developed.

"From there I went to Yale on full scholarship and then came here on full scholarship. I now have a fellowship and with luck, I hope to got a University grant to tide me over while I'm doing my dissertation when I finally decide what I'm going to do."

"Hazardville, Ohio! Where in the world is that?"

"Oh, way out in the boondocks, sir. My old man has a gas station and fuel oil service there. He is also the mayor. He has been the mayor for about twenty years now. He can't get rid of the job. Twice he refused to run, but the local citizens re-elected him with a write-in vote each time. I don't think the population has reached five hundred yet, but we have a booming economy based upon a chicken slaughterhouse and a grain elevator."

It was after four o'clock before Perkins finished talking and before Tyndal began clearing his desk of notes and papers to be taken home for reading and grading.

VI

The programs, which included biographical data as well as the Order of Service, were typed and mimeographed by one of the secretaries. Specific announcements of the services were mailed to Mrs. Brosnan's non-academic friends. The editor of the alumni magazine promised to carry an article with a picture in the necrology of the winter issue. The University daily newspaper carried a black-bordered announcement and a notification of the date and time of the services.

Despite all the preparation, Tyndal grew more and more apprehensive as the hour of service grew near. He cut his morning classes short and didn't eat lunch. Although Perkins had executed each of the details of the publicity and the arrangements flawlessly, Tyndal had rechecked him anyhow.

Tyndal had visions of no one showing up. Once he had the terrifying fantasy that some radical student organization might picket the service or seize the Commons for a demonstration against the irrelevance of the English curriculum. There was no question that many students had legitimate objections to the narrowness of English literature curriculum. But at the heart of his apprehensions was the fear of appearing foolish or ridiculous.

He picked up the programs in the departmental office and proceeded to climb the three flights of stairs to the Commons on the fourth floor of Wycliffe Hall. When he arrived a full half-hour before anyone was expected, he found Perkins at the far end of the room rearranging the heavy drapes over the windows. Perkins waved.

Tyndal sat down on the first chair inside the door and took out the two file cards on which he had transcribed in minute handwriting the substance of his comments to be delivered in just thirty minutes. After reviewing his speech once again he surveyed the room where William Brosnan was about to be temporarily recalled, then memorialized, and finally forgotten for all eternity.

The English Commons was a substantial room with dark red carpeting and heavy wooden paneling. At the far end of the room the windows, across which Perkins was drawing drapes, curved across the narrow structural bulge which, if viewed from the outside, formed a section of one of the stony turrets of a medieval castle wall, which in turn housed the English, classics, modern languages, and history departments. Around the room in recessed wooden panels hung the gilt framed portrants of some of the University's great scholars—the Great Men—whose accomplishments would stand as eternal reminders of the incredible excellence which was, in fact, the only tradition of the University. At that moment, it seemed to Tyndal that they were ikons of a sort, foreboding academic saints, whose posed and pompous, well-robed airs commanded a genuflection and a prayer, perhaps even a waft of incense from the intellectual novitiates of another and probably less significant era of academic history.

Perkins had re-ordered the furniture of the room. The heavy leather chairs and sofas had been moved and placed along the walls. Folding chairs had been taken from storage and arranged like pews facing a dark stained, heavy oak table which had been placed across the window end of the room and upon which lay a copy of the dissertation. To the left, near one end of the table was a metal pulpit-like rostrum with a small neon reading lamp. Only a few of the side wall lamps had been lighted.

Perkins came toward him and then turned toward the door of the storage and kitchen alcove, a small closet-size room directly across from where Tyndal was sitting. In a few moments, he appeared again bearing two candles, each in an ornate silver holder. As he proceeded to the far end of the room, Tyndal called after him.

"And what do you plan to do with them?" He spoke too loudly for the acoustics of the room and was startled by the barking harshness of his own voice.

"With what?" Perkins turned and grinned. "With the candles? Oh, I thought we could use one on each side of the dissertation."

"Are you going to light them?"

"Of course. Who ever heard of a memorial service without candles." He seemed to be searching his memory for an illustration. "Once when I was going to prep school I had to deliver a little speech of gratitude to the Elks or the Lions or one of the totem identification organizations back in good old Hazardville, I forget which one, for the two hundred dollar scholarship they had awarded me. It was at the end of Christmas vacation and before I was to deliver my talk, they had their annual memorial service for members who had died during that year. They had empty places set at the tables symbolizing the recently departed brethren, and at the head table were five or six candles, each representing the spirit of a loved one who had crossed the bar, so to speak. Well, at the end of the memorial speeches and the mumbo jumbo, the high potentate extinguished the candles one at a time and then one of the chief assistants brought a candle to each empty seat. It was really quite effective especially if you were a Moose or an Elk or a Zebra."

Perkins had turned around and had walked back toward Tyndal during his explanation.

"Well, what happened then?" Tyndal asked.

"Oh, nothing, sir. It was all over. I thanked them. They applauded their generosity. I left."

"Are you sure the candles will help?"

"Absolutely necessary, sir." He held them out for inspection. "I'll extinguish them at the end of the ceremony."

"Well, all right, I suppose, but only two candles. We don't want too much magic lantern business." He hoped his voice conveyed the right amount of esoteric irony. Perkins turned toward the other end of the room but after a few steps he turned back suddenly.

"Magic lantern business?" Perkins looked puzzled. Magic lantern? Magic lantern? Mann?"

"No.

"Conrad?"

"Wrong again."

Suddenly Perkins brightened.

"Joyce.

"Right."

"Dubliners."

"You're getting warm. Which story?"

"Not 'The Dead'...just before it...'Grace.' That's it. 'Grace.' Kernan, he of the thick clotted tongue."

"Alpha minus. A bit slow on the identification."

Perkins held out the candles again. He shrugged his shoulders and seemed to suggest with a twisting shake of his hands that the candles were of little importance.

"Mere tokenism, sir."

"All right. We just want to keep things in proportion."

"Right, sir."

The first to arrive were the Colemans, the neighbors who had assisted Mrs. Brosnan the night her husband died. Then came Mrs. Brosnan's friends from the labs, two doctors and several lab technicians, mostly graduate students' wives like Mrs. Brosnan. They stood indecisively just outside the door. When Perkins saw them, he hurried back the length of the room. As Perkins approached, Tyndal caught his attention by waving the programs and motioning him to take them. Then Perkins greeted the mourners and ushered them to seats.

Tyndal moved toward the front of the room and selected a seat close to the wall in the second row so that he could quickly and unobtrusively slip forward to the lectern, deliver his speech, and return to his chair. For the first time in his years at the University he studied closely the carvings which-formed a border around each of the panel units. After a few minutes he decided that the design was, indeed, intended to represent an endless chain of eternally fornicating hippos. He wondered why anyone would want to decorate the English Commons with such a design.

The room began to fill quickly. Professor Watling arrived, nodded at Tyndal, and sat behind him. Several couples, presumably friends of the Brosnans, arrived in pairs, sat briefly in isolation, and then upon recognition, moved together to form a cluster. Professor McAllister, who had flunked Brosnan in his first orals examination, took a seat in the last row. He did not appear particularly enthusiastic. He squirmed in his seat for several moments, then finally settled upon a comfortable position and stared absently at one of the portraits. Apparently, Professor Watling had done a bit of arm twisting. Tyndal thought briefly about the size of a full grown ewe in 1780 England. He wondered what the correct answer was.

And, apparently, Perkins had done some proselytizing also. Several graduate students filtered quietly in and began to fill the empty spaces between the whispering clusters of old friends and the faculty members who had already arrived and had taken up well distributed positions. By the time the Dean arrived punctually at two by the chapel bell, Tyndal realized the room was almost full.

He was seized for a moment by panic. He looked once more over his notes for reassurance. Then his panic settled into a less anxious state of gnawing tension. When at five after Mrs. Brosnan had not yet arrived, he began twisting in his seat, peering at the doorway, hoping that the fact of his scrutiny would produce the object of his anxiety. But, unfortunately, Mrs. Brosnan did not arrive; each minute they waited seemed unendurably long. He must have turned around several times, for Professor Watling finally leaned forward to tap him on the elbow.

"Shelbourne is bringing them. They'll make it."

He smiled briefly and then turned to fix his gaze upon the copy of the dissertation which Perkins had placed squarely between the two lighted candles.

Mrs. Brosnan and her two children finally arrived with Professor Shelbourne. Tyndal was surprised to discover how handsome the children were. The boy, dressed in a dark suit with a white shirt and light blue tie, was about ten years of age. Escorting his mother on one arm, he followed Shelbourne. Trailing was the daughter, a child of eight or so who clung to her mother's hand as they hurried to their seats in front of the room. After they were seated, Perkins closed the door and came forward to take his seat at Mrs. Brosnan's right just in the front row.

There were several moments of shuffling feet and turning heads. A certain anxiety, born of uncertainty and embarrassment, seemed to settle on the group. Tyndal peered toward Perkins who stared straight ahead. Professor Shelbourne turned around and seemed to be looking for someone, probably Tyndal or Professor Watling. Shelbourne took out a set of file cards from his pocket and began to examine them one at a time and then shuffled them in front of him.

Tyndal knew it was his moment to move. As he stood up and began walking forward, he was struck by the sudden realization that he had not seen the undergraduate who was supposed to read the poetry selections. He reached in his pocket to take out his note cards and placed them with a slightly trembling hand on the lectern as he turned to face his congregation. He looked out searching for Dawson's face. He tinkered with the reading light pretending to adjust it. He looked up once more, and after searching the faces collected before him, saw Dawson sitting three or four rows behind Professor Watling. The sense of relief he felt at the moment released the tension that had been building since morning. He spoke easily without either hesitating or stammering. Unconsciously he set the tone of the relaxed almost friendly formality that pervaded the entire ceremony.

He spoke rather eloquently of the revolution in higher learning that Professor Wren had spearheaded at the University. It is true, he summarized, that historical background and biographical information is important for the understanding of any work of art, but whenever scholars and critics become primarily concerned with background materials to the exclusion of the corpus itself, then it is time for re-evaluation.

The obsession with biographical and historical materials had misdirected the energies of two generations of scholars (even though much important information had been accumulated in those years), but the simple truth was that two generations of students had been directed away from the text. It was Professor Wren's great contribution, in addition to his obvious eminence as probably the finest Eighteenth Century scholar in the history of the University to have through his discovery in his later years of the great critics—of Aristotle, Longinus, Sidney, Johnson, and Coleridge— to have accomplished a re-direction of attention to the work itself. In his attempt to formulate the true principles of critical judgment as a branch of aesthetics, he had liberated literature from the dominance of history and had given it a new freedom and thrust as the handmaiden of philosophy.

As a result of Professor Wren's change in academic focus, tremendous new energies were released and critics discovered again the purity and architectonic brilliance of the masterpieces of western culture. A new generation of scholars and critics also discovered the great critics, and as a result of the need to know what critical problems had already been solved, it became apparent that a solid foundation in the history of criticism had to be laid lest energy be wasted by each generation formulating the same artistic principles over and over again in different words or out of a different dialectic.

And finally, it was in the context of this last new direction that Tyndal placed William Brosnan's original contribution to the knowledge of mankind—"The History of the Critical Evaluation of the Major Novels of William Dean Howells." He then read the abstract crisply and forcefully and returned to his seat.

Dawson carrying a small volume in his hand came forward immediately. He opened the book flatly on the lectern and began fiddling with his place marker. After what seemed to Tyndal to be an incredibly long rhetorical pause, Dawson began to read softly the lines from 'Lycidas' that Mrs. Brosnan had selected. Within several lines, however, Dawson was booming with all the emotional and inflectional intensity of the voice he was obviously imitating. His long, black locks rose and fell as he bobbed back and forth in physical reinforcement of the deep feeling evoked by Milton's majestic lines. Tyndal unconsciously bent over and pretended to be staring at the floor in contemplative appreciation of the emotion of the moment. But he was, in fact, so embarrassed by the artificiality of the delivery that it seemed he could feel his shame creeping hotly into his face. If imitation is the soul of art, he thought, then Dawson is surely one of the great artists of all time.

But by the middle of the reading Dawson seemed to have settled down. As Tyndal sat staring at the floor, he heard a note of restraint develop in Dawson's voice. He looked up and saw that Dawson's annoying mannerism of bobbing back and forth and switching his weight from foot to foot was virtually under control. By the end of the excerpt Tyndal felt that 'Lycidas' had moved the congregation. In spite of Dawson, it was possible that Milton had won the day for William Brosnan.

Then the ceremony, its order established by Professor Watling's reading and the return of Dawson, seemed to move rapidly toward consummation. Tyndal was impressed by the substance of Professor Watling's selections. Though he read for less than five minutes, Tyndal felt he had conveyed a fair sense of the "labor" of the dissertation. Professor Watling's reading was, in effect, a catalogue of fact, quotations, and references. He suggested through his representative paragraphs the empirical verisimilitude, the essential authenticity of Brosnan's scholarship.

There was only one interruption of the smooth flow of the ritual, and it took on, because of Perkins quick response, the effect of an interlude that implied the half-way point of the ceremony. Between Dawson's second performance and Perkins' reading, Mrs. Brosnan opened her purse and took out a cigarette which she placed between her lips while she searched for matches. She peered into the open purse and probed its depths with one hand several times without success.

Quickly and unobtrusively, as though it were an integral part of the rite, Perkins stood up, stepped to the table, and picked up one of the candles and while carefully protecting the flame with one cupped hand, offered the light to Mrs. Brosnan.

She raised her cigarette to the flame and like a feeding goldfish puffed and sucked her cheeks as her puckered lips nibbled the end of the cigarette. As she inhaled deeply, she nodded her appreciation to Perkins. Then, after working her jaw and lips for a few moments, she wiped from the tip of her tongue a shred of tobacco with her finger. With two or three gentle snaps of her wrist, she flicked it toward the floor.

Immediately, from behind him and across the room Tyndal could hear the rustling of relaxation. A few purses snapped open, the chairs creaked as members of the congregation shifted the weight of their bodies to more comfortable positions. He could hear the crackling of cellophane and the sounds of lighters and matches being struck as the smokers, following Mrs. Brosnan's lead, lighted cigarettes.

Later, he recalled the rest of the ceremony in snatches and fragments. He remembered Perkins' precise and articulate reading, Dawson's restrained rendition of passages from *In Memoriam*, and Professor Shelbourne's rambling, anecdotal reminiscences of the young William Brosnan. Tyndal remembered wincing when Shelbourne summarized his personal remarks by suggesting that "Bill Brosnan had always revealed in his written work a learned and sweeping prose style not unlike the Milton of Areopagitica."

And then it was all over. Perkins blew out the candles.

Tyndal himself helped fold and remove chairs. Perkins and several graduate students drew the heavy drapes to the side of the windows and rearranged the furniture. The mourners waited in the hall and talked with Mrs. Brosnan until Perkins called them back as guests of a departmental tea honoring Virginia Brosnan and children.

He remembered the Brosnan children darting joyfully about the room. He remembered that Dawson was the center of a great deal of attention from Mrs. Brosnan's fellow employees and that they engaged him to read at the next meeting of the Clinic's Cultural Club. He overheard Dawson promise to read not only his own poems (he allowed that he was a fledgling poet) but also selections from Dylan Thomas and T. S. Eliot. He remembered the firm elbow squeeze from Professor Watling as he whispered into Tyndall's ear, "A most satisfactory job, Don, most satisfactory." And finally, just before he left for home, he remembered that an ebullient Virginia Barton Brosnan, a copy of her husband's dissertation pressed tightly against her bosom, extended a warm and lingering handshake and professed her profound, sincere, and eternal gratitude. For ever and ever.

OF STREETCARS, STRANGERS, CHESTNUTS, AND CHILDHOOD

Once when I was a young man, not so very long ago, I lived in the Midwest— not in any obvious place like Keokuk or Muncie but way out on the irrelevant and sub-arctic edge—in St. Paul to be precise. Now I confess that having lived in St. Paul is no special recommendation unless you were a good hockey player or ski jumper or unless you lived out on Summit Avenue and stood in line to inherit a railroad or a lumber company or a brewery. I lived there by heritage not by choice and I left as soon as I could, which you must concede, if you have survived just one, let alone over twenty grim, cold Minnesota winters, is a sign of some degree of practical intelligence if not ambition. I also felt then a young man's foolish despair that because I could not skate or ski or inherit a fortune I didn't have much of a future and so I left for California to find one.

I was returning home one night on one of the old, screeching, lurching, yellow streetcars since retired to the junk yard in favor of buses. It was about two in the morning, and I had taken my usual position on the rear platform with my back warming against the waist-high radiators. It was bitter cold and the conductor had humanely decided not to open the rear doors unless someone specifically pressed the rear buzzer.

I say humanely on purpose because streetcar conductors were a strange and unpredictable lot. Most of what I learned about human nature before I was twenty years of age was based upon my observation of streetcar conductors. Here was harassed humanity in the raw: underpaid, understaffed, and under pressure. There were heroes and villains, saints and sinners—a complete spectrum of types and individuals to be observed and noted, admired and forgiven. But, alas, they are gone now, and I fear that our lives will be somehow less exciting, less fruitful because Progress has unsympathetically consigned the old cars to the junk heap and their conductors to oblivion. But enough nostalgia. I am for progress in history as well as in this story.

That particular night many years ago a drunk, loud and obnoxious, got on and came weaving down the aisle, muttering oaths and insults at the passengers seated in the main body of the car. He staggered onto the back platform, and as the streetcar lurched, fell to his knees on the concrete floor at the edge of the steps. He gripped the balance pole and tried to pull himself up.

I helped him get up and placed him with a thrust against the wooden railing used as a hand support located just above the radiator. He stood there stooping and rolling his head, his hands grasping the railing where I had placed them. When he looked up and spoke, I knew I had found myself a friend.

Out of gratitude or loneliness he tried to amuse me, and then amused by my amusement, he decided to insinuate himself into my confidence. In the course of his rambling, disconnected anecdotes, to which I responded with a nod and a smile, he became suddenly and unexpectedly both coherent and serious. He apologized for his condition and with glistening eyes confessed the depths to which he had fallen. In his youth he had been a model young man, religious, an altar boy in fact, destined it seemed at the time for the priesthood itself. "Until . . .until . . ," he began but he could not continue.

As he paused to regroup his emotional forces, I casually mentioned that I too had been an altar boy. He jerked back suddenly with a look of startled incredulity. He wound his hands in the air before my face, to clear away the cobwebs of his mind, I guessed, and then when his vision had cleared, scrutinized me for several moments as though his squinty concentration was a sufficient test of my integrity. He decided that I was a soul mate, worthy of his trust and most secret confidences. That night I witnessed for the first time in my life a grown man, his eyes lighting in enthusiasm, enter again into the days of his youth and speak to me as if the thirty years difference in our ages had been suddenly and absolutely wiped out. We were both equals, both boys again at the altar of God.

That night I learned from my drunken friend that I belonged to an unofficial brotherhood of men whose members (without plumed hats, emblems, or secret handshakes) recognize each other only in the discovery that each was an altar boy in his youth. My drunk in recalling his experiences, recalled mine: the awesome initiation at the first mass, the progression from the "easy" side through the ranks of dignity and prestige crowned by the role of censer or cross bearer at special rituals. Then to seal the authenticity of our brotherhood, almost as if I were required to give the secret sign, he demanded that I say the Suscipe. I stumbled through it, the one prayer I could never master. He smiled sadly in toleration of my incompetence and then delivered the prayer, drunk as he was, without a fault. He pressed the rear buzzer at the next stop and we shook hands solemnly. He descended into the darkness calling out as he left the final prayer of the mass, "Ite missa est," to which I automatically responded, "Deo Gratias."

Now I thought this was an isolated experience, the sentimental weakness of a single drunk, but the universality of this brotherhood and its emotional force became evident two or three years later when I was in the service. In a bar in San Francisco I met a college professor who I learned later was a famous economist and notorious atheist. He was just another drunk when I met him. Because he bought drinks for the house, I went up to thank him. I forget how we got around to it. We exchanged the usual trivia about our backgrounds. I think I told him that although my name was German, I was half Irish. He confessed that he was Irish and in his youth had not only been a Catholic but an altar boy for over six years. When I admitted I too had been one, we laughed and he bought me another drink for old times sake. I returned to my stool down the bar and he moved off to a table of his friends.

The bar was full of his colleagues and students. The professor drank heavily and wandered about the room carrying on, in sequence, arguments in the several circles of discussion that had formed about the bar. Everyone seemed to treat him with special courtesy and deference. As he drank more, he became more argumentative and abusive. He raged at the injustice of the human condition and the impossibility of solving the problems that kept man in bondage to suffering and disease.

Suddenly I found him behind me. As I turned, there he stood with tears in his eyes. He raised his hands in the manner of a priest and said, "Pax dominus vobiscum," and I answered, "Et cum spiritu tuo." A look of calm came over his face and he squeezed my arm in affectionate gratitude. Then he shook my hand slowly in ceremonious recognition of our fraternal bond.

He disappeared into the crowd. In a little while he loomed again behind me, this time throwing his arm over my left shoulder and demanding again an answer to a prayer from the mass. When I answered correctly, his face again conveyed that sense of relief, of calm certainty as if God were once again in heaven and all was right with the world. As the evening progressed, he bobbed in and out, arguing and gesticulating. Then he appeared again and said, "Gratias agamus domino deo nostro," and I answered, "Dignum et justum est," and off he would go again weaving his way through the crowd. I soon realized that I had become a point of order and stability in his drunkenness as his memory of a childhood of serving was a point of order, a psychological refuge, for him in a life and universe of injustice and disorder.

Now I mention all of this as a preface (the relevance of which will soon become apparent) to a simple story told to me one lovely spring evening in Rome a few years ago. It happened that, after the service and four years at a small Midwestern college, I grew restless and decided that England was the only milieu to continue my education. The details are unimportant. It was a bad year. I took some courses in theater in London and, vaguely dissatisfied, withdrew in early March. I headed gradually southward. With rapidly diminishing funds, I toured France and Germany and then made a pilgrimage to Rome as the last fling in a year of flings and wasted opportunity.

Once there I got in with an American crowd that saw little more than cheap restaurants and bars and bad abstract art. I had seen little of Rome. Two days before I was to leave to catch my ship in Marseilles, I turned to a cousin of my father's, a Benedictine priest, who had spent most of his adult life in the Vatican. I had promised my family I would visit him and now with time running out, I suddenly felt the urgency of family obligation. I hoped that he might show me in a day the Rome I had failed to encounter in a month.

He was gracious and kind and happy to hear from someone in the family, but he was extremely busy, gave me a list—the standard list with directions—of the things I should not miss and then gently dismissed me with the promise that if anything came up, he would contact me at my hotel.

That evening a note from him was delivered to my hotel. Although he still had no time, he knew of a parish priest from the Campania, an old friend, who was visiting Rome and who had consented to show me the city the next morning. I was assured that he spoke excellent English because during the war he had served in a liaison capacity between German and American authorities in the evacuation of religious from monasteries which had become military outposts. I was to meet my priest at six in the morning if anything was to be accomplished in a single day.

When I met him and we began our tour, I could sense that he was doing a duty out of obligation, and although he delighted in the beauty of the sculpture and painting, it was clearly a chore for him. I was a bore.

He was slight and short with quick deep-set eyes that seemed to flicker. He moved hurriedly from object to object, from building to building, from cab to church to cab to fountain. He never looked me straight in the face; when we spoke, his eyes were averted down or to the side, out of shyness I finally decided. We moved rapidly in the first few hours covering the standard and obvious. Occasionally he would step before a painting and in suspended rapport reveal to me its essence with such faith and force of spirit that I found myself swept along by the enthusiasm of this tireless, diminutive parish priest at least fifteen years older than I, but with a soul somehow centuries younger in eagerness and delight.

When I slowed him to a walk and finally to a rest to catch my breath, we sat and talked over coffee. I obliquely dropped the suggestion that I had been an altar boy in my youth, and the magic words worked again. He too had served at the altar in his village. Suddenly I was no longer a stranger to be instructed out of obligation. He looked at me directly for the first time. I was a compatriot, a brother who shared a special order of experience. I was worthy of his finest effort.

The rest of the day was revelation. All of the pat and easy generalizations I had learned in textbooks about the art and architecture of Rome came to life, and at the same time somehow became all wrong in the face of the real thing illumined by the faith and the love of this little priest. When in the early evening we decided to quit because the light was gone, we stopped in a little café, and I, exhausted, ordered some wine and dinner. I drank my first few glasses too quickly and discovered myself talking, answering the priest's questions about myself too readily. But it was a pleasant reversal of our roles of that day when I had asked the questions incessantly.

After another glass of wine and one thing leading to another, we agreed to exchange stories of our days as altar boys. I told my story first, in great detail, of the time we decided to carve our initials on the altar steps underneath the kneeling pad. Each boy carved his initials when there was no one in church and then covered the area with the kneeling pad. When old Father Ryan learned what we had done, he threatened to fire all of us from the altar and school to boot until he discovered after deciphering the initials that the son of the president of the bank was one of the culprits. Not wanting to bite the hand that held the mortgage on the church and school, he gracefully forgot the whole matter.

My priest laughed and asked, "The Irish are good businessmen?"

"Oh, yes. They give a lot up when they go into the church. There's not one of them I have ever known who wouldn't make an excellent accountant, banker, or car salesman."

"I am a very poor businessman," he shrugged.

"But you are a good teacher," I said, " and now you are going to prove you are a storyteller."

"My story is a long one," he warned.

"That's all right. Dinner has not been served and there is still much more wine."

As we sipped wine and later as we ate dinner, he told his story. He spoke an accurate and idiomatic English but it seemed he was recalling the story to himself in Italian and then translating it into English.

* * * * * * *

The Priest's Story

In the days of my youth before the fascist and the communist destroyed our faith and before the devastation of war ruined out countryside, there was great pride in our village. Our people were close to the soil and close to the church. They worked and prayed with a passion bred of the sun, and they argued and loved with the same intensity of passion.

The priest of our village was one of the people, not well educated and a man of the soil. He was like most of the men of the village, short-tempered and violent once his passion was aroused. He was always quarreling. He would have a hundred petty squabbles in a year because he thought that since he was the priest he had a right to instruct all on how to work the land or how to manage their business or personal affairs that were not usually the business of a priest. He always seemed angry, but nothing sent him into a rage more than the slightest mistake or carelessness by one of his altar boys at the morning mass.

When he was not working the earth of the little plot of land near the church, or arguing with his parishioners, he spent his time pondering ways to make the lives of his altar boys unbearable and their performance excellent beyond words. His soutane may have been spotted with food, his hands caked with the dried earth of his land, his temper disgraceful, but his service was perfect in every detail. Our altar boys were the source of our deepest pride.

Sometimes he could hardly wait until the end of mass to unleash a torrent of abuse on the head of the unfortunate boy who was ever so slightly late with a response or a bell. The earlier in the mass the mistake was made the longer he waxed in anger and the more violent his abuse. New altar boys learned very soon not to make mistakes before the Credo. One could survive, without too much loss of dignity, minor errors from the post-communion to the end of mass, but they, too, were to be avoided like sin.

No one served at the altar until he knew every word of Latin pronounced exactly as our priest demanded. We were terrified of him but more terrified of our parents if we were not successful in receiving his approval and permission to serve. Over and over he would drill us even if we had successfully passed our first trial. At any time of day we might accidently meet him, he would challenge us to respond properly to one of the prayers and then he would jump all over the mass to make sure we knew the answers absolutely, not just in sequence. No slurring of prayers was tolerated, no careless, hurried genuflections in our village church.

Because of our priest's temper and his exacting discipline, our village had the reputation of having the finest altar boys in the whole region, even far better, some said, than those in the cathedral, but if we were to make such a favorable comparison, we would be rebuked by our priest and told of the sin of pride which was the sin of Lucifer himself.

"But, Father, the priest in the cathedral at the seven o'clock mass had to change the missal from the Epistle to the Gospel side himself."

"But that is not ordinary," he would say, "that is not the general rule in the cathedral."

"But, Father, the boy did not pronounce his Latin correctly, and his genuflections were disgraceful."

"He was probably a substitute. Perhaps, there was a sickness."

"No, Father, I do not think so. He was there the next day and the day after that. All the time I was there."

"Is that true?" he would say and scratch his big stomach and shake his head thoughtfully for a while.

"We make mistakes here also," he would say. "We have our share of dumbheads, my children. Do not be too critical of one server in the cathedral. You should be there when the bishop says high mass."

"But they are priests who serve then. I think our altar boys must be as good as the priests, Father, and without half as much training." Then our priest would frown his darkest frown.

"Remember the sin of pride, my children. It was the sin of Lucifer himself. It is sufficient that our boys give honor to God. Their excellence is its own reward."

"Yes, Father, excellence is a reward in itself and when it is done for the love of God, all the more excellence. But our altar boys are still the best in this region."

"Yes," he would nod in agreement as his frown disappeared. "They are the best in the region. To say they are the best in the region is not pride. It is a fact. But to say they are better than those in the cathedral is pride, my children."

"Yes, Father, but. . ." and he raised his hand to silence all further debate.

Now among the servers in our village there was a boy of such an even and cheerful temperament that we all looked to him as our leader, as a foil to our priest who was humorless and volatile. His name was Eugenio and he stood a head taller than every altar boy even those two years older than he. We called him Big Eugenio out of respect and awe. A day was special if Big Eugenio said hello with his confident smile. To be counted among his closest friends was an honor, but then everyone thought he was Big Eugenio's closest friend because he had the gift to make everyone feel special and important. It was not that he was political; it was his natural compassion. He always had a smile or a joke. He was the one who made the life of a new server bearable after he had received the wrath of our priest because of some petty mistake. He always said the right thing.

"But Big Eugenio, Father said there can be no imperfection at the altar of God. There can be faults and mistakes in the rest of the world but not in God's church in service at the holy sacrifice."

"What did you do that was so horrible," Big Eugenio would commiserate.

"I did not see that he left the missal open at the close of mass. He waited for me to change it, but when I failed, he had to carry it across the altar himself and then return to the middle for the blessing and then back again to read." And the young server would hang his head in shame as he remembered his disgrace.

"Oh, that is certainly a serious error," Eugenio would say, shaking his head, and the spirits of the server would plunge, and then Eugenio would smile and say to his young friend.

"How old are you?"

"Eleven," he would answer puzzled.

"Only eleven years!" Eugenio would respond in surprise,

"And that is the only mistake you made?"

"Yes, but it was a grave error."

"Yes. Yes. I know," Eugenio would answer, "but such a circumstance, to return the missal to the gospel side a the end of mass, is rare. It, perhaps, does not occur ten times in a whole year."

"Yes, but we were cautioned. We were forewarned a hundred times by Father."

"Did Father tell you of the exception before mass?"

"No. Should he have?"

"He is not required to, but it is strange he did not. He has always told me."

"Is that so? Is that so?" the boy answered with rising hope.

"Certainly!" and then Eugenio would avoid accusing the priest of an error. He would say,

"Do you know the gospel in which Christ says, 'Let the little children come to me' and 'Unless you become as one of these children you shall not enter the kingdom of heaven.'"

"Yes, but what is that to me already eleven years old?"

"You are not long a young man. You are close in age to the children of whom Christ spoke." Then he paused and looked directly at the boy. "Why do you think the Church has young boys serve at mass and not older people? Look at me. I am only sixteen and soon I will be retired."

"I don't know. Maybe because we have nothing else to do so early in the morning?"

"I don't think God would do anything for such a slight reason, would he?" Eugenio said.

"No," the boy answered, ashamed at his ignorance.

"I will tell you," Eugenio continued. "It is that young men like you are closer to the perfection of childhood."

"But Father is a man and the Bishop is an old man, and the Pope is an old, old man."

"Yes, but they are specially anointed, picked by God and ordained to serve him, yes?"

"Yes, that is true. I never thought of that. But if we are more perfect, why did I make such a bad mistake?"

Eugenio answered smiling, "It is not in your serving that God expects your perfection."

"Ah, I see," the boy said. "Our perfection must be somewhere else." And the boy, newly enlightened, spent the rest of the day avoiding those venial and mortal flaws which alone disqualified him from the altar of God.

Eugenio himself was close to perfection as an altar boy. It was rumored that our priest had never abused him for even the slightest error although this was difficult to believe because of the temper of our priest. We felt privileged when we served with Big Eugenio. Our priest called on him for all the special occasions. Never was there a funeral without Big Eugenio carrying the cross. At benediction he was the censer bearer. We argued and sometimes fought for the honor of being his assistant with the incense boat. Sometimes he let us carry the censer after, of course, he had lighted the charcoal properly. At high mass our priest had Big Eugenio do virtually everything that required dignity and precision and Big Eugenio never failed him.

He was our leader in everything we did, outside of the church at school and on the village streets. We dressed like him, and because his tastes were simple, we escaped being fools about fashions. We imitated his walk and his style of kicking the football, and we always tried to smile with politeness and gentle compassion at everyone we met. Even the bullies respected Big Eugenio for they feared his just wrath if they ever antagonized him. They would receive little sympathy, and they would probably be soundly defeated and humiliated anyway.

Now among the boys of our village there was a great love of chestnuts. We carried them always and roasted them to eat at each and every opportunity. Nowhere was this love of chestnuts stronger than among our altar boys and none loved them more than Big Eugenio. It was he who began our most cherished custom, and it was because of this custom that there were always more than enough volunteers to serve the benediction. Our priest could not understand this eagerness, for he usually said a rosary and a litany before benediction. Sometimes it was a novena or the stations first. It was a long evening except for the most faithful, at least fifteen minutes longer than mass. Our priest suspected that it was because of our great love of song, for benediction was the one service at which everyone, not just the choir, could sing, and we, the altar boys sang loudly if poorly, following the lead of Big Eugenio.

Our custom was simply this: while the priest led the people in the rosary and the litany assisted by only two boys, the rest of the servers gathered in the sacristy about Big Eugenio's burning charcoal in the censer. The number varied depending on the service, but there were always at least two and there was an unwritten schedule or rotation to guarantee justice and an order or precedence of which Big Eugenio was the sole arbiter. We roasted our chestnuts on the charcoal fire and ate them as we responded antiphonally through the partially opened sacristy door to the prayers of our priest. Ah, it was a veritable symposium, our responses interrupted by the cracking and munching of chestnuts. It was a service of prayer and delight, climaxed by our grand entrance upon the altar for benediction and our loud and enthusiastic singing of "Tantum Ergo" as we followed the lead and the tempo set by Big Eugenio's rhythmic clanging of the censer chain. I can see it all now. Out we would all come in perfect unison. Ah, I can assure you that I have never had such faith as in those days of my youth even though now I am a priest.

Now it is in the nature of chestnuts to explode when they are not slit properly and roasted too long, and it is in the nature of our fallen world that error and circumstance should put an end to our simple joy.

It happened one night when I had the honor of carrying the boat as Big Eugenio's assistant. There were only two of us in the sacristy and two on the altar that night. Big Eugenio had arrived early to light the charcoal, and as soon as the rosary began, we placed some chestnuts on the glowing coals. Because there was room for only two or three at a time, Big Eugenio did his first. When they were sizzling hot, he took them off the fire and motioned to me. I placed mine on the charcoal while Big Eugenio took up my position and prayed and kept a watchful eye through the door.

They had not been five minutes on the fire when Big Eugenio bolted upright and whirled around.

"The censer, quickly, the censer. There will be no litany."

He grabbed the censer, loosened the chain, and dropped the cover over the charcoal. Father entered the sacristy and quickly changed into the vestments for benediction. He withdrew the cope from one of the vestment drawers and folded it neatly on a kneeler. He turned and said,

"Try not to throw it on me like an old rag and do not trip on one of the edges and fall flat on your face."

Then he turned toward the altar, pushed us into line, and gave the signal to proceed. Father was in a hurry.

Big Eugenio and I stood under the sanctuary lamp about three paces behind Father. When he stood to sing the chant, I whispered to Big Eugenio.

"Hey, Big Eugenio, the chestnuts." He did not move his head. With his eyes straight forward, he continued to swing the censer. Then he answered out of the side of his mouth.

"Good, eh! Very good." He did not understand what I meant.

"In the censer, Big Eugenio, in the censer." But he did not hear me, for the priest was ready for the first sprinkling of incense upon the charcoal.

Father turned around and we stepped forward. I opened the boat revealing the incense and the spoon, and Big Eugenio swung the censer high as he withdrew the chain and raised the top. Then Big Eugenio saw the two chestnuts on the coals. Father saw them too but seemed confused. His hand hesitated as he took a spoonful of incense. He spread it on the coals and the smoke poured off the charcoal. Just as he was reaching for a second spoonful, the first chestnut exploded, hurling the unburned incense grains into our faces and a loud and unexplained noise throughout the church.

Father was frightened. His hand shook violently and he withdrew in fear from the censer. In a moment he began to draw forward again, cautiously, peeking toward the censer as if trying to look at it from around a corner and stretching his shaking hand again toward the boat. I looked then at Big Eugenio and I saw he wore one of his most reassuring smiles. As the priest dipped into the boat and then carried his reluctant hand toward the charcoal,

Big Eugenio whispered, his voice full of confidence and encouragement,

"Courage, Father, courage! Only one more!"

What happened after that should not be spoken of so lightly, for it occurred in the presence of the Blessed Sacrament exposed upon the altar. It was not so serious itself, perhaps. It was only that it was a priest and in church. It is said that God does not tempt us beyond our strength. I am certain that if our priest sinned, it was but a slight offense and that Christ in his infinite compassion will understand and forgive at the final judgment. Big Eugenio never once uttered the slightest criticism of Father.

I remember vividly the sound of exploding chestnuts that evening, but it is the third sound that especially reverberates in my memory over the years as it reverberated throughout the church after Big Eugenio exhorted Father to stand his ground like a good soldier. It was the sound of flesh upon flesh, and the blow was delivered with such economy of movement that I wonder how anyone beyond the first few pews could have seen his arm move. It was a quick thrust, a sudden shot delivered from the shoulder, professionally as it should have been if our priest had been a boxer, and it left a red blotch on Big Eugenio's cheek that lasted for a half hour.

We left the altar that night with divided feelings. It was not that we did not appreciate Big Eugenio's suffering. After all he had endured the ultimate humiliation and pain inflicted by our priest on any altar boy in the memory of our parish. But we were startled and awed by the speed and accuracy of our priest's jab. We assumed, perhaps to mitigate Big Eugenio's humiliation, that an ordinary man could not have delivered such a blow.

In time, we invented an authorized, if apocryphal, version of the story of our priest's past. We speculated that in his youth our priest had probably been a professional fighter, perhaps famous in his region, a contender even, and that he had foregone a promising career in the ring for the priesthood so that he could redirect his energies in the service of God by making the lives of his altar boys unbearable and their performance excellent beyond words.

Big Eugenio endorsed our speculations with good humor. He often acted out in pantomime for newcomers how he received the blow. Then he touched his cheek and winced in testimony to our priest's prowess as a former boxer and as a stern disciplinarian.

* * * * * * * *

I drank a good deal during his story and at dinner. After we had coffee, I asked him as if by delayed reaction,

"And whatever became of Big Eugenio?"

"Oh," he shrugged, "I don't know. There was the war and he was conscripted. I was in the seminary. His family left our village for the factories in Milan. I have not returned for years myself."

Then he got up to leave. He had planned to take a night bus. He excused himself saying that he hoped to return to his parish in time for mass in the morning. He had already been away three days on his holiday. I gave him a small sum, all that I could spare, keeping only enough to pay for my meals and wine on my bus trip and before my ship sailed.

"I will use your kind gift for new surplices for the altar boys," he said with a smile on parting. When I left the café, I bought some more wine and returned to my hotel where I drank long into the evening. That night, moved by the wine and my priest's story, I,too, was restored to my youth at the altar of service and lived once again in the days of my innocence. I could see again, almost like a vision, St. Paul transfigured in my imagination, its skyline bathed in a silver light, the buildings glowing as if they had been scrubbed with celestial detergent.

A TRIP TO THE COUNTRY

On Friday night after his mother had packed, Matt helped his father load the car. His mother always prepared for any eventuality. She brought enough clothes and food along to survive the most remote of possible natural disasters: storm coats and overshoes for blizzards, rain gear for thunderstorms, a five gallon plastic tank of water in event of drought. Matt shook his head doubtfully when he picked up his third load. He exchanged knowing but tolerant glances with his father, who was waiting by the open trunk of the car, already almost full. Then he returned for the sleeping bags in the attic. They were not intending to camp out so late in fall, of course, but his mother insisted the bags and some extra blankets be brought along in event they became marooned along the roadside in a sudden cold snap or early snow storm. She remembered the Great Blizzard of Armistice Day in 1940 and the hunters who had frozen to death when the temperature dropped over sixty degrees in less than twenty-four hours.

    Matt didn't complain. He didn't care what his mother wanted to bring along. Now, they were going for sure. No more postponements because of rain. No more delays because of a last minute change in his father's work schedule. Now, they were going for sure. Since Monday Matt had monitored the foliage reports in the newspaper and followed the weather forecasts on the radio. The color was at its peak along the river road north. When it seemed fairly certain that the clear skies would hold at least through Saturday, Matt's father called Uncle Emil to make sure the annual autumn visit would not be an inconvenience. It never was, of course, but there were rituals to be observed, expectations to be respected.

Uncle Emil Besserman, his father's cousin, farmed a half section eighty miles north in the country around Elk River. Two summers before Matt had spent three weeks there, and every October since he could remember, his family had made a weekend trip to the farm to observe the trees along the river in the time of autumn color and to visit Uncle Emil, Aunt Tilly, and Peter, a full second cousin two years older than Matt. Although Uncle Emil was actually Matt's first cousin, once removed, he called him "Uncle" as a concession to an adult generation which commanded to a boy of fourteen an authority still unchallenged in its wisdom and unlimited in its practical opportunity.

They knew he was excited as he had always been before a trip but they hoped it was more than that. He seemed to be his old self again. They still felt guilty about the move in July. They had told him about the decision after it was an accomplished fact though they had instructed him in all the practical reasons for the move. The house was too large and expensive to maintain, especially now that his older sister Peggy had married and moved away. The value of the house had increased dramatically in a real estate boom and so had the taxes. His father had grown tired of fighting the traffic to and from work each day. Now when the weather was nice he would be able to walk the two miles to work or take a bus when it grew cold. Besides, his mother had never cared for the quasi-suburban neighborhood on the outer edges of the city. It seemed that all she did was drive the car for shopping, to school activities, to her community service projects. All her close friends remained in her old neighborhood in one of the old sections of the city not far from her childhood home, long sold by her parents in order to relocate in Florida.

It had all happened so quickly that he did not have time to object or to fully understand what had happened. They found the perfect apartment in the old neighborhood, sold or gave away to Matt's sister and other relatives the excess accumulated furnishings, and moved during his father's vacation in July. Besides, he had been swept along by his mother's enthusiasm and happiness. It was only gradually after the move that he began to realize what he had lost. He began to feel a quiet, brooding sense of injustice. He had been uprooted from the only home, school, and friends he had ever known. He took the bus back to visit friends and invited them to visit him, but everything seemed different, and after a few exchanges, the visits stopped. There was so much he had taken for granted, the familiarity and certainty of place, the quiet order of daily routine, the clarity of relationships now all irretrievably changed.

In the first few weeks he did not venture much into the streets. Their apartment had a wide sidewalk and a grassy boulevard with Chinese elms spaced at orderly intervals at the edge of the road, which was a main access route to the business center of the city. It was a wide road with three lanes in each direction, separated by a safety divider. In both directions on both sides of the road apartment buildings stretched as far as Matt could see. Matt's apartment looked down on the inbound lanes. At quiet moments it seemed pleasant enough, but there weren't many quiet moments. The lanes were full of cars and trucks rushing by, bumper to bumper, from before dawn into the late hours of night. Traffic signals two blocks away controlled the traffic. The cars would stream and then clump and then start up again in an endless confusion of noise. The next street over was a commercial street and bus route, full of exhaust fumes, stores, restaurants and bars, and pushing crowds that shoved and bumped along under overhanging signs.

In the early morning he watched the traffic from the living room window. The apartment building had a large service elevator and after he and the caretaker became friends, the caretaker let him operate the elevator in exchange for help carrying trash barrels. The work served to amuse him for a part of each morning. He ran errands for his mother and sometimes accompanied her on her excursions to museums and art galleries or shopping, but he did not explore his new neighborhood or venture the short walk downtown to wander the huge department stores as he had planned to do before the move.

Matt made one exploratory trip to the nearest neighborhood playground. When he arrived, it was deserted except for a few small children. There was nothing there to amuse himself with. It was more a joke than a disappointment. The playground was a narrow, uneven triangle of asphalt wedged between busy streets on two sides, and the windowless, brick, rear facades of adjacent buildings on the third. It was completely enclosed by a cyclone fence.

In time he made a truce with his surroundings and accepted his loneliness and disappointment as a kind of noble sacrifice he was making for his parents' happiness. It would be only a few weeks before school began. He was certain he would find friends there. His father drove him by the school once so he could get his bearings. It was an enormous red brick building that looked like cross between a factory and a prison. When he enrolled in early September, he discovered that it was something of both. The classes seemed ruled by clanging bells and bellowing authoritarian voices, male and female, over intercom speakers. He was overwhelmed and diminished by numbers. Everything was engineered by a distant remote control which seemed to haunt and intimidate even the teachers. He was often late to class, and except for a few tentative friends he was excluded from the groupings that formed quickly in the first few weeks based upon friendships of the previous year.

It was a few weeks after school had begun that he turned in his imagination to the memories of his trips to the country and especially to the summer two years before when he wandered the crop fields and the pastures and the woodland and marsh along the river that formed the boundary of the south quarter of his uncle's farm. It was the woods and marsh along the river that he recalled in precise detail. It was an untouched wilderness that had been too impractical to cultivate or clear for pasture. It was hilly and irregular and heavily wooded. Steep rocky embankments, almost cliffs, descended to the water and deep irregular ravines cut through the bluffs from the flat crop fields above to the river's edge. A marsh had formed from spring flooding in a low area and was covered with cattails and tall grass.

He knew the annual fall trip would only be a temporary escape from the geometrical limits of the city, from the clogged and sooty streets, the flashing lights, and blaring horns. He wanted to escape, if only briefly, from a world defined by law and order where a quarter of a million people had been jammed into an area hardly big enough for a thousand scrawny range steers. He longed to explore one last time before winter set in the open spaces of farm land, the brooks and ravines and ponds, the trees and rocks and anything that flourished without order or pattern, that grew or existed haphazardly as it had been cast down by divine caprice.

II

They left before sunrise the next morning. Matt's mother made him wrap in one of the blankets in the back seat until the engine warmed and the heater could be turned on. The car bumped along on the brick streets, stopping and then jerking ahead at intersections where traffic signals gave silent commands. Matt looked out at the cast-iron light poles that methodically approached them and then vanished quickly behind. He felt a vague pity for the early-rising factory workers, huddled under the street lights, waiting half asleep for busses. They were bundled in heavy jackets and coats against the numbing chill of the early morning, and Matt knew that they were going off to factories or offices where time was money and where they would be as intimidated as he was at school.

Two years before he had toured one of the factories with his classmates on a social studies field trip, designed to widen his horizons. He felt as though he had been cast into a dungeon, the walls of which teetered dangerously inward, pressing downward threatening to overwhelm and suffocate, and everywhere the whirling tangle of machinery shuttling massive arms of force back and forth. He decided then that some day he would live on a real farm, according to the impulse of the seasons when there was a time to sow and a time to reap and a time to rest. Before they left the city, the sun rose in a blue and cloudless sky. Although there was a new interstate highway north, Matt's father followed the old route in the river valley where the trees flourished in greater variety of color. His father drove slowly. Each bend in the road seemed to bring a new thrill to his mother. She had his father stop the car in those places where the view was perfect. Once they got out and walked back a hundred feet or so into a small woods of mixed hemlock and white birch and up a small rise to an cleared knoll with a view of a river bend. Then she proclaimed that the spot was a perfect location for a house. She was always building houses, finding perfect spots, searching for beauty in the world about her. She sent Matt back to the car for their picnic lunch and they ate there sitting on a blanket. Matt knew they would never build a house in the country. The trip was his mother's once a year venture into natural beauty. She found most of her beauty at concert halls or in art galleries.

To Matt his mother was romance and French literature. She had gone to college for two years with grand aspirations of majoring in French. There was always one section of the bookcase which was reserved for French novels and books of French poetry, which she occasionally read when the mood struck her though the pages remained uncut in about half of them. She had spent one summer in France before she married his father and she often spoke of that summer of glorious adventure as if it happened only yesterday, as if his father and sister and he had never occurred.

Although one of the reasons for the trip was to satisfy his mother's yearning for the seasonal beauty, Matt knew that his father enjoyed the autumn color as well, but he, like Matt, could not express his feelings as openly as she did. She, a woman and a major in French literature at that, articulated for them what they secretly felt but could not exclaim. Besides, his father was not a man of many words. His mother had ten words for every one his father uttered. Matt always felt sorry for his father whenever he groped for the right words. To Matt his father was masculine, but in the sense of "mathematics" and "machines," and those words seemed to reveal him in his essential character just as the words "culture" or "beauty" revealed his mother or "practicality" revealed his married sister.

The river road led back to the main highway about twenty miles from the farm. His father increased the speed of the car until they reached the gravel road where they turned back toward the river and Uncle Emil's farm. When they drove into the yard and up to the house, Matt saw Uncle Emil step out onto the porch. He shouted something into the house and as his father stopped the car and set the brake, Uncle Emil stepped down from the porch toward the car.

"Where the hell you been?" he shouted with a grin. "I thought you'd be here an hour ago."

Uncle Emil was a barrel-chested, thick-bodied man whose sleeves were always rolled just above the elbows, revealing the bulging forearms of a man who worked with his hands. He had a broad and high forehead with thinning straight black hair always combed flatly and parted neatly just slightly to one side of the middle. The grooves left by the teeth of the comb showed in his hair. Whenever he revealed any emotion or enthusiasm, one side of his mouth twisted with a slight curl of the lip, which left the impression that everything he said came out of the corner of his mouth.

Aunt Tilly and Peter appeared on the porch through the door.

"I was just telling Tilly I was about to send the old sheep dog after you." He laughed, and Matt and his parents laughed also out of courtesy.

"We just kind of poked along. Went along the river road so Ruth could see her trees and build a few houses along the way," his father answered and opened the car door to get out. The men laughed at the standing joke about his mother. Matt pushed the seat forward to get out on his father's side. His mother remained in her seat, talking to Aunt Tilly through the open window. Peter walked around the car and stopped. He leaned over and selected a stone and sent it toward the crib to the left of the barn. The stone went through the slotted space and muffled in the hard, dry sound of corn cobs.

Matt listened to his mother and aunt exchanging news and his father and uncle with their light banter. He was always able to understand his father's and uncle's friendship, but how his mother and Aunt Tilly got along so well was a mystery to him. His mother was so refined and delicate; his aunt so awkward and rough hewn, but there had developed over the years an unaccountable intimacy between them.

Matt looked past Peter toward the corn fields yet to be picked and the woods a quarter of a mile beyond, which rose on a gently sloping hill and then plunged down steep embankments to the river bottom out of sight behind the trees. Peter turned to Matt and said,

"You want to go hunting? I got a new .410," and then with disappointment already crossing his face and a touch of contempt in his voice, "or do you just want to go hiking and looking around at the trees and the birds?"

"I don't want to hunt, but if you want to take your gun along on a hike, I don't mind," he compromised. Peter, sensing there would be no competition in a hunt with one hunter and one spectator, shrugged and leaned over to select another stone.

Matt re-evaluated his cousin, trying to remember him as he had been two summers before and trying to know him in a way that would lessen the vague uneasiness he always felt in Peter's presence. Matt didn't want Peter to spoil his trip. During the summer that Matt stayed on the farm for an extended period, there was enough time to go off by himself, but he knew Peter would be his constant companion for this weekend. Matt couldn't always understand Peter. He seemed sullen and unpredictable. Matt often went out of his way to mention things he didn't care about himself but which he believed would strike some resonating chord in his cousin. But what seemed of certain interest to Peter for a few minutes would suddenly lose its enchantment, and Matt would become confused when he sensed that Peter's interest had changed so quickly.

Peter's face gave the appearance of age and maturity inconsistent with his undeveloped child's body. The skin of his face was stretched tightly over his bones and flesh, leaving a bluish hue under his eyes and around his mouth. Peter's first and most ready reaction was to scoff. He said little. Matt often felt ashamed, even effeminate before the lacerating thrust of his cousin's gaze and the curtness of his manner.

"You gonna show Matt the new animals we got?" he heard Uncle Emil addressing Peter. "I guess the way he likes the farm, he'll like them." He winked at Matt's father.

"Which ones?" Peter asked.

"All of them," Uncle Emil laughed. "Try the corral first. They might have stayed behind again. They'll learn in a few days that the cattle know where the feed is. You can always take him over to your ma's old chicken shed. They can't go anywhere."

Without answering, Peter turned and headed toward the barn. Matt followed him, his interest whetted by his uncle's teasing indirection. When they came around the corner of the barn, Matt saw three horses, one grey and one dark brown with a black mane, and one a blotchy-white and brown, standing near the water tank. The boys climbed and straddled the fence; two of the horses stilled momentarily, looked at the boys, and then trotted off toward the safety of the middle of the corral. The chestnut horse ventured to take a last drink and then shied quickly away toward the other two. From the distance their coats seemed to glisten in the sun.

"They look nice from here," Peter said, "but up close you can see they're covered with pock marks. Pa bought them at an auction last week. They're from an Indian reservation. They're still wild. They're supposed to run with the cattle to pasture, but they've been staying by themselves the past few days."

They climbed down the fence and began walking toward the horses.

"Didn't the Indians ever break them?" Matt asked.

"Yeah, once. But then they let them run wild again. Pa says they're worth more to the Indians sold at an auction than used to work stock or trained to plow."

As they walked toward the horses, Matt could see that their hides were horribly scarred. The horses shied slowly away from them and then suddenly galloped toward the far side of the corral.

"What'd your pa get them for?" Matt asked.

"I don't know. Another one of his businesses, I guess. I suppose he's going to breed them. They're all mares. It won't cost much to feed them, and I guess it'd be too much work to break and train them again. That one's a quarter horse and that one's mostly Appaloosa. The colts will bring a good price. Every kid around here wants a colt to train to work stock or for rodeos."

"I'll take one when its born," Matt offered seriously.

"It'll cost you over a hundred dollars, at least," Peter answered, squelching whatever dim hope Matt felt.

"What other animals you got?"

"Pa's been feeding a hundred mink since last spring. He got sick of all the work with chickens and he wasn't getting twenty cents a pound, so he converted the old hen house on the other side of the barn and got the mink from a breeder. He just feeds them. He's going to see if he makes any money before he starts trying to breed them himself or he gets in too deep."

"Are they like wild ones?"

"Yeah, except for the color. Wild ones are dark brown. These are kind of blue. Their color's called sapphire. A cross-breed or something. I trapped some real mink last winter but I didn't get enough to pay for the traps."

"Let's go see them."

"Are you sure you want to? They stink terrible, and besides I got to feed them later this afternoon. You can see them then if you help me with the chores."

"Couldn't I just look at one first? I've never seen a live mink before," Matt laughed to cover his eagerness.

"I guess so, but let's go back to the house first and get my shotgun. The mink are on the way to the woods if you want to go that way first. I'd just as soon walk out through the pasture anyhow. I might get a shot at some gophers."

It was almost noon by the time they left the house. Aunt Tilly had lunch ready and Matt had to eat something and "visit" a while before they went off. Peter carried his gun, and wore an ammunition belt around his waist. They went to the mink shed first. As they approached the entrance, Matt smelled the musk.

"Whew! You weren't kidding when you said they stink."

"Pa knocked all the window casings out and cut away the planks on the sides and the end to let the air come in and out so that the temperature and humidity would be like nature, but I think he did it so they wouldn't suffocate on their own smell."

Matt waited in the entrance until his eyes adjusted to the darkness and his nose became accustomed to the smell. He saw four rows of wire cages extending the length of the building and separated by two wide aisles. He could hear the gushing sound of water through the troughs that ran down each row of cages. He could hear animals pacing back and forth on the wire mesh. Peter leaned his gun against a support post, and picked up a pair of thick leather mittens from the top of one of the first cages.

"I'll show you one real close in the light outside."

Peter reached into the cage and caught a squirming animal, one hand firmly gripping the mink's neck just below the jaw and the other around the underside of its hind legs, withdrew it from the cage, and walked several paces out of the shed. What Matt beheld was like a vision. In the sunlight the mink's fur seemed to glow silver-blue—a color of such rarity and purity that it seemed unearthly. Matt squinted and rubbed his eyes.

"Is it real?" he asked startled.

"Sure it's real. Touch him. Feel the thickness of the pelt. It's got two layers, the underfur and the guard hairs."

Matt hesitated.

"You'd better hurry. I can't hold this squirming crybaby much longer." Matt touched the fur gently with the back of his hand at first and then caught the thick pelt between his fingers and tested its texture. He ran his hand along the length of its back several times. As Peter returned the mink to its cage, Matt shook his head in disbelief.

III

Tired but still excited and full of wonder, he climbed back up the hill beyond the river embankment to the corn field, yet to be harvested, and disappeared into the rows of tall golden stalks. Peter followed him at a distance, carrying his gun under one arm. They walked up the rows that would end a half mile further on in the stubble of an alfalfa field adjacent to the pasture that led into the barn.

All that he had hoped for had been realized. In three hours they had stalked the river bottom and a large pothole marsh and the woods. He caught glimpses of kingfishers flashing from reed to reed and beyond the reeds at the open center of the pond, squadrons of blue and snow geese landing and departing to and from the corn field above, which they could strip if the farmers did not frighten them away.

In the woods they wandered off the trails and climbed the rock ledges covered with moss. Each new rise or outcropping he mastered served as a different perspective from which he viewed where he had been and where he was going. The woods were a mixture of white pines, hemlock, red and white oak, maple, and white and grey birch. As he walked, he was continually surprised and delighted by the new combinations of color and line that rose before him and then changed and shifted as his perspective moved. He looked up frequently to the sky through the cross- patch tangle of limbs and swaying white pine needle clusters. He discovered once, coming over a rise, a flaming maple of such brightness and subtly flickering shades of scarlet that when the wind gently touched and fluttered its leaves, they seemed to brighten as though they were hearth coals stirred by a bellows. He stood momentarily stunned by the tree's beauty, savoring the privacy and purity and brevity of the moment. Then he moved on regretfully when he heard Peter's footsteps behind him.

At the outset Matt rushed ahead, following the capricious dictates of his senses. Peter had followed without enthusiasm, aiming his shotgun at arbitrary targets along the way but never firing. But whenever Matt stopped to examine anything closely, Peter became his tutor. In the shadowed intimacy along the river and the edge of the marsh, he caught up to Matt and revealed his factual understanding of all that Matt worshiped as mystery and wonder. His learning derived from a high school general science course and his hunting experiences, and though Matt pretended to defer to a higher order of truth, he privately dismissed all the labels and distinctions and gratuitous observations as superficial or useless.

Still Peter brought Matt's attention to refinements of detail that he would never have noticed on his own: the minute differences of shape and structure of leaf by means of which species of trees were distinguished; the wintergreen that lay buried under the fallen leaves which Peter picked and broke and gave to Matt to chew; two speckled trout in a still, sandy-bottomed backwater pool along the river, which they viewed from above after crawling noiselessly out on a rock ledge that hung out over the water from the bank. Later on the edge of the woods, they discovered at eye level, sitting on a bough of small white pine, a Great Horned owl. The bird sat there unmoving, staring back at them, blinking occasionally. Matt watched for several moments and then began to laugh at what he took to be the owl's ridiculous behavior. It didn't fly out, it didn't attack. It just sat there looking at him with absolute eyes. Was it terrified? Confused? Angry? He couldn't tell, so he laughed. Peter stepped alongside him and reached up to detach a small object from a branch below the owl.

"He's just finished digesting his dinner," Peter explained, and handed Matt a tiny pouch of milk-white skin. As he received it, he could feel through his finger tips the hardness of its contents.

"What is it?" Matt asked.

"Open it and find out for yourself."

He gently tore it open in his hand and discovered the intact and polished-clean skeleton of a mouse, cushioned as though packed for shipping in its own fur.

"The bones and fur don't go through him," Peter explained. "After the flesh has been broken down by digestive juices, the bag forms around the bones and fur and he spits it out."

Matt was confused for a moment and then shook his head, marveling, and placed the tiny remains in a pocket of his jacket as a souvenir of his trip.

When they hid in the tall grass along the edge of the marsh and watched ducks, darting among the reeds close off shore, Peter seemed almost excited as he described the various species—wood, mallard, teal, black—their distinguishing characteristics, speed of flight, and feeding habits. The earliest to hunt were the teal, in early September, and he had shot eight the first day with his new gun. One species of duck, when wounded, was known to dive to the depths of a pond or lake and seize with its bill a sunken branch and literally drown, commit suicide, rather than surface and be hunted. Matt learned that the mudhen was the lowest order of duck, the mongrel, stupid and inedible and not worth the effort of hunting or conserving except as food for the weasels. In time, however, Matt wearied of Peter's facts and then became saddened by the encyclopedic indifference of his observations.

It was then, while walking along the corn row, perhaps a quarter of a mile from the barn, that they smelled it. It had been carried on the wind but it was a heavy, overpowering stench that could not have originated as far away as the barn. Matt stopped and waited for Peter to catch up. When Peter drew alongside, he noticed it too.

"Something's just been ripped open. That's guts. The last time I smelled that was when my Pa gutted a deer two seasons ago."

"But it isn't deer season yet, is it?"

"Naw, not for another month."

As they walked ahead together, the smell grew more pungent and oppressive.

"It's coming from somewhere ahead past the end of the cornfield."

"I can't think of any reason anything would come from that direction. A pack of wild dogs might get a sick cow, but our cattle are in a pasture almost a half mile from here and we've got a mean bull running with the herd."

At the end of the cornfield they dropped into a drainage ditch and climbed up the other side into the mowed hayfield that sloped upward gently and then downward again to another drainage ditch that separated the field and the barnyard pasture. Though the sun was still high, its light was yellowing and Matt could feel the chill of the breeze as it swept up the open field.

They walked up the small rise. At its crest they would see the farmhouse and barn in the distance, partially hidden behind several rows of spruce that served as a windbreak on the north side of the barnyard and as a machinery storage area. Below them, perhaps two hundred yards away, a pick-up truck was parked on the far side of the ditch, and they could see over the top of the nearside mound the heads and shoulders of two men, leaning over and working their arms vigorously on something obscured from Matt's view at their feet in the bottom of the ditch. Halfway down the field it became apparent that the stench was coming from the ditch. Peter began to run ahead.

"That's Mr. Arneson's truck from the locker," he shouted behind him. Matt broke into a slow trot, following Peter for a while, then he slowed to a walk. He watched Peter climb through the barbed wire fence on the edge of the field and then climb the mound of the ditch just beyond. At the top, he stopped suddenly, stepped back a foot or two and seemed to go rigid as he stared into the ditch below him.

In his haste, Matt caught his jacket in the barbed wire and spent what seemed minutes disentangling himself. As he climbed the grassy mound to Peter's side, he felt himself beginning to gag on the gaseous stench that saturated the air around him. Then he stood beside his cousin and peered into the bottom of the ditch. He was breathing heavily. Each inhalation stung his nose and mouth and brought nausea to his throat.

Below them, stretched on its side as though staked to the earth, was a massive heap of flesh, shimmering scarlet in the sunlight. It was several moments before he could sort out in his mind what lay before him and what had happened. In time he saw the gray, blood-spattered hide lying in a crumpled tangle where it had been discarded, three or four feet below him and to the right. When his senses had focused, he realized it was the carcass of one of the horses he had seen in the corral earlier that afternoon. It had not been dead long. Its dwindling life-heat was still steaming in the chill air. It had been gutted and stripped of its hide by the two men, dressed in hip boots and rain jackets, who were beginning to butcher the hind quarters. The sheath of muscles, fibroid and glistening red, that bound its frame had gone slack. The surface seemed to ripple in a panic of quivering counter motions, each muscle of the animal jerking spasmodically and desperately.

They crossed the ditch to get upwind of the smell. As he climbed the other side, Matt noticed a rifle leaning against the rear bumper of the pick-up truck. They walked along the mound toward the truck. Revolted as he was, Matt had difficulty keeping his eyes off the slaughtered animal. He watched the men work. Each wore a steel mesh glove on his left hand. They cut the meat into chunks and pitched them into a battered milk can. There were several more cans on the truck platform, and two round shallow metal wash tubs, two or three feet in diameter, lay on the ground.

The boys stood near the truck for several moments, silently watching the butchery when one of the men looked up and saw them. He straightened up and smiled at Peter.

"Why hello, Peter. Where'd you come from?"

"From the woods and the river bottom. On the other side of the corn field." Peter pointed across the field toward the corn.

"Too bad you didn't come by earlier. We could have used some help holding this old mare still. She sure seemed to know what the rifle was all about." The man laughed and leaned back over the animal and began to cut again. His partner, dour and uncommunicative, worked on the flank at a steady pace, cutting flesh with dexterity and pitching the slabs into the receptacle.

Matt raised his eyes and looked down the ditch. On the ground twenty or thirty feet away, he noticed several blackbirds had gathered around the lumpish pile of organs that the men had cleaned from the animal and dragged to the side. Two of the birds had ripped the intestines open with their beaks and were already feasting on its contents. He looked up to see in the distance a few crows venturing near along the treetops of the cottonwood windbreak that ran for a hundred yards or so along the east edge of the pasture. They settled finally into the top of the nearest trees to await, patiently, their turn at the carrion.

Matt and Peter carried one of the tubs of meat across the pasture to the barn so that the men from the locker would not have to take time out from their work to haul a load to Uncle Emil, who was waiting to grind some fresh meat for the minks' evening meal. The men wanted to finish before dark. Their task was slow, they explained, because Peter's father wanted the chunks small enough to be frozen in pre-measured plastic bags and small enough to fit into his grinder. By the time they reached the barn, the boys' muscles ached from the strain of the load, especially Peter's because he had to carry his gun under his free arm. So much blood had drained from the chunks of meat that they had difficulty preventing it from slopping over. Near the end of their trip, they could carry the load only several feet at a time before they had to set it down. The blood sloshed against the sides for several moments at each stop.

They delivered the tub to a wooden butcher's table in a section of the barn that had been partitioned off after the war and refurbished as a meat locker and small chicken slaughterhouse. Uncle Emil, who had never been satisfied with his role as a farmer, had installed a walk-in freezer and had over the years used his facility for various business schemes. Once he had prepared poultry directly for retail outlet in several supermarkets in the city until he was undersold by a national food supply company. For several years, he skinned, dressed, and froze pheasant and duck and geese in season for hunters from the city who used to hunt the fields and ponds before the pheasant population had been decimated by several wet springs and an overpopulation of fox; and most recently, his mink, which in spring he had contracted with a breeder to feed until the late November pelt harvest.

They went across the barnyard into the house. Peter put his gun away in the gun rack in the hallway. In the kitchen Matt found his mother and aunt talking over coffee. The table was still loaded with food—sandwiches, cold chicken, cookies, and cake—left over from lunch, which Aunt Tilly had also served to the men from the locker when they arrived in the middle of the afternoon. Peter and Matt were invited to eat again because supper would be late. Upon tasting a piece of chicken, Matt discovered how hungry he was. He had been so excited at noon that he really had not eaten very much. Now, he ate three chicken legs, two sandwiches, and some cookies.

They went upstairs to Peter's bedroom where Matt found his pajamas, comb, toothbrush and paste on his bed. He put them away in the drawer in the dresser that Peter indicated was his. Matt had stayed in Peter's room every time he had visited. He felt that the guest bed was almost his. The room was long and narrow and the walls at shoulder height slanted inward, following the roof line. Peter's bed was at the far end of the room near the window. Matt lay down to rest while Peter removed the shells from his gun belt and placed them in a dresser drawer. When Matt closed his eyes for several moments, he realized that the delight and fulfillment he had experienced in the early afternoon had been eradicated by the searing memory of the slaughtered horse.

Later, he helped Peter with his chores, the last of which was feeding the mink. It was a practical, almost scientific operation.

Each mink was caged separately. The cages were wire mesh on all sides. A trough of continuously running water ran through each cage. Uncle Emil ground the meat into metal vats which Peter placed on a small cart. He shoved the cart down a wooden ramp out the door and across a space of open ground to the entrance of the shed and down the rows of cages. He stopped every several feet to measure from a vat with a metal scoop the correct amount of food, which in turn he pressed through the wire to a waiting mink. It was not necessary to open the cage either to feed or clean the animals. The food, which looked like hamburger, was pressed though the wire mesh. The animals' droppings fell through the wire of the bottom of the cage to the straw covered floor, which was swept and hosed down periodically, and then covered again with fresh straw.

The musk made Matt's eyes water the first several minutes, but as they worked, he grew fascinated watching the animals eat, and he grew indifferent to his own physical revulsion to the animals' smell. Though the horse meat had been ground and mixed with cereal and tripe, the mink ripped and tore at their portions, their teeth flashing savagely. They gulped the food in a matter of seconds and then, temporarily satiated, resumed at a lower rate the endless pacing that had intensified with their first smell of the fresh horse meat.

When they had finished feeding the animals, they returned to the locker area of the barn to wash the equipment. There they found Uncle Emil and Matt's father. Uncle Emil had dismantled his grinder and was washing the blades under the faucet of a deep sink. As he washed, dried, and reassembled the grinder, he explained his mink venture to Matt's father.

The boys pushed the cart to the sink, and when Uncle Emil had finished, filled it with hot water and dumped the scoop and vats into the water. Peter used a scrub brush to remove the particles of meat that did not loosen in the water. They worked slowly because this was their last chore. It was dark out already. Soon they would go into the house and eat supper. As he worked, Matt listened to his uncle. Occasionally he looked up toward his father, who stood, puffing a pipe and asking questions, by the butcher's table across the room, where Uncle Emil was reassembling the grinders.

The mink were born in late March or early April. When they were weaned, the breeder farmed many of the mink out to feeders like Uncle Emil. The secret of success was the diet, which included in progressively varying proportions cereal, milk, fish, tripe, and red meat—chicken heads, rabbit, or horse meat—whichever was the cheapest. The percentage of red meat necessary for development of the fullest coat increased as the mink grew older. By August, the animals had developed a special substructure, nourished primarily by red meat, out of which the thick, rich coat of fur blossomed. Uncle Emil had luckily heard about the Indian horses being auctioned. The purchase and feed and slaughter fee would finally cost him about eight cents a pound, much cheaper than what he had been paying wholesale for rabbit.

The mink would be slaughtered in November, shortly after Thanksgiving. Uncle Emil retrieved a wire mesh from a nearby workbench and showed Matt and his father how he would shove the mink head-first into the device encasing the entire body; then the front half was quickly bent backward snapping the animal's neck. Then their hides were prepared for curing and tanning. Their bodies, stripped of hide, were sold to a rendering company which ground the remains into another food formula which was then sold as hog feed. Matt felt suddenly ashamed of the interest verging upon fascination with which he followed his uncle's explanation.

IV

He woke to a thunderclap overhead and flashes of lightning on the ceiling. He looked at the clock on the dresser across the room and saw during one of the brief intervals of light that it was 3:30. He heard a few isolated drops of rain and then suddenly a roar of water beating a few feet from his head.

He had slept dreamlessly since about midnight. After dinner and dishes, they had played cards for a few hours and then he had convinced Peter to play a while longer. He did not want to be alone. He welcomed any diversion to prolong the evening, but Peter finally went to bed. He listened to Peter's short-wave radio at low volume. He moved the dial across the arc of numbers. He stopped to listen to one half of a ham radio contact. For a while he listened to code and although he couldn't understand it, he liked listening to the rhythm of the signals. But physically exhausted he soon fell asleep, and his mother turned the radio off on her way to bed.

Now as he lay in the darkness listening to the sound of the rain, he felt a strange detachment toward himself. He knew he would recall in detail what he had seen, and although the image of the quivering flesh flashed into his mind repeatedly, it seemed as though a second, critical self had emerged out of the shattering of his simplicity. It was as though he were a divided self: the one consciousness sensitive, wounded, despairing; the other distant, critical, reproachful.

His senses had betrayed him. They had led him to beauty and joy but as easily to ugliness and disgust. One brief, horrific vision had obliterated all the loveliness that his senses had conveyed to him in the several previous hours. He had never before witnessed a death in nature. The most he had ever seen was the squashed remains on the early morning highway of raccoons or rabbits or birds that had been run over. But he knew violent, unpredictable death occurred all the time and that the death of one animal meant life to another. He knew, for example, at that very moment, that the entrails of the horse in the pasture drainage ditch had been since nightfall, and would be for several days, a community feast at which all manner of bird and beast would eat its fill.

He had been properly instructed. In school he had been shown film strips of food chains. The chain began in the water with a single cell organism being consumed by larger more complex organisms, and they in turn being eaten by still larger ones; small fishes were eaten by the larger, and then the birds ate the fish and in their turn were consumed by land animals in a great organic cycle.

He reproached himself for refusing to see nature for what it was. He was angry that out of loneliness and weakness he had blindly sought emotional refuge in a fantasy. He didn't want to see predators and food chains and fear and the terrible struggle for life. But he had witnessed the blood and muscle of the less favored animal being transfigured, virtually before his eyes, into the incredibly beautiful fur coat of another beast and he was appalled to discover that he had been fascinated by the efficiency of the process. Nothing was wasted. Even the body of the mink would be ground and fed to hogs, which man, in his turn, would consume so that, in time, his own flesh would be made up of the flesh of wild beasts.

He lay in the darkness brooding. Occasionally he dropped off to sleep, but he was soon startled awake by fitful dreams that had caught up and distorted fragments of his imaginings. The rain had dwindled to infrequent and brief spattering on the roof, and Matt could hear the whine of the rising wind as it pushed the rain line through the region.

It had stopped raining by the time he got up. He ate breakfast with his parents—one of Aunt Tilly's enormous offerings of juice, cereal, fried potatoes, ham, eggs, hot rolls, and coffee. Uncle Emil and Peter had already eaten and were out in the barn packaging the horse meat and storing it in the freezer. The men from the locker had finished the butchering after dark, using the headlights from their truck to see by. At about nine o'clock, they had delivered the vats and cans of meat to the cooler. Now Uncle Emil and Peter were finishing the job.

After breakfast Matt waited for Peter to return to his bedroom. He looked out the window, surveying the flat farmland for miles around, and could not believe the dreary, colorless scene before him was the same countryside that had thrilled him so the day before. When Peter returned from the barn, Matt agreed to accompany him to the gravel pit where they would carry bottles and practice shooting.

They each filled an ammunition belt with .22 longs. Peter loaded an extra belt with .410 shells and then took two rifles and his shot gun from the gun locker. In the ell behind the kitchen they found a trash barrel full of empty soda pop and beer bottles and some food jars from the kitchen and stuffed them into a gunny sack. With their load they made their way across the barnyard to a small Ford tractor with a grain wagon attached. Matt climbed into the wagon, and Peter handed the sack of bottles and the weapons up to him; then he climbed up onto the tractor seat and started the engine.

The gravel pit was about a mile away in the northwest corner of the farm. The State Highway Commission had purchased the rights to the sand twenty years before to maintain the county roads. Uncle Emil thought he had a bonanza for a few years, but the grade of sand that met state specifications was soon exhausted. Now, it had become a dump for hard trash—old cars and broken machinery.

They drove out of the barnyard to the gravel road that fed, a quarter of a mile away, into the county road. After almost a half mile Peter turned off onto a muddy car path along a line of trees, up a small hill and down again to the edge of the excavation. Matt bounced violently in the wagon, sometimes needing to hold on with both hands. He was certain the bottles would all break, but most survived the trip.

Peter took several bottles and at two foot intervals pressed them into the soft sand and half way up an embankment about fifty feet away. Then he turned to where Matt was standing, pacing off the distance as he walked. He took up his rifle, loaded a clip, thrust it into the magazine and proceeded to blast each bottle with a single shot in a left to right rapid fire sequence.

Matt was impressed by the performance. His admiration increased when, during his turn, he failed to break any of his bottles in fewer than five attempts. But under Peter's guidance, he made refined adjustments of arm position and sighting so that his second round of shots showed marked improvement.

The last several bottles were used in a makeshift trap shoot. Matt stood behind Peter and about thirty feet to the right. Peter stood with his gun at his waist. Then he shouted "pull," and Matt flung a bottle into a high arc. Peter waited until the bottle began to descend; then in a single motion of raising, aiming, and firing he disintegrated the bottle into an amber puff of powdered glass.

Matt had no success at shooting the bottles with the shotgun so Peter finished them off and, as a gesture of pity for Matt's ineptitude, he let him drive the tractor back to the barnyard. Peter put the guns in the wagon and climbed behind Matt on the axle where he shouted shift and power instructions into Matt's ear as they drove along.

Matt found the tractor easier to drive than the family car, which he had driven a few times under his father's nervous tutelage. On the county road, he drove with the throttle wide open. By the time they drove into the barnyard, he felt he was in control, that he had already achieved a certain professional competence. They parked among the spruce in the windbreak and then walked back along the corral past the barn toward the house.

They ate dinner in the late afternoon and began preparing to leave immediately after his mother helped with the dishes. Matt loaded the car with Peter's help. The trunk, already half filled with his mother's natural disaster emergency supplies, was quickly filled. The amount of food that Uncle Emil and Aunt Tilly had readied to send along was enormous. Both boys made several trips loading the packages of frozen meat, eggs, canned vegetables, squash, and apples into the back seat. Some of the food would be picked up in a day or two by Matt's older sister. Finally, unceremoniously, they parted. Peter disappeared upstairs to his room where he planned to clean the rifles and his guns, and Matt squeezed in the back seat among the boxes of food and waited for his parents while they drank a last cup of coffee in the kitchen.

As they left in the early evening darkness, he closed his eyes and tried to sleep, but the ride on the gravel road was rough. His father drove intently. His mother would not speak until they had been underway for a while. They were always nervous about driving unfamiliar roads at night.

He stretched his legs and thrust his hands into his jacket pockets and looked at the fields fading into darkness. In his right pocket his fingers touched several small, sharp objects. He closed his fingers around them and withdrew his hand, opened it, and peered at several tiny disengaged bones. He reached once more into his pocket and withdrew the entire remains, fur and bones, and inspected them closely in the dim light; once again he saw in his mind's eye the slaughtered horse, it's quivering mass of flesh steaming in the late afternoon, cold-yellow sunlight. He lowered the window a few inches, thrust his forearm through the crevice and opened his hand into the wind.

Once on the highway he closed his eyes, shifted his body sideways to a more comfortable position, and in time fell asleep to the rhythm of the wheels thumping against the tar insulation in the joints between the great slabs of poured concrete. Later he awoke to the uneven, bumpy whir of tire on brick. He looked out the window and saw the blur of light, and then when his eyes had focused, he could read the neon signs of bars and hotels and restaurants. He saw the changing traffic signals and the flashing headlights of cars and trucks. He looked up into the tall black apartment houses and saw the irregular checkering of lighted windows. He was almost home, in the city again.

THE PARTNERSHIP

Sometime during the early months of 1944, when I was twelve years old, I came of age, morally speaking, under rare and special circumstances. I didn't realize at the time that anything was extraordinary even though, as a matter of objective fact, I spent the last years of my childhood in a world gone absolutely mad.

For the two previous years, resounding imperatives, blaring from the radio, and thundering and intimidating newspaper headlines had infused my wakening conscience with an unquestioning faith in the National Purpose. If there was dissent, it was conducted discreetly out of earshot of children or limited to a criticism of the diligence or manner with which we pursued our military objectives. Everyone,—unless you were a conscientious objector or a coward, subscribed to a single, clearly defined moral absolute: if you weren't falling on a live hand grenade or diving your plane into the stack of a Japanese cruiser, you felt, or should have felt, somehow insufficient or inadequate or even guilty, depending upon how far you were from looking down the barrel of an enemy gun, and although it was my duty as a loyal citizen and a Catholic to pray for a speedy end of hostilities, I secretly hoped the war would last long enough for me to grow up and be part of it all. I often acted out in my imagination the roles (usually inspired by a recent newspaper or magazine account of some heroic accomplishment) I hoped to play when my personal historical moment arrived. Sometimes I was a tough marine cut off behind enemy lines or a fighter pilot forced to bail out over enemy held territory. I was usually reported missing in action. When I finally arrived home, to everyone's happy surprise, I was impeccably dressed in a pure white officer's uniform. I don't recall ever expecting to be killed in action, though the circumstances surrounding my disappearance were often as dangerous as they were obscure.

I was trying to grow up then as quickly as possible in a small Midwestern city about as far away from the foxholes and the cockpits as you could possibly get. My sole contribution to the war effort had been foraging the city dump for tin cans, newspapers, and rubber which I dutifully delivered to gas stations and collection centers. My father worked for an airline that, because of war contracts for the remodification of B-24's, had been thrust into the forefront of the war effort. My mother had my younger brother and my aging grandmother to take care of, my older brother had high school and baseball and a job. I existed somewhere on the edge of their concern, diminished by those awesome newspaper headlines and the terrible historical urgency that filled everyone's conversations with so much anxiety and hope.

I lived then south of St. Paul along the Mississippi River in a packing plant center notorious for its smell and the violence of its bars, more than sixty of them stretched out along Concord Street, which ran along the railroad tracks at the base of the huge river bluffs. Just beyond the railroad yard was the river and beyond that an enormous shallow-water backup, formed by years of spring flooding, called Pig's Eye Lake. The streetcar line ran along Concord Street northward and connected the packing plants and the rail stockyards center to downtown St. Paul about five miles up-river. Thousands of workers rode them daily to and from the three shifts a day that Swifts and Armours ran in order to meet war production demands. We lived above the business district, securely insulated from the hustle and bustle of the marketplace and the violence and the drunkenness of the bars, on quiet, nicely ordered, tree-lined streets. But it was impossible to escape the ubiquitous smell of the packing plants, the squeal of the hogs, and the plaintive moans of the cattle that drifted upward to us on an east wind.

Half way up Grand Avenue, which connected the residential neighborhood on the hill and the marketplaces of Concord Street, was the Hollywood Theater. It had originally been called the Ideal

Theater, but its name had been wisely changed in the early thirties for obvious reasons. The City Council never got around to changing the name of Grand Avenue though there was certainly as a great a disparity between its name and what it had not become as there was between the Ideal and what had been going on inside its walls for twenty years.

Throughout the war years I went to movies at the Hollywood once, often twice a week. On Sunday I sat through two features so that as part of my patriotic duty I could clap and cheer and stomp my feet during the newsreel whenever President Roosevelt or Old Glory appeared on the screen, which occurred simultaneously, as I remember, with extraordinary frequency. Often I trudged home from the movies dejected and forlorn. I had seen another News of the Week in Review in which brave crews of sailors fought fires erupting through bomb holes in the deck of a dangerously listing aircraft carrier. Sometimes it was Marines amid the tattered palm trees and devastated vegetation of a former tropical Eden, forging ahead relentlessly behind a flame thrower, flushing out the enemy. But the vision that touched me most deeply was the shot of a bomber crew member leaning out the open window of a B-17, giving a grand thumbs up to the cameraman as the plane taxied in line, waiting to take off on yet another raid deep into enemy held territory.

By May of 1944, it became increasingly apparent the enemy could not hold out until I grew old enough to arrive and deliver the final blow. The Russians had broken the Wehrmacht on the Eastern Front. Italy had already surrendered. In the Pacific we were taking island after island. The Japanese fleet had been crippled and would, after the defeats of the summer and early fall, resort to the Kamikaze. I believed at the time that every American who had laid down his life for his country was a hero of the first magnitude, and I was assured by Sister Marie Bernard that such a self-sacrifice would be rewarded by an immediate admission to heaven, without the usual stopover in Purgatory. Any "Jap" who did the same thing, of course, was a suicidal maniac, but such was my belief then in the absolute moral rightness of our cause.

With victory clearly in sight, we were urged to redouble our efforts on the home front. Thousands of troops and tanks ships and planes were poised in England ready to invade Western Europe. They needed the support of every able-bodied American. In an agony of frustration I scoured the town dump once again although I knew it had been stripped long ago of useful materials. Whenever I went anywhere, I traveled the alleys, stopping to forage the trash barrels in hope of discovering some treasure inadvertently discarded that might be needed in the war effort, and which I could, as a service to my country, deliver to the proper collection center. My efforts proved futile. I languished on the brink of despair, deprived by the accident of an untimely birth of a share in the National Glory.

II

And then as I despaired of finding any opportunity of serving my country in its hour of greatest need, opportunity found me, or rather I became the beneficiary of the trickle-down economic boom that had begun with the first war plants and the draft in late 1939 and early 1940. In a gradually deepening and expanding job market, it had finally, at the peak of our war manpower commitment in June of 1944, scraped the dregs, the bottom of the barrel of able-bodied workers, and found me. Or rather I had grown into that opportunity naturally and inevitably as thirteen and fourteen year olds the summer before had grown into the job market in 1943, and many had, especially if they were at all mature physically, grown into virtual full-time summer employment at gas stations, restaurants, and motion picture theaters. Boys and girls barely in their teens assumed forty to fifty hour a week jobs in the packing plants from which their parents had been laid off less than ten years before. My older brother, though only sixteen, worked as the senior developer in the darkroom of a photo processing company that handled a good share of the over-the-counter films in St. Paul.

Beginning in early June, I found myself with two summer jobs that I would not ordinarily have held for three or four years. The first job, which was really an expansion of an already existing duty, began about a week before the end of school when I received mimeographed assignments for summer serving from Sister Frances before she mysteriously disappeared with the rest of the nuns, like migratory birds, for the summer only to return just as mysteriously and with clock like precision during the last week of August. I was listed to serve the seven o'clock mass alone no less than seven of the twelve weeks of summer. When I was not serving daily mass, I was listed "on call" for funerals, and finally I had been assigned most of the eleven o'clock Sunday masses during June and July.

Though I pretended to object, I knew well enough the boon that had fallen to me. I would have rights to all weddings during the weeks I served daily mass, a duty for which it was customary to receive a gratuity from the bridal party. Father O'Callahan always paid us for service at a funeral, except during the school year when we got out of class for over an hour—a reward which Father knew we all believed was sufficient unto itself. And those of us with most of the early morning daily duty had been assigned the eleven o'clock mass on Sunday, preferred because after mass we joined the ushers in the counting room to count and bind, in packages of one hundred, the opened collection envelopes. For this service we received fifty cents each and a Tampa Havana Corona from Father's own box, which I later sold to my father for a quarter.

I had inherited the privileges of altar boys ordinarily two or three years older than I, and the simple duty I had taken for granted for two years had suddenly become, because of the scarcity of servers, important, at least in my own eyes, Sister Frances's eyes, and those of permissive old Father O'Callahan, who was rapidly growing out of his usefulness as I had yet to grow into mine. Besides, I liked to serve. I liked the smell of the church, of melted wax and of the incense that had accumulated in the cassocks. I like the sound of the mumbled Latin that Father and I exchanged. And, above all I loved the green vestments, the flickering candles on the altar, and the golden bowl of a sanctuary lamp with its red candlelight that was suspended from the ceiling by a metal cord, swaying twelve to fifteen feet in the air just a few paces behind us as we knelt at the altar.

My second job, which became the center of my life that summer, was to assist the parish gardener, Joseph Wagner, or simply Joe "Wagon" (as he had been called by two decades of school children who watched him through the playground fence as he weeded and trimmed and watered the rectory flower garden), in the cutting and gardening services he had contracted for the summer and then found impossible to accomplish by himself.

I was not his first choice. My mother, who conducted the negotiations by phone with his mother, a retired home economics teacher who had taught my mother in her sophomore year of high school, assured me that Wagon had tried to hire a bigger and stronger helper but had failed to do so because all the older boys had easier, better paying jobs. Apparently he had seen me serve early mass and had mistakenly concluded that I was reliable. My mother knew that my early morning reliability was the result of her prodding and nagging and threats of violence. I'm afraid she didn't try to sell my services too hard. I listened to her conversation from the next room, and punctuating the elliptical nostalgia they exchanged, I heard myself characterized as small for my age, either sickly or lazy, of limited endurance and uncertain resolution. I suppose she was just covering me if the work turned out to be too difficult, but I was, nonetheless, disappointed by her assessment of my potential. She did negotiate solid conditions for my employment, however. My duties as an altar boy, a prior commitment, would take precedence so I wouldn't lose any of the money I had hoped to make serving, and I would receive, despite my limitations, an equal share of the wages for each job I worked.

III

In early June while the greatest armada of ships and planes and men the world has ever known assembled off Omaha Beach, I began work with Joe Wagon, weeding Father O'Callahan's circular flower bed on the side lawn of the rectory first and then moving on to two lawns half way across town.

I don't recall having any reservations about working with Wagon, though I should have had or probably *would* have had under ordinary conditions. He was, as my mother put it depending upon her mood, "slow" or "not very scholarly" or "not all there." I believe he was in his late forties. He looked something like Humphrey Bogart, if Bogie had had bigger ears that flopped a bit. His hair was sandy and cut short, almost into a crew cut. He wore work clothes of light grey or dungaree blue. On Sunday mornings, though, he wore a dark suit, white shirt, and tie to the seven o'clock mass, at which he sometimes took up the collection when a regular usher failed to attend.

I suppose everyone thought him strange. He had not married. He had not finished school. If he was different from other men his age, like my father, who wore suits and worked in offices and had families and ambitions, he was different in a good sense. He was known as a devotedly religious man, one of the few parishioners to attend daily mass where he prayed in a back corner of the church with a mournful sweep of his head, back and forth, and an elaborate clutching and unclutching of his rosary beads. He attended most weddings even though he didn't know anyone in the wedding party. He stood, beaming, behind the line of the wedding guests on the church steps as they threw rice on the newly married couple. He attended most of the funerals, especially of older members of the parish who had been forgotten, at which he looked somber and mournful. He was a ubiquitous presence at social gatherings in the church hall where he stood against a back wall with folded arms. He could be depended on to put up and take down chairs at virtually every meeting. He was so dependable about the chairs that the church janitor no longer considered seating arrangements as one of his duties. I saw him as a man of faith and devotion and a steady worker. If he was strange or different, his strangeness was not degrading as it was for crazy Bicycle Harvey or for old Snowball, the only Negro in town, a punch-drunk alcoholic whose bondage and degradation were perpetuated by patronizing gratuities of cash and liquor and food and a jail cell to sleep in.

After a week or so we settled into a routine. After mass and breakfast, we met at our first job about eight o'clock. Usually, we used the owner's lawnmower and rake or hoe or clippers, but there were a few jobs for elderly widows whose lawn and garden tools were beyond repair and then Wagon brought his own, which were stored neatly about the walls of his garage. Wagon repaired or sharpened or oiled all the equipment we used for no charge as part of our service.

We took turns mowing and clipping and hauling the grass away. While he mowed, I clipped. We weeded flower and vegetable gardens together on our knees, pitching the unearthed weeds into a bushel basket and then taking turns emptying it. It took me a while, especially the first few weeks during the rapid early summer growth, to distinguish the weeds. He didn't say much. I learned by watching what he uprooted. If I threw away more plants than weeds, he never told me. After the plants had taken hold, it became easier. I simply broke the soil with the hoe around each plant or down a row, assuming that any new growth then was a weed. The vegetable gardens were easier. There was more room to work the hoe. Much of the weeding in flower beds had to be done by hand all summer.

We had a dozen or so regular customers. Doc Eaton's was our fanciest job. His side yard was enclosed by a thick, squared hedge about eye level high. The lawn was bent grass like a golf green, neatly edged. When it rained, it had to be cut twice a week. It was the only lawn we regularly weeded though we did cut out dandelions on every job. Wagon kept the hedge trimmed. He had done the basic squaring in May. We worked the flower garden behind the kitchen together. Mrs. Eaton served us a soft drink about ten o'clock. We drank it on the patio in the garden. We sat briefly on the wrought iron chairs arranged around a matching iron table which in turn was overshadowed by a huge umbrella. Its pointed shaft fitted through a hole in the middle of the table and had been driven into the ground.

We weeded several victory gardens. They were located on the city land across from the Roosevelt Elementary School, fertilized and plowed by order of the City Council as its contribution to the war effort. In May, families had signed up on the plot map tacked to the bulletin board in the lobby-hallway of the City Hall, just outside the council chambers. We maintained the gardens of those who were away at vacation homes for the summer. They came in occasionally to harvest the vegetables.

Wagon came to work each morning with a copy of the St. Paul *Pioneer Press* in his back pocket, which he sometimes read during the mid-morning break. He was a slow reader putting his fingertip under each word, sometimes under each syllable and silently shaping each sound with his mouth, but he could read, and what he read he remembered. I read twice as fast as he did and forgot what I read just as quickly. But when it came to figures, Wagon wasn't just slow or 'not all there'. He wasn't there *at all*. It was painful for him to figure our income the first week in order to pay me my share. He had never had to keep books before, but now that he had a partner, he felt he had to make an accounting. He wrote the totals down in a column and then began the slowest toting of numbers I have ever witnessed, and when he was done and asked me to check him, it turned out he wasn't even close.

I kept the books after that. He even wanted to pay me for my mathematical services, so relieved was he to get rid of the burden of numbers. But I insisted my weekly bookkeeping be considered one of my duties. Each Saturday noon, Wagon read off the names of our customers from a small notebook. He printed everything in large, uneven capital letters. He must have used a soft lead pencil, for the names were so smudged I could hardly read them. I wrote up the list, and then he dictated the sum we had been paid. I added the list and divided it in half, and he paid me in cash from a canvas bank deposit pouch.

I knew within a few days I was being paid more than I was worth. Wagon worked steadily, unrelentingly throughout the morning. I worked in spurts—furious burst of energy, the peaks of which occasionally matched his normal output. I needed frequent breaks. I suppose I got up from my knees or left a lawn mower at the end of a row several times each morning to find the hose, and, when the water had run cold, to slurp long mouthfuls and then run the water over my head. Wagon might pause from whatever he was doing to watch me for a moment, but he rarely broke his rhythm once he set to work until the midmorning break when he had some water and sat down for a few minutes.

There were times when I matched his effort for relatively long periods of time, especially when we worked with hoes side by side down adjacent bean rows in a Victory garden. Once I locked into his rhythm, I didn't want to take a break no matter how tired I became. I couldn't explain it at first. I thought for a while it was the pride I felt in keeping up with him or sustaining my effort for a long period of time, the feeling the long distance runner must feel, even the loser, when the race is done and he realizes that he actually finished the prescribed distance.

Plausible as those explanations seemed, it became clear as the summer wore on that the satisfaction I felt was in the work itself, and I didn't come to grasp that until I understood that for Wagon working was like singing or dancing or praying.

IV

Wagon had two pastimes—passions would be the better word—that he offered to share with me as a fringe benefit of our partnership. The ruling passion of his life was baseball. He was a devoted fan of the St. Paul Saints in the old American Association. We listened to the games on his portable radio whenever we worked in the afternoon, and he read, in his slow and laborious fashion, the newspaper summaries during our morning breaks. He knew all the batting averages and pitching statistics though he couldn't compute them. I doubt that he ever understood that the batting average was a mathematical expression of the relationship between the times at bat and the number of hits.

Though we were interested vaguely in the Cubs, the major leagues were too remote, except at World Series time, to be of any abiding interest, so we identified with the Saints. Wagon followed them with the same relentless intensity with which he worked. I was only a lukewarm baseball fan. My passion was football and the Golden Gophers of the University of Minnesota whose national pre-eminence under Bernie Bierman had apparently gone to war along with Lucky Strike green; but in time I came to share some of his devotion as a logical consequence of our daily contact.

There were the Columbus Red Birds, and the Toledo Mud Hens, the Louisville Colonels and the hated Minneapolis Millers. I really can't explain why everyone was so irrationally devoted to the Saints. A few of the players went on to the majors. In the late 40's Duke Snider played for them briefly and Walter Alston managed them before moving on to Brooklyn. But we supported them and believed in them as we supported and believed in the war effort. There really wasn't any difference. Loyalty to the Saints and to the National Purpose sprung from the same spiritual source. I never thought much about it at the time, but I'm certain that I would have suspected a rabid Miller's fan capable of treason. Fortunately, I had little capacity to formulate paradoxes then. I certainly had no capacity to resolve them. I know *now* it would have been possible to be a loyal American and not be a lover of the St. Paul Saints. In my childhood those loyalties were inseparable.

Wagon took me to Lexington Park to several ball games that summer. I was startled at my first night game when I walked up the ramp and stood staring at the field, which had been transformed by the banks of lights into a radiant, almost mystical, verdure. I witnessed also that night the excitement of a night crowd, an excitement, I learned several years later, that had been generated out of the fact that half the fans were drunk on a local beer whose sign occupied most of the left centerfield fence. It was a St. Paul beer and was one of the sponsors of play by play broadcasts, which Wagon listened to on his portable during the game.

That first night I brought my glove along just in case I might get a chance at a foul ball. We bought reserved tickets just beyond the first base bag and about twenty rows up. I was disappointed when he led me to our seats. The foul balls that came our way during batting practice seemed to sail well beyond us into the right field corner or fall short into the net or the box seats. By the third inning, however, I discovered the practical wisdom of our seats. I didn't get a foul ball, but I did get a ball, a direct catch of a wide overthrow of first by the Saints' shortstop, an erratic seventeen year old rookie named Brown, who because of the war found himself playing on a level of competition beyond his ability as did several of his teammates, who were, as the song lamented, "either too young or too old."

The Saints won most of the games I saw that summer. They were always hitters' games, enlivened by errors. Twice a strong wind was blowing from behind the plate toward left field. On those days even a mediocre hitter could rattle the roof of the old roller skating Coliseum beyond the left field wall.

Wagon never said much. He clutched his radio in both hands, jumping up when the ball was hit sharply to the outfield. He rocked back and forth, shaking his head from side to side when the enemy was at bat. He pumped his radio in both hands over his head when the Saints scored a run, and he leapt up and stamped his feet if a Saint hit a home run. I scored the game in his program for him. He kept and, I believe, seemed to cherish the results of my nervous scrawl. He studied the smudged box score two or three times on the streetcar ride home. He let me sit next to the open window out of which I leaned to catch in my face the air we rushed through. After a night game, we didn't get home until eleven o'clock. I was surprised and disappointed to discover the city had gone to bed before we had left the ball park. Except for a few night shift workers, the loop was deserted when we waited to transfer at Seventh and Wabasha to a southbound car.

Besides the baseball games I rode the streetcar with Wagon on three other occasions but in the opposite direction. We took the Inver Grove car away from the city to the end of the line, hiked across the old train bridge below the boat docks and down the far side of the river to a series of small islands, the last of which was little more than a treeless sand bar in the middle of the river. There we pursued, more with quiet reflection than enthusiasm, Wagon's other recreational passion—drop line fishing for channel cats.

I helped Wagon set up two drop lines baited with chunks of bacon rind and weighted with enormous machine nuts, four inches across and an inch thick which we swirled about our heads and let fly toward the middle of the channel. On the way, Wagon had cut two stiff willow switches, which we thrust a foot or two into the sand and to which we attached the lines. Then I found a comfortable dune and waited and watched down river for one of the oil barges which daily plowed upstream to the terminals at the foot of the St. Anthony Falls in Minneapolis fifteen miles upriver. When one had worked its way upriver abreast of us, I waved at a crew member on a barge or at the captain himself in the tug, and sometimes they waved back, and I was thrilled and diminished by the enormous size of the several barges locked together ahead of the tug as they passed us. I had never seen them closely before—only from a distance of the bluffs. From there, they had seemed like toys.

One line was theoretically mine and one was Wagon's, but whenever a cat hit my line, Wagon handled it first to test whether it was small enough for me to haul in. We pulled a few in each time, which we then cut loose. They were black and shiny and fierce and defiant. They were all head and spur and whiskers and I was relieved when Wagon got the hook out or cut the line and I could take my tennis shoe off its back and slip it with my toe back into the water. I had heard of channel cat that weighed over fifty pounds, but we didn't catch any over ten or fifteen pounds. We didn't care because it was fishing that was important, not catching.

Once, we were on the sand bar when the old Capitol sternwheeler came by on its daily excursion from the Robert Street landing in St. Paul to the locks at Hastings. I had grown out of excursion trips, or rather I was beyond the day-time family picnic ventures and not yet ready for the shorter but more romantic midnight cruises in the moonlight. Sitting in the sand waving at the passengers along the railing, I felt strangely nostalgic and superior. Though I preferred my island in the stream to the steamer ride, I longed to see once again the old spiral bridge across the river below the government locks at Hastings. When I first rode on the Capitol, my grandmother instructed me to observe the spiral bridge closely. It had brought architectural fame to our obscure corner of the universe and was to be considered with seriousness and pride. She never explained why it was so special. Several years later an engineering student at the University explained to me that the spiral bridge was a kind of architectural joke, famous as a ridiculously complex solution to a simple problem, but despite the expert opinion, there was great resistance to its replacement a dozen or so years later.

V

I didn't spend all my time working or serving. When it rained, we didn't work. I hung around the house groaning about nothing to do until I drove my mother half crazy. She sent me outside to play in the puddles or find a friend. Instead, I went over to Wagon's garage and watched him clean or sharpen tools or work on one of the several handyman jobs he saved for rainy days.

One of his continuing summer projects was the recanvassing of the Boy Scout canoes. He stripped the old canvas off and applied the new with a coat of a resin glue. Then he sanded and dried the surface and soaked the canvas again and then sanded it again when it dried. When he finished one, the scouts would take it away to paint and return with another scratched and patched wreck for Wagon to renew.

Around the walls of the garage and hanging from the ceiling were all sorts of tools. There were hand scythes and tin shears; sets of files and saws, pliers, wrenches, screw drivers, hammers, and chisels; and power tools—a lathe and a drill—and soldering irons and rakes, lawn mowers, and clippers. I don't think there had been a car in the garage in ten years though there were still a few fading oil blotches down the middle of the concrete.

Wagon left the garage doors open. I sat just inside on an old saw horse and watched the rivulets of rain going by in the alley and listened to the sounds of the tools he worked. I never helped him. I just sat and listened and talked baseball or nonsense while he grunted agreement or the pain of his labor. When the Saints were on the road, we listened to the radio broadcast. The announcer took the results off teletype and relayed the play by play between the click-click-click of a relay ticker. I have always suspected that the clicks were simulated and that the announcer was on a telephone. The announcer occasionally tried to be dramatic and faked excitement, but he didn't have to. A telegraphic rendering of the factual play by play was enough for us. We were true fans.

On hot afternoons when I had finished working, I went to the swimming pool at Loraine Park in the south end of town. There I took up with some school friends who had in turn taken up with some older boys from the junior high school. Though we could all swim, we spent most of the afternoon in the shallow end of the pool tormenting a bevy of budding beauties who affected hostility but who became sulky if we strayed off to the diving board.

But we always returned to pay them the homage they deserved. We bombarded them with running cannonballs or splashed water in their faces. Though most of the girls were my age, they were all a few inches taller and about five years thicker. Two older boys from junior high, Eddie Mason and Sputzie Gillespie, who were sexually more progressive and less inhibited (certainly more inquisitive) than the rest of us, spent most of their time along the edge of the pool where they tried surreptitiously to sneak a glimpse of the female mystery as girls climbed out of the pool. They were forever jumping in water, stalking the edges of the pool, or climbing up ladders behind unsuspecting victims.

They returned to the rest of us with vivid descriptions of what they claimed to have seen. We were an attentive and appreciative audience, though we sometimes pretended to disbelieve in their witness, sworn to be true by strong oaths and threats of violence. Their versions of the female "thing" were based more upon invention than observation though most of us had no evidence or experience to contradict their testimony. Nature had apparently bestowed upon the female of the species such a marvelous proliferation and variety of "things" that for a year or two after that summer, whenever I happened to glance in a neighboring urinal at school, I grew temporarily depressed when my observation verified once again the rather prosaic sameness with which the male had been neglectingly endowed.

After supper twice a week I went to the American Legion baseball practice at the high school field. My older brother was the starting first baseman and the team's only left-handed relief pitcher. I became, in due course, the unofficial, practice bat-boy. Actually, bat-boy is a misnomer. What I did was shag balls hit to the outfield during batting practice. Most of the players were too lazy to chase the balls. They all wanted to bat, or pitch, or play short stop. If a hit ball didn't come right to a player, he threw a glove at it and sent me hustling. Toward the end of practice, they just lay down and picked grass and told dirty stories and let me cover the whole outfield.

It was a good team, despite the practices, and I followed the games with some enthusiasm. It was, after all, the American Legion and the National Pastime and my brother was almost a star. I attended most of the home games, which were played Sunday afternoons at the field adjacent to the swimming pool in Loraine Park. I even went to a few away games when my father had enough gas saved for a Sunday trip.

My brother was a solid .300 hitter, a modestly gifted first baseman, but an erratic pitcher with uncertain control. He threw a natural hook and a nice breaking curve that came in on the hands of right handed batters, but it was a matter of pure chance if it made the strike zone consistently. Whenever he came in to pitch from first base in a close game, we knew that victory was in doubt.

He used to get nose bleeds when he was excited or over exerted himself running the bases. He swung late most of the time and hit soft liners to the opposite field over the third baseman's head. He ran wildly for second, and after sliding into the bag safely, he called time out to sit on the bag while his nose bled. He always suffered his nose bleeds stoically. He tilted his head back for a while and pinched his nostrils shut. Everyone advised him not to swallow any blood lest he become sick and have to leave the game. In time, someone usually found some cotton, and he stuffed his nose and stayed in the game. We always gave him a hand when he got to his feet and put his cap on. The small puddles of blood that stained the bag or the drops that dribbled off his chin, staining the front of his uniform, made everyone feel a little more heroic and important. His shedding of blood was almost as satisfying as a beaning, which, as every second-rate ball player knows, is *the* cathartic moment in baseball.

Once, for a week I even became a teacher as Wagon and I temporarily reversed our roles as mentor and student. He wanted me to teach him the mass—the movements and Latin responses of the altar boy—so he could understand and appreciate the holy sacrifice more fully. It took me about three days to discover what he wanted, he was so shy and hesitant about imposing himself on anyone, but once I discovered the general topic he wished to discuss I could easily find out what he wanted specifically by asking a series of questions to which he could answer yes or no. In truth, most of my conversations with Wagon followed the format of a game of Twenty Questions or Animal, Vegetable, or Mineral.

We practiced the Latin mainly when we weeded gardens. First I pronounced the priest's words and then the server's. He then repeated the server's words. He knew some of the prayers from reading his missal, and though he quickly learned to recognize the priest's words and committed the server's responses to memory, his pronunciation remained atrocious however much he practiced. His rendition of the "Confiteor" was grossly comic.

I gave up correcting him. I simply drilled him until he knew every response. Then I began explaining the secret signs that the priest gave the altar boy, signs undetected by the laity in the distant pews, that told the server when to change the missal from the Epistle to the Gospel side, when to get the cruets, when to ring the bell. He sat in one of the first pews one morning at mass to catch a closer glimpse, but he missed the signs I had told him to observe. Finally I suggested that we run through the mass on the altar. I would be the priest and he could be the server.

He was reluctant at first but then decided it was the only way he would learn. He came back to the sacristy after mass one morning. After Father had left the church, I took him on to the altar where I had hoped to give him a trial run. But once we left the sacristy door, he underwent a strange transformation. He fixed his eyes on the tabernacle and he began to tremble. Every time I turned my back and went to the altar to demonstrate the priest's movements, he fell upon his knees and mumbled what I assumed were prayers. He responded to the priest's prayers I delivered at the foot of the altar in a halting, yawning stutter. I explained everything in detail, step by step and went through the priest's motions, and he nodded in apparent understanding, but then I had to coax him with the Latin and push and shove him about the altar to walk him through his moves. When we arrived at the Offertory, I suggested we give it all up and try some other time.

He nodded and began backing off the altar toward the sacristy door, his eyes still transfixed upon the tabernacle. He genuflected twice as he backed away toward the door, and once off the altar, he stopped for several moments in the sacristy and leaned for support on the sink. He breathed quickly and heavily for perhaps a minute, and when he had caught his breath, wordlessly departed. He never mentioned learning the mass again. I didn't understand what had happened to him then. I really didn't *care* to understand until years later when once in a rage of self examination and discovery, I groped for a while with the meaning of his terror as a possible key to the meaning of my despair.

VI

I began to accumulate vast quantities of money. By the end of July, I had bought two War Bonds for $18.75 each and was well on my way to a third. July was a bad month for the old and the infirm and a busy one for lovers. It was a good summer for altar boys.

Because Wagon often finished a job when I had to serve, I convinced him that any money I received the rest of the summer for serving weddings should be shared. In the second week of our agreement, after I had contributed modest sums to our weekly total, an incident occurred which momentarily tested my resolve.

It was a sudden wedding. No banns had been announced. Ordinarily a mixed marriage, hastily arranged, was performed in Father's office in the Rectory, but the bride's family were long-time parishioners and wanted a church ceremony though there would be no mass.

It was scheduled for two o'clock in the afternoon. I worked for an hour or so after lunch and then rode my bicycle to church. There I found Bernie Fitzgerald, the other server, already dressed and fidgeting in the sacristy. He was two or three years younger than I. He had never served at a wedding before. Since there was no mass, there was little we had to do to set up the altar. We opened the communion railing gates and put on the church lights. I instructed Bernie in his sole responsibility—to hold a small plate upon which the best man would place the ring for the blessing. My job was to carry the holy water.

It was a hasty and careless ceremony. The bride and maid of honor wore street dresses and picture hats and were crying. The groom and best man were soldiers. There were ten or fifteen in the congregation, all sitting in the first few pews on the bride's side. There was no music. Father instructed the wedding party in every step of the ceremony—now kneel, now stand. He read the prayers in great haste and in a monotone. When he blessed the ring, he sprinkled holy water over everyone. In the middle of the blessing, Bernie dropped the plate and ring and scrambled to the floor to pick them up. When he had retrieved them, Father decided to bless everything again. The groom took out his handkerchief to wipe the holy water from his face before placing the ring on the bride's finger and repeating the vows after Father.

When it was over, we returned to the sacristy where Father gave me his rope and we ran outside around the church into the vestibule where we breathlessly untangled the rope and stretched it across the end of the center aisle.

The bride and groom had walked slowly up the aisle. When they came to us blocking their way, the groom turned to the bride and half around to the best man.

"*Now* what the hell are we supposed to do? I thought it was all over."

"The best man is supposed to pay us for serving," I said. "It's an old custom."

"How much are we supposed to pay you?"

"Oh, anything you want."

The best man dug into his pocket and brought out a coin.

"Here, kid, get yourself some crackerjacks."

The groom put his hand out to stop his arm.

"Christ, don't be such a cheapskate. Let's do something right today." He took out his wallet and withdrew a bill.

"Here, kid. Go buy yourself a nice piece of ass."

The guests caught up with the wedding party. I ran to the vestibule door and opened it. Everyone stepped into the sun on the church steps. The best man disappeared. In a few minutes he reappeared around the corner, driving a battered old Chevy and parked at the foot of the steps. The bride and groom and the maid of honor got in. There were some unenthusiastic wishes for happiness shouted after them. Someone threw a handful of rice, and then they drove off, with black smoke billowing from the tailpipe.

As we walked back around the church to the sacristy, I slowly unrolled the bill and showed it to Bernie.

"Ten dollars," he shouted. "My brother said we'd only make a buck or two at the most."

After we changed, we walked silently to a drug store where we intended to exchange the ten for two fives. Though I suspected what the soldier had meant by "a piece of ass," I decided to avoid mentioning anything about it to Bernie, I suppose, in order to protect my own rather precarious innocence as much as to think the best of anyone who had bestowed upon us the most liberal gratuity in the history of altar service in our parish.

I had no idea what was going on in Bernie's mind at that moment though I have since found it necessary to ascribe to him an absolutely innocent state of mind in order to account for what he said about a block later, after I had given him for the second time the bill to scrutinize in wonder and disbelief. As he opened the bill and stretched it in his hands, he shook his head and asked me, and so far as I could tell, without a hint of sarcasm or irony.

"Will we have to spend it the way he said? Will we have to spend it all on a piece of ass? Or do you think we could spend some of it on ice cream or something?"

"Oh, I don't think he meant we have to buy exactly what he said. I think he was just making a suggestion. You know, like when your ma or pa tells you not to take any wooden nickels. They're just giving you advice."

I wasn't very convinced by my explanation, but Bernie nodded, apparently satisfied I had given him the answer he wanted to hear. He unfolded the bill again and stared at it for several moments. Then he stopped on the sidewalk and waited for me to stop and turn back toward him a step or two. He handed the bill back to me and asked,

"What's a piece of ass?"

Now I have never been very clever. I always think of the perfect retort a day or two later, or not at all. But I was superb that afternoon, so much so that I sometimes suspect that I was inspired by a special grace. How I managed to answer Bernie's question that afternoon is beyond my comprehension, and thus beyond my explanation, but answer him I did with what seems to me today to have been an absolutely brilliant response. My answer came out automatically without any reflection whatsoever. I *knew* what I had said only after I had said it.

"Well, a piece of ass is a fancy cut of meat, like steak. My ma gets one every so often when we save up enough red stamps. The butcher and my ma call it a rump roast, but most everybody else just call it a plain old piece of ass."

"Is *that* what it is?" Bernie cried in relief and delight, his face brightening.

"Yeah. That's why I think he was just suggesting something fancy for us to spend the money on. We couldn't get a rump roast if we wanted to unless we had the red stamps. I figure he was just telling us to spend it on something high class, like going to the movies or a ball game."

He fell happily silent for the next two blocks.

After we changed the ten, I went by our afternoon job, but Wagon had already finished. I found him in his garage sharpening a lawn mower. On the way, I was tempted to change the five and give Wagon only one or two, since that was a usual tip, and pocket the rest for lavish private spending. Though I walked slowly, I arrived at Wagon's still undecided. Now I don't wish to create the false impression that I was struggling manfully against selfishness and dishonor. I would have kept all of the money without a moment's hesitation if I had been blessed with a quickness of wit or the capacity for instant rationalization. I simply couldn't master enough mitigating excuses to decide. I have come to consider myself, to speak philosophically, as the moral obverse of Hamlet. Where he had too many motives and reasons to act resolutely, I have always had too few; as a consequence I have not always done as much evil as I might have.

I offered him, rather sadly, the five dollar bill. He declined it, stating simply that it was too much. He offered to release me from my promise because I had anticipated earning only a dollar or two on weddings and that if I had expected to make as much as five dollars, I would never have made the promise to start with. As slow as Wagon was in reading and math, his profundity as a moral philosopher was impressive. Had *I* thought of that reason in time, it would have been enough for me to keep the whole five, but coming as it did, after the fact, I refused. I argued, I *insisted* that he keep the money though I wavered in my resolve as I was insisting. In due course, he gave in. He released me from the obligation of contributing any further wedding income since the five dollars would cover the rest of the summer. In time, that sharing became the crowning, unselfish gesture of my childhood.

VII

During June and July of 1944, the beachheads at Omaha and Utah widened and deepened. The massive German counter-attack never materialized. In the middle of June, the invasion was slowed by ten days of gale force winds that prevented the landing of more supplies and man at Arromanches, the artificial harbor of old ships and concrete piers, towed across the channel and sunk by the British because the Germans would hold Cherbourg at any cost. But nature relented and the weapons and ammunition, the tanks, trucks, and troops poured in. Caen fell to the British finally in late July and the American paratroopers and infantry, regrouped, cut off Cherbourg. Then in August with two armies assembled and poised for the breakthrough, one pointing south to Rennes and Nantes and the other westward toward Brest, my homefront partnership with Wagon ended as suddenly and unceremoniously as it had begun.

I was told by my mother one evening in the second week of August that Wagon no longer needed my services. I didn't feel disappointed about being let go. I had been growing tired of the routine. In truth, except for his excitement about serving mass, he was exasperatingly calm and changeless and methodical. To a restless child of twelve he was about as dull as the middle innings of a scoreless ball game. Besides, the grass had stopped growing and the gardens were all firmly established. I had done my job.

Two days later I was shipped off by bus for a vacation to a lake about twenty miles north of St. Paul where a friend had spent the summer at his family's cottage. For two rainy weeks we fished for bullheads and crappies among the reeds along the northwest shore of the lake. In the evening we walked a few miles into a small village and bowled or went to a movie.

By the time we returned for the opening of school, my summer of work with Wagon had already become an infrequent and distant memory. Over the next few years we exchanged nods after mass or whenever we met on the street, but after I started high school, he didn't seem to recognize me any more. In a few years I left home first for college and then finally for the service. I returned after that only for short visits.

As I look back on that summer of work and serving, I now realize that I would never have known Wagon or received his influence so openly if I had been a year or two younger or older. In many ways, I had already grown beyond him. My reverence for the mass had already eroded. Even then it was little more than an exercise in aesthetic mumbo-jumbo. I was not intimidated by the Real Presence as Wagon had been during our trial run at serving. Soon enough the austere morality and penitential regimen of my Catholic childhood would give way under the influence of the real world and the marketplace.

Over the years I forgot about Wagon and our summertime partnership. I remembered other summers much more frequently and with greater clarity. Had it not been for a letter I received from my mother perhaps two years ago, it would have remained part of my buried life, that vast, mostly irrecoverable dump-heap of my lost days.

After my father died several years ago and my mother sold our home and moved into an apartment, she took up writing letters as the primary occupation of her widowhood. Her letters were witty and gossipy. She ran into her old friends or my former teachers and read the newspapers and passed along what she had gleaned. Her letters were sometimes snide even envious, but I enjoyed reading them even though I couldn't remember half the names that she passed along.

One of the features of her letters was a vital statistics section appended to the body of each letter. Over the years it grew longer and longer until it represented a quantity of information almost as large as the letter itself, and the obituary notices in the vital statistics postscript grew proportionately larger as my mother, time passing her by, grew old beyond weddings and babies and divorces.

The list was not comprehensive. She passed on to me what interested her. She had the odd habit of identifying in detail for my convenient recall persons I knew very well, and she failed to identify, perversely enough, recent decedents I couldn't remember for the life of me.

Near the end of one of her obituary postscripts, hurriedly jotted almost as an afterthought, was the brief mention of the death of Joseph Wagner and the casual tack-on identification. "You remember him. You cut grass with him one summer until we made you quit because people began to talk. . . ." There was nothing more, nor did she mention him in any subsequent letters. She didn't have to mention any more. She knew that I would understand *now* what "people began to talk" about then just as she knew that I would have had no idea what people had talked about in 1944 had she told me then.

Since that letter, and perhaps also because we are all eddying now in the backwater of what we have come to believe was an absolute moral and historical moment, I have scrupulously recalled my summer partnership to determine if it too was tainted according to the cynicism that passes for wisdom among men. I have done so in the knowledge that the world is full of ambiguity and complexity and injustice and confusion and imperfection and that we are overburdened with enthusiastic fools who run about shouting simplistic solutions to complicated problems, but I know too that it is just as wrong to find complexity or conspiracy or perversion in simplicity and innocence.

I know also that we remember or forget what we want to remember or forget. I don't remember that the river was polluted when we went fishing that summer, but it probably was. I don't recall the squalor of the city dump when I foraged it for war materials. I don't remember black markets or profiteers though I found out later that they abounded and grew rich out of the slaughter of innocents. I had never heard of genocide or saturation bombing, and Hiroshima was simply the inexorable consequence of the treachery of Pearl Harbor.

Conceding that I remember what I *need* to remember, I assert that Joseph Wagner was a good man. I don't pretend that he was a man of wisdom or complexity. His virtue, his strength, was instinctive not reflective. He had a steady and constant disposition to do good, to do his duty to his country, his fellow man, and his God, as he saw it and as it occurred, and he taught me by his silent example all I have ever known about partnerships. And so, I celebrate the memory of that summer of work and serving and baseball and fishing when simplicity was enough, though I am often perplexed that the God of my childhood, Whom I loved and feared and Who granted me the grace of a selfless partnership, should have permitted, to begin with, the terrible waste of war and the horror of the Final Solution.

GIFTS

Jardin du Tabor
Rennes, France

The pound sterling is now at a dollar and a half, holding steady and keeping us within our budget. We are expecting the dollar to reach eight francs, but 7.4 was enough last week to pack Paris with Americans, Germans, and Japanese even before the summer season begins. The government has restricted the amount of money the French can take out of the country this year, so we have met larger crowds than usual for the month of May in our tour of the usual historical monuments and shrines.

We spent April in Bury St. Edmunds, east of London, visiting the small towns and cities along the train route from Norwich to Cambridge. Each day during our walks in the Abbey gardens, we paused at the tombstone of Abbot Samson and read the inscription, trying to sympathize as best we could with the monastic authority against which our ancestors, the peasants, revolted so passionately. Though it seems a shame that there is so little of the great Abbey left, we cheered in our hearts the spirit of the commoners who dismantled it stone by stone after the dissolution of the monasteries to build homes.

Half way through our stay, we discovered a small, walled rose garden dedicated to the citizens of Bury St. Edmonds by a United States Army Air Corps Bomber Wing in appreciation of the kindness of the English during the last years of the war when the Americans flew missions deep into Germany out of a nearby air base. It seemed a noble and generous gift, in a sense our gift also, and we felt at home there among the rose bushes and vines as if the garden were American soil like the cemetery above Omaha Beach, which is in fact American soil ceded to the United States by a grateful French government. Although the roses were not yet blooming, we began to stop by each day and rest on the bench and browse along the graveled paths to read the identity plates that designated the species and color of each plant. Sitting there for a few minutes each day made us feel closer to the English, whom we spoke to each day in the market and the pubs and on the trains, and closer too to America. The early English spring reminded me of my childhood home in Minnesota, where each year in late April and early May the first spears of perennial green in my father's flower garden would begin to push through the earth, and he would gather his tools and begin working the ground for his annuals.

It rained almost every day during April in England, as it has rained here in Brittany several times each day through May. It rained when we visited Cambridge and Newmarket. It rained when we were in London and Portsmouth. It rained at St. Malo, at Cap Frehel, and during our trip along the Loire from Anger to the Atlantic. It rained when we attended the 12:15 mass in the Abbey at Le Mont St. Michel. There was a thunderstorm during the mass. I expected a lightning bolt to strike St. Michael up there above us, balancing on the pinnacle of this architectural wonder, but the crashing light illuminating the glass above us moved by quickly, and by the time the mass was over the sky was blue, and great mountains of clouds swept by us as we stood on the ramparts outside the cloister, awed by the vast sweep of sand laid bare by the disappearing tide.

The Abbey church, beautifully restored, is now administered by a small band of Benedictine nuns in jeans and sweaters, who, after leading tours through the Refectory and the Knight's Hall, return to church, don beige robes and assist the priest celebrate mass for world peace, ecumenical union, and the brotherhood and sisterhood of mankind. The mass is conducted in several languages, depending upon the national composition of the pilgrims of the day.

After mass we found a cloistered flower garden where we joined a large tour group to test our ability to understand French, but the tour guide spoke so rapidly that we could manage to grasp only an occasional familiar word or cognate that we proudly clung to and translated so slowly that we missed the substance of the guide's lecture. We soon gave up listening, and when the group moved along, we remained to rest. We sat along the stone sill of one of the gothic archways and admired the lovely plots of flowers interwoven among patches of grass and pebbled walks the color of sand. We took pictures of each other with flowers in the background and we relaxed and laughed at our poses as though we were home and not months from returning there. I wondered who brought the soil up here for the garden, who had plodded, bent double with sacks of dirt, up the winding, stony paths to this cloistered place in the sun. Peasants? Monks? Prisoners when the Mont was a prison? Aesthetes?

Here in Rennes it rains hourly each day. There are two weather systems, one from the Atlantic and one from the Channel that converge here, the weather crossroads and capitol of Brittany. Perhaps, there is such a condition as *beau temp tres sec* here. The barometer in the small house we are renting says such a reading is possible though the black needle has hovered in the uncertain range, leaning toward *mauvais* for two weeks now. *Beau temp* may simply be an illusory suggestion of the ideal, like 120 MPH on the speedometer of a car that cannot safely reach sixty. We come to this garden each day, captivated by its beauty as we have been by the countryside surrounding Rennes, which is itself like a delicately proportioned garden. We have already done our duty to the gods of high culture and history and art and have studied the scriptural revelations according to Michelin. We have paid homage to the hallowed monuments of our Western European heritage, secular and spiritual. Our interest in the churches and towers, fountains and bridges, cathedrals and chateaux, universities and great arches over broad tree-lined avenues has waned. They all seem remote, someone else's holy origins. We have gradually become touched by this good, green earth and the growing, living sculptures and tableaux in gardens and parks, patches of meadow, trim crop fields, and rows of trees in cities and farm yards now blossoming everywhere.

I like to sit along the edge of the greenhouse that is set as though on a dais above the formal garden and fountains. I can look straight out across the tops of trees that rise from the lower slope of the garden to the upper floors of the high-rise apartments beyond the park. Though we are thousands of miles from America, the flowers of this garden with its formal and geometric arrangements of sculptured shrubs and shaped trees remind me of my father in this month of his birth and death.

Sometimes it doesn't rain. I can see blue sky between the racing clouds and sweeping splotches of sunlight that break through and bathe a flower bed momentarily before moving on. It is as though some divine stage manager has called for area lighting. It can be spectacular when it floods a field of yellow colza in the Brittany or Normandy countryside, a yellow that only Van Gogh should be permitted to paint, or when it brightens the flowering gorse above the cliffs at Cap Frehel along the rocky Brittany coast.

But it is the flowers that I come to see each day, several times a day. No, not the flowers, the arrangements of the flowers, the distillations of someone's idea of order and beauty in stunning mosaics of color and design. It is something like this that my father must have been groping toward as though it were his incarnational duty to arrange anew each year as many species of flowers as God in his goodness had bestowed upon mankind and for which Father had space and climate to grow. He began at first along the south side of the house, then in a widening arc out from the front porch, then in terraces in the back yard and finally, with special shade tolerant species on the north side on the day we returned upriver from our trip to Grandmother's childhood home, and he continued with escalating vigor after her death a year later until his own death ten years after that.

Since we disembarked at Calais two weeks ago and worked our

way westward from Paris in our rented Peugeot, through Picardy along the Seine to Honfleur then along the coast to Normandy, I have been afflicted by a persistent confusion of time and place, as though I have become a displaced person among these artifacts of what should be my cultural heritage. We spent most of one day at the American Cemetery above Omaha Beach, silently wandering up and down the rows of crosses and tablets. I felt strangely serene among the dead heroes of my childhood, sensing the sacredness of this garden of trees and lawn and the sacrifice of young men, some just a few years older than I but now forever younger in their eternal rest. Is it the trip along the river, the spring rain, the flowers in this garden, the memories of death and victory that have produced this dislocation in time, unpredictably sudden flashbacks to that summer long ago after we returned from our Great Weekend Pilgrimage along the Mississippi to Winona, my father's greatest triumph as a driver? I smile now at his anxiety and timidity. He was not meant for travel. He made only one long trip in his life, to California by train, and then he returned to St. Paul to live out his life safely near his childhood home. He was not meant for all the machines that never seemed to work for him. He did not belong to the world that shaped him, then abandoned him and passed him by. He was meant to grow flowers and reflect on the nature of things.

II

We moved into my mother's childhood home three years after my grandfather died. It took Grandmother that long to admit that finally, at almost eighty years of age, she was beginning to feel some minor symptoms of mortality, that she no longer felt she would live forever as everyone expected her to do. For the first two years she lived alone, refusing to compromise her independence despite the burdens of maintaining an eight room house in a state of incipient disrepair. Then, in what must have been a gesture of bravado or recklessness (half in defiance and half in denial of her destiny as though she really could start all over again) she leased the house furnished to the newly appointed principal of the high school and his family, so that they could get a feeling for the community before buying a home. She moved downtown St. Paul into the old St. Francis Hotel where, two generations before and fresh from normal school, she had lived for a month at the beginning of her first year of teaching. To her disappointment, the once elegant St. Francis had become shabby in decor and clientele. She made no friends and began keeping to her room after the second week. She regretted not having spent the year in Pasadena with her sister-in-law or in St. Petersburg with old friends, but she knew the trip would have been too much for her alone. She did not want to stray too far from Grandfather's grave and her own undated tombstone. Besides, though she seemed so indestructible, something could happen to her. She told us how once on one of her trips to Florida she had witnessed the loading of several caskets into the boxcar of a northbound train in the Jacksonville train station. She dreaded the terrible anonymity of becoming, as she put it, mere cargo.

She stayed on at the St. Francis on a month to month basis because it was cheaper than the weekly rate. She visited us on weekends and stayed over for three days at Thanksgiving and Christmas, but because our house was small and my father intolerable for personal and political reasons for longer than a few days, she returned to the privacy of her small room at the hotel. By January she had become satisfied by her central location during the deep-cold winter months though she continued to maintain her distance from her fellow residents.

We visited her often that winter. Her hotel was located at the principal streetcar transfer point in the loop and so we dropped by going and coming from basketball or hockey games or on trips to the West Side where relatives on my father's side lived. Sometimes we sat in the lobby and visited while we warmed up or in the coffee shop where she took us for hot chocolate or we crammed into her tiny room on the third floor where it was necessary for one person to sit on the bed, one in the only chair, and one on the window ledge overlooking Wabasha Street. From the ledge we took turns peering down through whirling snowflakes at the crowds below, flowing off the curbs to board the streetcars. At times in the late afternoon a dozen or more streetcars were queued up as far as we could see up Wabasha Street, forming a river of yellow machines in a canyon of precipitous brick and granite.

In February she caught a cold that turned into pneumonia. She spent a week at St. Joseph's Hospital, a few blocks from the hotel, and despite the care of the good sisters, she admitted to my mother a certain loneliness and declining vigor. She regretted the double rent she was paying at the hotel and the hospital. She did not want to spend her life savings on hospital bills. She did not want to die alone. She invited us to move into the family house with her when the principal's lease expired even though it would mean she would have to tolerate my father, the only person alive who still dared to contradict her in her own house.

My parents accepted her offer immediately. We were tired of moving around. A honeymoon trip to Los Angeles to visit my father's older brother extended itself into several years when my father took a job as a teller in a branch of the Bank of America, which managed to survive the Bank Holiday and the uncertain years that followed. My older brother and I were born there, but the deepening and apparently unrelenting hard times dampened my parent's spirit of adventure. We returned to St. Paul, to more secure and supportive environs, to family and old friends. As the years went by and the winters seemed to get colder, they regretted having left California and often recalled those idyllic years with nostalgia and lyrical distortion.

My father changed jobs several times, trying to get settled again. He was a part-time accountant for a beer and whiskey distributor and then for a Chevrolet dealer. He was a bookkeeper for a year or two with one of the commission firms in the stockyards and then finally with a large airline where he hung on through the war contract years and survived the post war lay-offs. We moved three times whenever the rent went up. Once we moved from an otherwise perfect home when my mother discovered mice that wouldn't go away despite the traps and poisons my father placed strategically about the house. Moving about became particularly disheartening to my father. While in California he had developed a passion for growing flowers. During those unsettled first years after returning to Minnesota, he put in a flower garden each spring. Each evening during the summer he hurried home from work, changed clothes and plodded along on his knees, down ordered rows, uprooting weeds and delicately cultivating the soil around each plant. Then after supper, he stood watering the garden into the darkness with that loving, soft spray from the nozzle turned almost shut. But it was unsatisfactory planting on rented land. Whenever we moved, he had to dig up and replant his perennials. He was willing, even eager, to live with someone whom he disliked and who in turn held him in open contempt.

We returned with mother to her childhood home in September after Grandmother's year at the St. Francis. It was clear from the very first day that Grandmother had no intention of abdicating any of her authority. She was a formidable woman, tall and lean, severe and distant—a schoolteacher of the old school first, a grandmother last and least and reluctantly. She was a liberated, career woman before those terms came into use. She had taught school for fifteen years when she first met her future husband. He was a contractor who had built many of the older homes in town— the city hall, two elementary schools and the original structures of the packing plant that, as years went by, earned a certain notoriety for our home town. He was a successful business man and politician already in his second term as County Commissioner when Miss Kate came to town as the new fifth grade teacher in the old Washington School. After their marriage, she became virtually a partner in his political career, though she remained a Democrat and he a Republican in state and national elections. She gave speeches to women's clubs in his behalf and distributed apples and potholders at rallies throughout the county.

My mother was a late, only child. When she was three, they built a new home on the frontier of the growing town. It was on a bluff with a good view of the Mississippi and the packing plants and stockyards which sprawled along one of the river bends. Gradually, when improvements came, a neighborhood developed as car dealers and doctors and commission men built homes in what became for a while a distinguished part of town. Though Grandfather was the contractor and builder of the house, it was built to Grandmother's exacting specifications. Though he whimsically referred to her as the "boss" to his cronies and business associates, the house represented to her the only time in their forty odd years of marriage she had wholly dominated him.

Grandmother moved back in a month before us in order to reestablish her domain before we moved in. She had serious second thoughts after she was comfortably resettled and tried to back out of the agreement, but we had already given notice and had moved many of our packed boxes into the cellar. As the day of our arrival grew nearer, her doubts and misgivings intensified. She could take us all for a few days at a time or one at a time, but a permanent invasion and occupation was another matter.

She was particularly apprehensive about living under a single roof with my father. At best she only tolerated him. She ignored him most of the time and at worst argued with him. He was, to her eternal disappointment, a first generation American of German ancestry. His father was an obstinate immigrant from Leipzig who had refused to speak English despite his forty years in America. Her pure Irish stock had been blemished and diluted when her only daughter had chosen my father, she suspected, because of his talent as a good dancer and semi-pro hockey player, qualities greatly admired in a generation Grandmother never understood.

He had little else to recommend himself. He never finished high school though he had become self-educated by reading and by apprenticing himself to a bank at seventeen. Still, he lacked official credentials (though Grandmother conveniently forgot that Grandfather had none either). My mother had had for her time a lavish education. She completed two years at St. Catherine's College majoring in piano and library science. She never did much with her education except play the piano during holidays and make book markers for us, but there was a social and educational disparity between my mother and father that was implicit in Grandmother's resentment of him. My father never amounted to very much in the world of high finance though Grandmother admitted it was not all his fault. In retrospect, banking had been an unfortunate career choice in the late Twenties.

They were also political adversaries. Our family celebrations at Thanksgiving and Christmas were marred by their political debates. She was a New Deal Democrat, a theoretical liberal; he was a Hoover Republican, a conservative disillusioned by the times and the sad fact that all human endeavor was flawed by human frailty. Besides, he read voraciously on every side of every issue and was much more informed than she. Grandmother preferred to argue principle rather than specific policy or personality.

But when we moved in, the expected daily confrontations between them didn't materialize. He became, ironically, her silent ally in the territorial disputes and jurisdictional friction that erupted the very first day between Grandmother and my mother. Where Grandmother had expected sympathy, she found a mirror of her own stiff-necked independence. Where she expected opposition, she found kindness and understanding. She didn't help her own cause by issuing edicts and commands so rapidly and repeatedly in the first few days that we entered the house and moved about only with the greatest of trepidation. We were forbidden to venture even close to her precious heirlooms, mostly English bone china which I understood to be some kind of polished fossil material from extinct dinosaurs. She had her chair in the living room, her place at the table, her bedroom and her daily regimen, which was only remotely connected to our daily regimen. We could do nothing right. We were too noisy, too rambunctious, too finicky at the table, too inquisitive, too disrespectful. We were banished from the attic and Grandfather's trunk from which we had appropriated defunct stock certificates, business ledgers, and copies of discharged promissary notes and deeds of transfer. The new world of my mother's heritage that promised so much adventure and exploration in that last month before we moved diminished dramatically in its romantic possibilities. My mother bore the brunt of those first weeks of friction. She was also the buffer and chief negotiator in the often severely strained relations between Grandmother and the rest of us, except my father, of course, whose withdrawal to his bedroom in the evening to read the paper and listen to the radio was conspicuous. He avoided Grandmother completely except to run her errands, help balance her checkbook, or supervise the carrying out of her commands for repair and maintenance of the house, menial tasks such as hanging the storm windows implemented by his reluctant vassal-children.

Throughout that first fall Mother and Grandmother argued constantly over issues of authority, particularly in the kitchen. Grandmother put things away after cleaning up in one cupboard, Mother in another. Grandmother was growing forgetful. She put water on for tea, then lost herself in a newspaper until confronted by Mother with a red hot kettle boiled dry. On bad days when she forgot the lighted stove two or three times, Mother wanted to know whether Grandmother intended to kill us all along with herself or only herself, and if so, could she at least warn the children. Sometimes they screamed at each other. Grandmother recalled instances of Mother's failures of responsibility since early childhood like failing Spanish, for example, or denting the fender of the car when she was learning to drive. By November, Grandmother developed a temporary affection for my father, and once when he arrived home from work and after she had had a particularly violent disagreement with Mother, she folded her newspaper, and welcomed my father, who was taking off his coat, with the pre-emptory demand: "Whatever possessed you to marry *her*?"

For a while Grandmother maintained a separate schedule. She bought her own food, claimed separate shelves and drawers for her dishes and pots and pans. She ate breakfast after the rest of us had left for work and school, and ate lunch and supper before us. She washed her own dishes, and weather permitting, did her own shopping, but this was her final assertion of independent authority indoors. By Christmas her meal hours and menus gradually and subtly merged back into ours until she was simply another member of the family under the tyranny of Mother's authority in all household matters.

In three months we had eased in gently about her and taken over most of the house. We must have been difficult for her at first, but we were some consolation also. My older brother Hank accompanied her on the streetcar to shop in St. Paul. I took long walks with her up and down neighborhood streets, viewing the houses Grandfather had built and estimating how they were holding up.

In late March, two days after the fourth anniversary of Grandfather's death, Grandmother awoke with a weakened left side. Her speech was slightly slurred and she seemed confused and disoriented. The doctor diagnosed "a slight cerebral accident," which father translated for us to mean a "stroke." Mother took care of her at home. The doctor saw no reason to expose her to staph infection and hospital incompetence. The paralysis was only slight though the disorientation seemed profound for some time. She began a saltless diet and regular medication. She recovered rapidly physically, made it downstairs and around the house in two weeks, and, by the time the snow and ice had disappeared, she ventured with the aid of a cane two blocks to the drugstore.

But the confusion remained, as though the clogged or broken artery had cut off the blood supply to the present. It wasn't simply a matter of wandering reflection, of remembering moments from the past. I became a younger brother of sixty years ago or a nephew of thirty years before. She returned to the present for meals and reading the newspaper, but she was more often living again on the farm of her childhood over a hundred miles down river. She carried on one way conversations with her brothers and sisters and with Ma and Pa. She called me Alan sometimes and asked me about California, which I had left before I was four, but there was a logic of sorts in her questions because I was born in California and a nephew named Alan did live there.

With the warm days of early May, she set out on walks, prescribed by the doctor, of gradually increasing distances. One of us usually accompanied her, but she discarded the cane and made her way independently with relative vigor and stability. Once upon returning from one of her trips, she held my arm as we walked around the yard as she inspected the poor state of the lawn given the four or five years of neglect since Grandfather's death. It was worn and patchy. She told me how she and Grandfather had fought the battle against the weeds and Queen Anne's Lace forty years before when they first built the house and struggled to claim from the primal fields some semblance of order in the form of a trimmed lawn—the symbol of civilization on the disappearing frontiers. After Grandfather retired, the lawn became each summer a competitive battleground where he sought to outdo his neighbors and re-assert the pre-eminence of his status one more time. The next day in what must have been a response to the awakening promise of spring and her own increasing vigor she acted impulsively. She ordered a load of loam that was delivered the next morning and dumped in the back yard, presumably to be spread, rolled and seeded by my father.

When he understood what she wanted him to do, he looked as though he had been struck a physical blow. He had assumed he would be given charge of outdoor matters. He had taken care of the house all winter. He wasn't against a decent lawn, but he had planned to cut his flower garden in at least four feet out from the foundation. He had been planning his garden all winter. In early spring before the earth had thawed, he had visited the Observatory in Como Park to study the spring flower show. He had already planted some of his bulbs along the foundation, but it had been a late spring. He really couldn't have planted any earlier and if Grandmother had her way, he wouldn't plant at all. I assume there was a confrontation of sorts, somewhere beyond my hearing, for the load of loam remained untouched where it had been dumped in the yard for over two weeks and we could feel the tension, the impasse that settled gradually over the house. The inevitable confrontation between them, deferred for almost year, had come to pass.

III

"Right there," he said and stabbed his forefinger at a point on the map approximately fifteen miles south of St. Paul along the river where two red lines formed a Y, merging and proceeding southward as one. His glasses reflected the light from the fixture above the kitchen table as he rubbed the back of his neck with the hand not being used to designate the intersection he feared might become our doom. "That's the danger spot. I can't remember for sure, it's been so long since I've driven that way, but you can rest assured there'll be some raving maniac roaring through the stop sign just about the time we're halfway into the intersection."

My father's anxieties weren't just paranoid musings. Given his incompetence and bad luck with automobiles as owner and operator, there probably would be some madman, blind drunk, roaring through a stop sign and bearing down on our car while yet another raving maniac, driving a cattle truck or moving van, came plunging straight at us as we stalled indecisively at the center point. He shouted to my mother in the living room, asking her if she remembered about the stop signs. I couldn't hear her answer because Father had walked to the kitchen door and put his head around the corner to listen. I was sitting at the kitchen table across which we had spread out a road map. He disappeared around the corner and I could hear the murmur of their voices. When he returned, we resumed our imaginary trip south along the Mississippi River through Hastings, the county seat and home of the spiral bridge and one of the state mental hospitals about which we joked endlessly and tastelessly, Red Wing, Lake Peppin, where the river became as wide as a lake, to Wabasha and finally to

Winona and the small village of Homer just beyond, which was for all practical purposes the very beginning of time since it was there on a homestead farm that Grandmother had been born and raised.

"The highway drops straight south after Hastings, away from the river, then it turns east right there," he pointed again, "and rejoins the river at Red Wing. After that it's river bottom and bluffs all the way—steep hills, blind curves, and narrow bridges."

"Could we go across the spiral bridge? Across and back just to say we did it?"

"On the way back, maybe. If we make it back, that is."

"I suppose it'll rain," I suggested gloomily to let him know I sympathized with his despair.

"Hell, it'll probably snow. Rain on the way down, a snow storm on the way back. That's my kind of luck."

"It's a little late for snow, isn't it?" I tried to be a little hopeful.

"Not in Minnesota. It's never too late or too early for snow in Minnesota. I've seen it every month of the year but July."

"Well, Pa, there aren't any intersections after Red Wing, and all the towns seem pretty small."

"They don't show the gradients on the map. It looks nice and flat with easy curves, but I've been that way before."

"Grandma says it's beautiful, the most beautiful section of the most beautiful river basin in the world."

"I suppose she's seen all the river basins too. Ask her how many of them she's driven."

"We don't have to go that way. See. We can go straight down to Rochester and take Highway 14 east to Winona."

"I suggested that, but she wanted the river route. It's her trip. I've already agreed. It's too late." He folded up the map and handed it to me. "You hold on to this. I know the way, but I like to know what town comes next and how far we've got to go in between."

This reconnoitering of the road map was the final step in our preparation for a weekend car trip down river, an event from my father's perspective of heroic dimensions not unlike Perry's dash to the Pole though in truth it was to resemble more the Joads' plodding pilgrimage to California. Nor were the dangers we might confront entirely real— elements of an objective order of things. They were obstacles of my Father's imagination, proceeding from his ineptitude as a driver and the questionable reliability of our car—a twelve year old, fading green Plymouth he had been nursing into its old age since before the war. For almost ten years he had been putting money into it to keep it going. Now it was worth little as a trade and nothing on the open market. He had too much money invested to let it go for junk. Besides, he felt a certain affection for it, they had been through so much together.

He had taken the car to a garage and had the mechanic go over everything. The carburetor had been adjusted, the oil changed, the points and plugs cleaned, the brakes checked. He picked up an extra rim at a junk yard and stored a second spare in the trunk. Now we were going over the route itself, Highway 61, which ran from Duluth to New Orleans along the Mississippi. I had become his sounding board, assistant navigator, and subdued advisor, for which assistance I had been promised the front seat in the absence of my older brother, who had to play two American Legion baseball games over the weekend and was staying with a friend.

In his gloomiest moments he expressed anxieties of certain disaster with some justification, and it wasn't just that the highways were full of raving maniacs and drunks. In all fairness to him, it wasn't all his fault. Born at the turn of the century he grew up with the car but never really adjusted to it. Part of his problem was beyond his control. He was the victim of an imperfect automobile technology, one perhaps adequate to California or Florida or the Deep South but hardly ready for the Minnesota winters until long after the Second World War. Perhaps it was just that he never had enough money for a new car or new tires or new batteries during the Depression. And then when the war came and he had enough money, there were no new tires or parts or cars. I don't know. What I do know is that I became something of an expert patching inner tubes, holding carburetor flutter valves open with a screw driver, jump starting the old Plymouth or its successors, all lemons, in the bitter early morning cold. He had learned through experience not to trust the automobile, and I had learned through observation to respect his distrust and to sympathize with his impotence. In the whole of my life I have discovered that there are few moments more hopelessly frustrating than sitting behind the steering wheel, head bent disconsolately, of a car that will not start and that there is no moment more terrifying than the sudden realization that you have no brakes or no traction on a road slick with ice or impacted snow. Those moments, fortunately rare in my life, were commonplace in his and at least partially the basis of the anguish he must have felt as we prepared to depart. He had made only one voyage further than fifty miles from St. Paul, a fishing trip to northern Minnesota before the war.

My mother prepared for the trip with an equal amount of anxiety, but her concern was profoundly different. My father feared other drivers, mechanical failure, poor road conditions. She feared Father because quite simply he was a terrible driver, temperamentally unsuited to the concentration and anticipation necessary to negotiate the narrow two lane highways and clogged urban streets of those early and middle years of the rise of the automobile in America. I believe he drove a car out of some vague obligation to his manhood or sense of honor and not out of any love of power or speed or convenience. He was a classic "gawker," easily distracted by sights along the way and a conversationalist who had to look at the person he was talking to, usually someone in the back seat. He was also prone to sustained periods of introspective withdrawal when he lost all sense of external reality and drifted across the middle line or swerved onto the shoulder of the road until my mother screamed at him. At a long stop signal his mind quickly wandered, and we would have to urge him along after the light changed since he had developed a deliberate if not arrogant insensitivity to honking horns.

He had had his share of minor accidents. Once he caught his front wheels in the streetcar rails during a sudden snow storm and slid into the rear platform of a streetcar, smashing his grill and bending his hood askew. He tied the hood down with a clothesline and drove it that way until spring when all the damage of winter had been exacted before having it repaired. But he miraculously escaped the serious accident we all feared. As the years went by, Mother became more and more certain that their time would be up every time they went out. His eyes were bad and his reactions slow, but he insisted on driving everywhere except during the brutal months of January and February when he commuted by streetcar to work on snowy or sub-zero mornings. He was a cautious, deliberate driver but so much so that the traffic often backed up behind us on the highway, making us a menace to impatient drivers who wanted to drive somewhere near the speed limit. As I grew older, I hated to drive with him because of the humiliation I felt as car after car passed us, their occupants sneering as they drove by. If he were still alive, I couldn't bear riding with him. Today, everyone guns by a slow driver, revving the engine, flipping the finger, mouthing obscenities.

At seven the next morning I left him standing by the open trunk of the car and walked slowly past the untouched load of loam toward the kitchen entry of the house. He had removed the car from the garage and parked it along the edge of the alley. We had just carried the ice chest from the house and stowed it in the trunk. I was returning for the first load that Mother had prepared for Father to pack away. He had been up since five. From my bedroom I could hear him downstairs pacing from the kitchen to the living room, back and forth, before I drifted off to sleep again.

He lighted a cigarette and began walking around the car inspecting the tires. He wore dark blue, pinstripe trousers, a white shirt, and a tie. His hat, a summer fedora, was made of finely textured white straw with a broad, dark-brown, grosgrain band. I remember thinking at the time, as I turned my back to him, that he looked distinguished, dressed already for a stay in the hospital or for his own funeral. Someone, surely,—the rescue team, the doctors and nurses in the emergency room, the coroner—would treat him with respect after he had been removed from the wreckage of our car to an awaiting ambulance or hearse. We would all be treated with respect. My mother wore a white linen dress with large maroon balls of varying diameters floating about, and Grandmother wore her silk, navy-blue polka dot like a starry night with white lace trim. They wore similar hats, misshapen pillboxes set askew with black veils, and each had a pair of white gloves at the ready. I had to wear Sunday trousers and a white collared shirt stiff with starch, already itching though I had been dressed for less than a half hour.

In the kitchen I stood beside the table waiting for my first load of food—sandwiches wrapped in tin foil, baked chicken sealed in cellophane pockets, jars of olives and pickles, potato salad. Mother stood beside the open refrigerator with two lists in her hand, one of which she was checking off against the meals she had prepared for my brother, who though he would sleep over the night at a friend's house had been instructed to take his meals at home. She closed the door and turned toward the table and began a final inventory of her preparations. Then motioning me closer she began filling my arms with the objects that would occupy the deepest recesses of the ice chest, to be partially covered by ice cubes just above the cans of beer Father had already buried under the ice. When I returned for my third and final load, Grandmother was in the kitchen finishing a cup of tea and a piece of toast. Mother sent me to the dining room for the two small suitcases, one for Mother and Grandmother and the other for my father and me. They followed me out of the house and across the yard to the car. While I stored the suitcases in the trunk, Mother helped Grandmother into the back seat. I closed the trunk and took my place in the front seat, in the "death" seat my brother had advised me the night before in his vain attempt to temper my eagerness to replace him. Father lighted another cigarette and circled the car slowly three or four times, drawing deliberately on his cigarette and inspecting everything once more. Then he threw down his cigarette, twisted it out with his foot and took his place in the driver's seat. He started the engine, shifted into low, and gripped the top of the steering wheel with both hands. He paused, waiting for my mother to speak as she always did just before we set out on another adventure with my father at the wheel. I was surprised by the gentleness in her voice.

"Don't gawk, Rudy," she said. I expected her to have delivered a long list of instructions. He waited for several moments and when she kept her silence, he let the clutch out slowly and we lurched forward on our epic journey along the river to the village of Homer where time began for Grandmother almost eighty years before.

IV

Late Sunday afternoon I sat on our front steps, looking across the river basin toward the silhouette of a ski jump chute rising on the eastern horizon out of one of the hills of Battle Creek State Park. To the left beyond the river I could see the East Side of St. Paul just beyond the shallow backwater of the Mississippi called Pig's Eye Lake. As soon as we had arrived home, Grandmother had gone to her bedroom to rest. My mother was in the kitchen putting things away, and Father was methodically dismantling the load of loam into a wheelbarrel and distributing it along the foundation of the south side of the house where he had begun to prepare the soil to receive the seedlings of his first permanent flower garden.

We had not died at a dangerous intersection. We had not plunged through the railing of a narrow bridge into the depths of a rocky gorge. We had not wandered across the center line into the path of an onrushing tractor-trailer or swerved off the shoulder and rolled down an embankment into the swirling currents of the mighty Mississippi. It had not rained. It had not snowed. It had been a clear, cool, sunny early June weekend. My father did not gawk except when, coming around a turn, we caught our first glimpse of Lake Pepin. He pulled over and parked, and we all got out and gawked in awe at the river that had suddenly become a widening lake like some bay opening into an ocean, its steep bluffs like headlands diminishing in the distance. Later as we continued, whenever three or four cars backed up behind us, he pulled off the road and lighted a cigarette. He negotiated the steep descents in low gear and we climbed the heights, steadily and confidently, as the road, cut in terraces, wound upward from the river's edge. It had been his masterpiece as a driver and he knew it as did my mother who acknowledged his accomplishment with respectful silence.

From the time we stopped for lunch in a state park twenty miles or so from Winona until we started north toward St. Paul early on Sunday afternoon, Grandmother became our narrator and guide, giving coherence and focus to what I now remember as a kind of surrealistic montage of visual scraps and pieces—fragmented and disordered images of the Polish church, my first glimpse of Byzantine architecture; the cemetery where I saw Grandmother's maiden name repeat itself down rows in gray and rose monuments and headstones and where I walked, knee-deep in shooting grass and weeds, down the shallow troughs between the gently sloping mounds to read the names and dates; and the image of Grandmother herself in a rage sending Father to find the caretaker and to register her complaint that the perpetual care she had paid for ten years before, the receipt for which she withdrew after some searching from the depths of her purse, had produced the effect of eternal neglect. But Father could not find the caretaker and so we drove to our hotel and Grandmother's anger subsided.

My father and I shared a room on the third floor of the hotel next to Grandmother and Mother's room. We ate dinner and breakfast in the hotel restaurant, but I cannot remember what either the lobby or the restaurant looked like. I can recall only the view from the single small window in our room that looked out across the flat, black rooftops of an adjacent block of commercial buildings. Each building was two stories and shared a common wall with its neighbor that extended a few feet above the tarred roof surfaces, creating the effect of a steeplechase or a race course of hurdles across the top of the stolid brick buildings.

All that afternoon and in the evening after dinner until it grew dark, we drove up and down streets searching for places where Grandmother had lived, mostly with relatives, during the school years when she stayed in town. We found her high school and the original classroom buildings of her teachers' college, buried in among the newer structures of what had become a large institution. Finally, on Sunday morning after early mass at the cathedral we drove to the top of the bluff west of town to the flat farmland above the river basin and down a straight gravel road between rows of new corn and fresh green fields of early oats, clover, and alfalfa to the small white schoolhouse where we parked and walked around the yard out to the swings and teeter-totters and back to the front steps to try to see through one of the windows into the class rooms. Then we followed Grandmother's directions to drive perhaps another mile down an intersecting gravel road underneath the wires at the edge of the road, strung from pole to pole and vanishing in the distance. Then she commanded us to turn at a mailbox up a driveway of muddy ruts to a farmstead obscured by a circle of trees, a wind shelter under which rusting farm machinery and junked cars had been abandoned.

Only the image of the white clapboard farmhouse set off from the barnyard by a wire fence remains whole and coherent and vivid in my memory, and I remember it as stark and ugly and lonely, a foreboding American Gothic that had replicated itself from Ohio to the far reaches of western Nebraska. Beyond the house through an opening in the trees I could see the forested river basin and beyond that the rolling hills of Wisconsin. We waited in the car as Father walked through the gate of the fence up to the front door, removed his hat, and knocked. We watched as the door opened and he spoke to someone inside. In a few minutes he put his hat on, returned to the car, opened the back door, and offered his arm to Grandmother.

I did not stay long in the living room where a young couple served coffee and answered Grandmother's questions. The room was small and narrow with high ceilings and crowded with too much furniture and an old organ installed in Grandmother's childhood upon which the oldest daughter of the farm couple was learning to play. It had survived three changes of ownership. Its power was supplied by two pedals near the floor that had to be pumped by the player's feet. My mother played a few tunes, but her legs grew tired so I crawled underneath and worked the pedals with my arms. While everyone talked and drank coffee, I returned to the yard where I was attacked by barking dogs. I scrambled to the roof of the car and sat quietly until the barking stopped and the dogs retreated. Then as I sat waiting, I tried to imagine Grandmother as a little girl living here in this house on this flat and treeless land, and all I could think of was her trudging down that gravel road to the schoolhouse a mile away, perhaps in a snowstorm, bundled in layers of warm clothes and leaning into the wind-driven, biting snow, knowing then, as she surely must have, that the only way out of this desolation was through the schoolhouse. Had I been twenty years older sitting there on the roof of Father's old Plymouth, beholding for the first time Grandmother's birthplace and childhood home, I would have felt differently. I would have thought : So, this is it, so, this is where Grandmother's itinerant and displaced Irish immigrant parents, longing for permanence, took possession of the earth for the first time here in the New World. So, it was here that they sunk foundations for a house and barn and outbuildings, planted trees for a windbreak, plowed, seeded, cultivated, and harvested the earth. It was here that they raised a family that, to their dismay and regret, grew up and left the land after only one generation, dispersed to the four winds only to gather again upriver briefly in St. Paul and Minneapolis, and finally where within a generation they lost each other forever in the labyrinthian anonymity of the city.

They emerged at last from the house, Grandmother holding Father's arm. I slid down from the roof and opened the car door for her. She stopped at the gate and turned around as she let go of Father's arm. She looked at the house one more time, then turned back to the car. As she took her first steps, she seemed to stumble.

I saw on her face a brief grimace of grief or pain, I could not tell which. She closed her eyes and took a deep breath as Father took her arm again and helped her into the back seat.

We sat silently as Father re-negotiated the bluff highway down through Winona and turned northward on Highway 61 toward home. Grandmother began talking, a rambling anecdotal narration, as we left the city limits, and she did not stop until somewhere between Red Wing and Hastings when she gradually drifted off to sleep. She told us how Ma and Pa had come to Minnesota, how Pa had come first, walking off his mill job in Scranton and taking a train as far as his money would take him—Toledo— and then riding the rods to and out of Chicago westward to Dubuque where he caught a Burlington freight northward along the Mississippi to Winona where he stayed with his mother's brother until he took a lumbering job for a year on the St. Croix and lived in Stillwater until he saved enough money to send for Ma. They were married in Winona and they began their life on a homestead grant of 160 acres just south and west of town where they built a house and began farming.

She told us how Henry, her oldest brother, left first and joined the army and served during the Spanish American War. After he was discharged, he returned to Minneapolis and married a divorced woman and left the church and remained in defiance of its authority to his death, though he relented on his deathbed until the priest who arrived to hear his confession insisted that he renounce his wife before he would grant absolution, and Henry told the priest he would plead his own case before God and trust in His mercy and so he was not buried from the Church.

Grandmother was the next to leave, though going into Winona to complete high school and normal school was hardly leaving since she returned on weekends and during summer vacations to help with the chores. Tess, two years younger and lovely and romantic, actually left before her. Tess was pregnant at seventeen, married at eighteen, and left for St. Paul with two little children and her feckless and lazy husband, still only a boy, before she was twenty. She had another child by twenty-three, contracted TB by twenty-five, and died in a sanitarium before she was thirty.

And then, inspired by Henry's example and using his home in south Minneapolis as a staging area or beachhead (something of each), Grandmother left the farm finally and irrevocably to seek a higher destiny, followed by George and Gene, each to escape the farm work and Pa's tyranny. Gene, three years younger than Grandmother, joined the railroad and worked his way up to be an engineer on the Hiawatha, one of the great passenger trains that ran from the Twin Cities to Chicago along with the Burlington Zephyr and the Northwestern 400 (which made the trip in 400 minutes, Grandmother instructed me when I wondered out loud why they couldn't think of a better name like Zephyr or El Capitan or The Broadway Limited or, best of all, The Super Chief). Once Gene became briefly a newspaper hero of sorts when during a violent summer downpour in central Wisconsin he had been stopped by switchmen a mile short of a section of track where the rain had washed away the supporting ties, leaving a gap between rails. He climbed down from his cab and walked a mile in the rain to inspect the tracks. Then he walked back to the train, climbed into his cab and told the trainmen he thought he could make it through. Without consulting any higher railroad authority he backed the train up several miles and charged the washout at full speed, jumping the separated rails with the force and speed of the engine and carrying with the impetus the bumping and swaying passenger cars to safety and a punctual arrival in St. Paul. It was in the papers everywhere and one of the stories was about how a passenger, eating a turkey dinner, was splashed with cranberries as the diner was dragged, bumping and thumping across the washout. He wiped his face with his hand and believing the cranberries to be blood began to scream and race up and down the aisle in panic until he was subdued by the porters.

Gene married Eva and they had two children, Clayt and Wilbur, and they lived near Lake Street not far from Henry, who had married the divorcee named Bess and adopted her son from a previous marriage, who later was one of the first Americans to cross the Rhine with the Signal Corps in 1945. Henry worked for the *Tribune* selling advertising and knew reporters and columnists who came to his house especially during prohibition because Henry and Bess had a kind of salon, a continuous open house where the reporters sometimes brought celebrities to have a drink almost any time of the day and night. Mother was very pretty when she was young and a little bit wild when she went to St. Catherine's and got arrested once when the police raided one of F. Scott Fitzgerald's parties on Summit Avenue in St. Paul. When the police called Grandfather and told him, he let her stew all night in jail before he bailed her out because she should have known better than to go anywhere near that "goddamn drunk."

George married Lena and had two daughters and lived off University Avenue in St. Paul where he worked as a bartender nights and a salesman of girlie calendars days in the gas stations and night clubs along University and out Rice Street. He dressed fancy and thought he was a sport and a ladies' man until the paternity suit straightened him out once and for all and gave Lena a little peace of mind in her later years. She was a waitress in the night club where George worked, a farm girl from over in Plum City, Wisconsin, but her cousin was a lawyer in St. Paul and when George wouldn't answer her letters, she called Lena and told her that she was going to file a paternity suit, and hysterical and ashamed, Lena called Grandmother. She and Grandfather drove to Plum City and took one look at the child and offered the woman an out of court settlement because it was the right thing to do and because Lena and the girls, Catherine and Patricia, would have been humiliated. They settled for more than the woman would have been granted by the courts if she had won, which she certainly would have had she brought the child into the courtroom because only an outright liar would have dared deny the resemblance. Grandmother thought it was strange that the child looked more like her brother George than either of the girls, who didn't look like Lena either and nothing like each other. Patricia was a beauty who looked like a movie star. After high school she began working at the Emporium demonstrating cosmetics on customers. In a few years she was already an assistant buyer and had more young men trying to court her than she knew what to do with. She went to a convention in Chicago and met an executive from Marshall Fields and accepted his offer of a job as a model of stylish clothes and as a demonstrator of make-up in the store. Pretty soon she was appearing in advertisements and fancy displays. My mother cut her picture out of magazines and kept them in a small scrap book that we looked at once in a while as a reminder that someone in our family had become famous even though nobody ever knew her name.

But poor Catherine was ugly as a mud fence and worked for ten years after high school making scotch tape at Minnesota Mining. She finally got a beau at twenty-nine when she met a soldier stationed at Fort Snelling. He was no bargain, but Grandmother figured that Catherine wasn't anything special either though she was a sweet person. They were married when he received his discharge and they moved to his home in Muskogee, Oklahoma and had several children and apparently lived happily ever after, which was better than Patricia who was divorced twice and didn't have any children and had to spend her life living in Chicago, which Grandmother felt was too big a price to pay for her success in business and a little passing fame.

Another of my mother's cousins had anonymous fame like Patricia. His name was Alan, the second son of Tess and her shiftless husband Will Seeger, who came to California and lived with us for a year and was credited with rescuing me from my crib during an earthquake. When we returned to Minnesota, he stayed on in Los Angeles and got a job as a cameraman at RKO studios and became an alcoholic and went through a wife and two jobs before he stopped drinking. Once he was in a movie as an extra. It was a famous war movie about the heroic American troops at Anzio. Alan played a German soldier who was killed near the end of the movie. Grandmother and mother went to the movie two or three times but they couldn't tell which German soldier he was. They didn't show the faces of any of the German soldiers clearly. Besides they wore padded uniforms to make them look big and they wore Nazi helmets pulled down over their eyes. Grandmother and Mother finally decided that Alan was one of the two machine gunners shot when the Americans overran their nest. My mother liked Alan who was two years ahead of her in high school and was president of his senior class and had the lead in all the plays, which helped her popularity because he was her cousin and paid attention to her and taught her how to dance the two-step and the Charleston.

The last to leave the farm was Tom. Poor Tom, the simpleton and Grandmother's favorite because he was God's child. He worked the farm until Pa died and Ma sold the place because Tom couldn't run it alone and they moved into Winona until Ma became infirm and had to move upriver for Grandmother to take care of her. Tom came along and worked in the packing plants for a while, but then he was laid off because of the Depression and drifted off, wandering from town to town along the river, taking jobs here and there and then leaving suddenly without a word. Grandmother invested Tom's share of the inheritance for him after Ma died and when he showed up one spring not looking well, Grandmother convinced him to stay. He took a room at one of the places for truckers down on Concord Street and Grandfather got him a job in the summer months for the city, mowing grass in the parks and playgrounds. In the winter he shoveled walks here and there and when he took sick a few years later, Grandmother doled out his savings until that was gone and paid his hospital bills and took him back to Winona and buried him in the family plot along with Ma and Pa and Tess when he died just short of his forty-seventh birthday.

Then she told us her last story about Doctor Clayt, Gene and Eva's oldest boy, after Father pulled off the road at a roadside stop near the northern end of Lake Pepin and we got out of the car and stretched and Father drank one of the warm beers that were left in the iceless cooler. Mother and Grandmother had some hot tea from the thermos they had filled at breakfast and they offered me an ice-cold bottle of pop when we went through Red Wing or Hastings. They offered me one of father's beers (that I suggested might wet my whistle) in about eight years.

I didn't think she would start up again. I thought she was asleep after our stop near Red Wing, but she was only dozing a little and she began her last family story, a tragic story of promise and overreaching and shame, as we entered the home stretch and Father, now certain we would make it, speeded up and took curves and steep grades with what was for him wild abandon. She began in bewilderment, still wondering how it all could have happened. There wasn't a suspicion in anything he did or said that he was involved to the extent that he was, indebted was the better word and compromised and surely frightened when he finally realized to whom he was in debt.

Doctor Clayt was the pacesetter of his generation, the first of the family to be born and raised in Minneapolis and the harbinger of good things to come. He was a brilliant student of science in high school, a pre-med major at the University, and finally a graduate of Marquette University Medical School, where he swore to uphold the ideals of his profession in an oath administered by the Bishop of Milwaukee, a great uncle by way of a Wisconsin branch of Grandmother's family. His practice was instantly lucrative. He was a good man, gentle and courteous and sympathetic with his patients, and he loved the good things in life. He drove a La Salle and he had hunting and show dogs that he kept at a kennel with a trainer and he went big game hunting in Canada for caribou and deep sea fishing off Florida for marlin and sailfish. Within a few years he had a grand suite of examination rooms in his office downtown and he bought a large Tudor style home out on Minnehaha Parkway where he lived with his wife and two children. It had a beautiful yard with perfect bent grass and square hedges of yew and a big garage called a carriage house with an apartment upstairs where a gardener lived who took care of the place in the summer so he could live there free the year round because times were hard then for common laborers.

That's what they believed first about the gardener whom Grandfather met once when they were leaving after a visit. They met on the walk when the gardener was trimming the hedge. He stopped cutting while Grandmother and Grandfather walked by. When Grandfather complimented him, the gardener took off his hat and smiled and called them *sir* and *Mam* with great courtesy. Later, during other visits that summer when they dropped by to visit Doctor Clayt after they had had a picnic at Minnehaha Falls, Grandfather and the gardener became joking friends and Grandfather offered him a job to put in bent grass and hedges at our home, but the gardener respectfully declined, saying that gardening wasn't his real occupation and that he only worked for Dr. Clayt between big jobs, which were irregular in his profession and besides he didn't feel comfortable working anywhere but in Minneapolis.

It all came out when Tommy Gibbons, who let Jack Dempsey stay with him for fifteen rounds in Shelby, Montana, cleaned the rackets out of St. Paul in his first term as sheriff and ambushed Dillinger out on Lexington Avenue where he was visiting one of his women and shot him in the leg though Dillinger got away because somebody took the bullet out of his leg and didn't report the gunshot wound. That somebody was Doctor Clayt and Grandfather engaged the lawyer who got him off with a suspended sentence. There were witnesses who came forward and an investigation and a trial with extenuating circumstances, (Doctor Clayt and the nurse were forced at gunpoint), but then he didn't report the wound, giving Dillinger time to get away. Then it came out about his gambling debts and how the mob in Minneapolis was using him because of all he owed them trying to get rich faster than being a doctor was going to get him there. His losses at cards had been heavy and they let him pay some of it back by letting two friends of the man who ran the gambling parlor stay in

Dr. Clayt's carriage house and pretend they were gardeners. One of the men was a Mr. Kelly and the other was a Mr. Nelson.

Later after the pain and shame had subsided and Dillinger's gang had been broken and he had been shot finally and for good in Chicago, Grandmother and Grandfather could laugh about it all a little bit. Grandfather was able to admit that he had once offered a job to Machine-Gun Kelly but that he had been turned down, fortunately, because Tommy Gibbons had cleaned up Ramsey County and confined the criminal element to Minneapolis where it belonged. They weren't sure they had ever seen Babyface Nelson over at Dr. Clayt's, but once Mr. Kelly had a helper raking leaves and Grandmother swore that he looked just like the pictures she had seen of Babyface Nelson in the papers.

Grandmother fell silent for a few minutes and I guessed the story was over so I asked her what ever became of Dr. Clayt and she said that they did some plea bargaining or something like that she didn't understand and he was put on probation. Then the state board took away his license to practice medicine and suggested he leave the state and start over again in some other profession. Then I asked where he went, and she said "Oh, out to California somewhere, of course," as though that's where every doctor went who failed to report a gunshot wound to the police after extracting a bullet from the leg of John Dillinger.

V

I must have inherited the genes, apparently recessive in my father's generation, that drove my ancestors westward on that great adventure across an ocean and halfway across a continent before coming to rest along the Mississippi, for I left home at nineteen, never to return except for short visits and funerals and even then I was making plans to leave as soon as I arrived. I retraced my parents' journey to California, and during a war went beyond them westward throughout the Pacific and to Japan and then returned eastward past St. Paul and Chicago, past New York and Boston (wherever my Irish and German ancestors entered America) to Ireland and England and beyond there to France. I returned in time to the monuments and mausoleums and artifacts of Europe, to the obscurity of the myths and megaliths of my wild Celtic and Germanic ancestors.

It has not been a consciously chosen pilgrimage to origins, though that is what I have done, in fact, returned through the course of a life well beyond my family's vague remembrance of those obscure and distant beginnings, if legends and tales were the beginnings. My travels have brought me here to this lovely garden in Brittany and I am, in my mind's eye, once again in Minnesota sitting on the front steps looking down toward the river, hoping that the summer of uneasy truce between my father and grandmother has not been breached.

It is August now. The days are growing shorter. My father has just returned from work to discover that Grandmother has mutilated his garden, making bouquets for the neighbors as an excuse to visit and bore them with her thrice or more told tales. He is talking to my mother on the side lawn in a repressed and violent whisper. I cannot hear what he is saying, but his arms are flailing. He points along the side of the house to a flower bed I cannot see. Then he walks over and kneels down beside what used to be a row of zinnias, leaves trampled, decapitated stems bent askew. He stretches his arms out before him, his hands open in supplication. It is such a wonderful dumb-show that I smile inwardly despite the melodrama that is unfolding before me. They come back across the lawn, my father striding angrily, my mother following and calling after him in a voice that is at once pre-emptory and pleading.

"Don't say anything to her, Rudy. She didn't mean any harm. She just wanted to share them with the neighbors."

"Didn't mean any harm!" My father stops before reaching the steps and turns around. "Didn't mean any harm?" he shouts incredulously. "She's ruined the whole garden. She didn't even cut them with a scissors, just yanked them out and threw away the stems and the roots as though she were pulling up weeds. And she walked all over the snow carpet and the colias."

"The bouquets were beautiful, Rudy. She was so proud of them. She was proud of you too. She called you a horticulturist."

His face softens a little, but he makes another sally. "Why didn't she ask them over? I'd have given them a guided tour."

"She wanted to visit them today. It's the coolest day in over a week. I think she knows that they hide sometimes when she comes. They pretend nobody's home. I think she thought they wouldn't turn down a gift, the flowers, and that they would let her in. She spent an hour at Lundeens and had tea, and a half hour at Schumakers helping Florence arrange the flowers in a vase. She hasn't had such a good time in weeks. She can't always get out, especially when it's hot. It was perfect today, and she came home with a smile that was positively beatific."

My father stands now hesitant and confused.

"Where is she now? I just want to talk to her, to tell her how to cut selectively without ruining the whole design. She probably didn't know that it's all a plan of species and colors and sequence. I just want to tell her."

"She's resting in her bedroom. I put the fan on. I think she may be asleep now."

"Can't I tell her when she wakes up?"

"Let her alone, Rudy. She's been happy for the first time in weeks. She's so disoriented and distracted most of the time and she cries all the time, remembering what isn't any more and will never be again."

My father is pleading now, already past anger and half-way through the mourning that will be resolved when he decides to clean out the mess, drive to the greenhouse and replant with mums or whatever would bloom in fall.

"Why the hell couldn't she have asked me? I'd have cut them for her. I know it's her land, that I'm the outsider, that she never liked me and doesn't now, thinks I'm some kind of circus freak, but she didn't have to trample everything."

"She didn't do it on purpose, Rudy. She doesn't hate you, she doesn't know what she has done. She just wanted to make some bouquets, the flowers are so lovely." My mother pauses, her voice gentle now that she knows she has won. "She's dying, Rudy. She hasn't much time left and the flowers made her so happy today."

He did not say what I know he could have said: "She's been dying for two years now. That's why we moved in here, to be with her at the end, to help her through.She knew that. We knew that.She was dying last fall, too, when you fought with her every day, finally stripping her of her life's authority." He did not say that though he had every right to speak.

Grandmother died less than a year later. She shriveled so much that she seemed like a doll, a shrunken figment of her former self. During her last two months I refused to visit her though she often called my name from her bed in a mindless chant whenever she happened to think of me. I did not want to witness her final lunacy, to trespass against her last right to privacy. The undertaker and his assistant carried her down the stairs on a small pallet with an undercarriage of collapsible wheels that they unfurled on the walk. It was early in the morning, perhaps six or seven o'clock. My mother awakened us to witness her removal, but I could not see her. She was wrapped in an oilskin cloth and she had become so tiny, I remember thinking at the time that if she could have lived another month or so, she would have disappeared entirely, evaporated and saved everyone the bother and expense of the wake and funeral that few attended, time had passed her by so completely.

I was living in Connecticut when my father died. I did not visit him in his last months either. It would have been useless. In January he felt the beginnings of the paralysis in his hands and feet and then the pitch of his voice began to lower until he could no longer produce intelligible sounds. He began to have difficulty swallowing. Unused to such strange symptoms, his doctor tested him for cancer of the throat, because one of my uncles had had cancer of the larynx, and when the x-rays proved negative, my jubilant parents went home to celebrate, but he gagged on the whiskey and water he tried to swallow hastily after toasting his own good health.

Though he could manage to swallow solids for a while, he soon could no longer swallow liquids. He went to the University Hospital for observation. The neurologist noted extensive atrophy of muscles in his limbs and throat. The diagnosis was surprisingly swift, given the rare symptoms: amyotrophic lateral sclerosis, Lou Gehrig's disease.

At first he responded positively to the ACTH, achieving a brief remission of some of his symptoms, but he regressed soon after each treatment. The disease was irreversible. For a short time, my father became something of a medical celebrity. They wheeled him into the amphitheater several times during his few weeks at the hospital, where contingents of white frocked doctors gathered to observe him and discuss his symptoms. I heard that he seemed to enjoy this brief notoriety, but he deteriorated rapidly, the sclerosis moving quickly to the breathing centers of his brain and spinal cord. Soon he could not draw enough air to light his cigarette. He could not write. He could not speak or walk. His mind was acutely alert, however, his anxiety increasing as he became aware of each nuance of neurological or muscular deterioration.

At the wake, an atmosphere of subdued sorrow was mingled with subdued relief. My father's doctor appeared early in the evening. He was a kind, compassionate man who apologized for his impotence. "I wish it had been cancer," he mourned. "We might have been able to do something." Everyone was glad it was over, including my father who, once he could no longer draw on his cigarette, gave up the will to live and prayed daily for a speedy end. It had been mercifully quick, just four months from the appearance of the first symptoms, which in this insidious disease are always terminal.

The wake itself was held at a new funeral home. The building had been formerly a New England style tea house and restaurant. It was a lovely low building of flagstones and beams. There were windows everywhere and paneled inner walls, long mahogany tables and pewter lamps and a walk-in fireplace along one inner wall to the left of my father's casket. The atmosphere was almost festive, hardly mournful. I overheard one of the neighbors remark that "Rudy would have liked it this way. Colorful with flowers and everything," but I know my father would have preferred live plants to the cut bouquets then dying about the room. When I left our house for the last time on the morning of the funeral, it was cold and windy though the sky was clear. I walked around the house through the unweeded rows of an unplanted garden. Only a few scattered perennials were growing without his care.

Now years later I sense the essence of his spirit about me here in this garden in this foreign land. The species he grew were undramatic, ordinary—hollyhock, bearded cockscombs, iris, nasturtium, asters, marigolds, snapdragons, zinnias, alyssum, geranium, pansies, daffodils, tulips, petunias, straw flowers, begonias—"horticultural banalities" according to one of my snobbish friends who cultivates and cross fertilizes exotic species of orchids in his solar greenhouse, but they grew tall and lovely, breast high zinnias, hollyhocks whose zenith blossom was beyond my father's reach. It is virtually all I can remember of him after twenty years, the most enduring legacy that survives his demise.

As I sit here in this lovely garden, I think of our weekend trip to Grandmother's childhood home. I suspect now that they struck some sort of deal back then. I suppose it was a selfish trade-off, a bartering, each having something needed by the other though I'd like to think I became the beneficiary of acts of self-sacrifice, gifts exchanged as gestures of previously unexpressed respect if not a grudging love finally realized by natural enemies. I also like to think they gave me two gifts that have sustained me during times of confusion and uncertainty as fixed points of reference, the spiritual bedrock, the still point of a turning world, beyond which I have no need or desire to journey.

By braving the terrors of the highway and an imperfect technology, the raving maniacs and sharp turns and steep hills of the highway along the Mississippi to the bluffs of Homer, my father gave me Grandmother's heritage—stories of Ma and Pa and brothers and a sister all dead, of nieces and nephews scattered to the winds, and times forgotten except by her. And Grandmother, in relinquishing the last vestige of her earthly authority to my father, gave me his sense of the beautiful, that majestic procession of flowers—from daffodils to marigolds to mums—that marched, in regal splendor, through the summers of my childhood and youth.